I0626849

CATHRYN PETIT

A Spell of Wanderlust

I♥Y Green
Publishing, LLC

First published by ILY Green Publishing, LLC 2019

Copyright © 2019 by Cathryn Petit

All rights reserved. No part of this publication may be reproduced, stored or transmitted in any form or by any means, electronic, mechanical, photocopying, recording, scanning, or otherwise without written permission from the publisher. It is illegal to copy this book, post it to a website, or distribute it by any other means without permission.

This novel is entirely a work of fiction. The names, characters and incidents portrayed in it are the work of the author's imagination. Any resemblance to actual persons, living or dead, events or localities is entirely coincidental.

First edition

Editing by Antonia Reed

This book was professionally typeset on Reedsy.
Find out more at reedsy.com

To my mother, Elsie, my greatest cheerleader through life. I couldn't have done any of this without you!

Contents

Acknowledgement

Much indebted gratitude to my editor from across the pond, Antonia Reed, for her insight and keen eye.

I

Summer 2018

One

Chapter 1

*D*eep purple streaks whizzed through the room at dizzying speeds. Her brain could only read fire and glistening metal, enveloped by the high-pitched sound of Zaghareet calls that were bouncing off the walls and driving the energy of the room into a frenzy.

She watched as the purple-and-fire blur cleared back into form as the tempo dwindled. The slowing motion allowed the stunning redheaded woman to come into focus. She was balancing two glistening swords on her head while performing figure-eight hips up, before turning them downward into Mayas and then corkscrews as she alternated chest and hip circles. All the while, the swords held steady.

Jewell had realized something special was happening just moments ago, when she'd descended the steps to the studio and found the door ajar. She hadn't been able to put her finger on what it was. Music had been pouring from the space, nothing seemed particularly unusual.

She had put the feeling down to timing. It had been a few weeks since they last gathered. In June, Maggie had once again marked the end of their session with a required performance for the students to showcase their new choreography and skills. Then they launched into their annual summer recess. The free time had allowed Jewell to get so tangled up into knots and sheets with Kage that the magic of what her troupe continued to create in this room had been temporarily pushed from her mind. Now, the same undeniable force that had pulled her down those stone steps that very first day in Southbridge beckoned her again.

When she had stepped into the room, she found the majority of her group already there. She would normally have gone over to greet the others, but had been too captivated by the hypnotizing stranger whirling like a brightly colored dervish in the center of the room.

Now, the dancer was sweeping her arms inward with a grace only the most accomplished of dancers achieve, then away again in contrasting geometric shapes. Jewell stared in amazement, mesmerized not only by the dancer's ability to keep the shining blades stable on her head, but also the way she made such simple movements look like art. Her arms flowed as if no bones filled them, and her fingers fluttered like the petals of an aquatic flower. Her face was soft, and Jewell almost felt butterflies when the performer's strangely calm eyes met hers for a moment. This woman had the earthy confidence and inner peace of a born dancer.

Jewell thought about the jitters she felt while waiting in the dressing room prior to her own performances. Her face felt like stone with a plastered-on smile. That was until...like a beacon of light, she would glimpse Kage in the audience grinning encouragingly up at her.

The music climaxed into a finale as the performer spun in a fury, keeping tightly in place. Then she dropped to the floor, landing with her legs in a wide hero pose, her upper body erect. The swords plummeted from her head and she deftly snatched their handles in mid-air. Gasps echoed throughout the studio. The students glanced from one to the other.

"Well, Lord a mercy, if that wasn't ever something," Della Rae said.

"It was," Sherry said, her eyes fixed on the dancer who was now rising to her feet.

"Your costume is beautiful," Candi said, forgetting to close her mouth after she completed her sentence.

"Oh, this girl has the costumes," Maggie said.

Jewell silently admired the deep purple chiffon sweeping like a Grecian robe around the visitor's petite yet shapely body. The costume's silver accents gleamed in the Sacred Veil Studio lights like highly lustered pearls. The silver bangles garnishing her wrists and forearms clanked out musical notes as she laid aside the swords. Maggie and her students applauded wildly.

"Now don't try this at home, kids," Maggie joked as Gabby burst through the door, her uncombed mousy-brown hair flying behind her.

Breathlessly, Gabby asked, "What'd I miss? What'd I miss?"

"For those of you who were late," Maggie announced, clearing her throat and firing glances at Jewell and then Gabby, "this is my friend, Aniela. She's visiting from California and I thought you'd enjoy her show. Was I wrong?"

The group cheered again. Aniela beamed, walking up to the students and offering them each a business card. Jewell noticed that her full, heart-shaped lips were the exact same red as her hair.

With a soft, sweet voice Aniela said, "If you ever visit Southern California, please let me know. I'd love you to stop by my studio or come eat at the restaurant where I dance. I hope it's alright if I stay and watch tonight." Jewell could only marvel at how her gentle air contrasted her vibrant performance.

The students filed into their usual three-row formation. Jewell was in the middle row on one side of Becca with Z on the other side bubbling with enthusiasm, her tattoos and piercings proudly on display. Nicci and Candi were already engaged in whispers at the front, and Della Rae, Gabby and the somewhat stage-shy Sherry were in the back.

The break from class had left Jewell feeling rusty. She and Becca had planned to get together to dance, but between their respective romances and work, they hadn't made it happen. Fortunately, glimpses of their classmates showed them to be just as unpracticed.

After the class, Della Rae invited Aniela to Rhita's for their usual after-class ritual, along with the enthusiastic agreement of the others. Aniela graciously declined, saying she planned to stay to observe the advanced class.

"Can you make it tonight, Gabby?" Becca asked. "Celebrate us girls being back together?"

"No, I gotta get home to my brood. Kevin and the boys are planning an ice-cream party after dinner. I reckon I'll be peeling them off the ceiling before bedtime…Kevin included." A snort escaped with her jovial laugh.

The two-block stroll to Rhita's Daily Perk took place in the same formation the group had established when Jewell first joined the class. Memories of that first night clipped through her mind and she realized just how monumental a transformation her life had undergone.

First, she broke away from Josh and his agoraphobia, moved to Florida, stumbled into Maggie's bellydance studio, embarked upon new friendships and a full social life, became part of a bellydance troupe, started a new career, was followed by a ghost, returned to Washington and found Josh dead, worried she had caused his death, met a cowboy, dealt with a blackmailing brother, discovered Josh's death was of natural causes—nothing to do with her medications, and then, of all things, she participated in a seance to boost the bellydancing ghost of Clara Tessa Berg onto her next spiritual level. What a ride!

How could the girl who sat in her Washington apartment gazing out the windows at the birds have ever guessed what a tumultuous six-month period awaited her? Sure, once that initial drama ceased, she welcomed the sense of normalcy that had settled into her life. Although she enjoyed the quiet of the last twelve months, she wondered if there wasn't some kind of balance between earthshaking and commonplace.

They arrived at the coffee shop. The familiar comforting aroma of vanilla and cookies greeted her, and Jewell read the new signs the owner must have added since their break. The hand-drawn boards mixed well with the shop's rustic interior.

Despresso: the feeling you get when you're out of coffee.

Coffee: if you're not shaking, you need another cup.

They stood in line to order and Jewell pulled Aniela's business card from her pocket. She daydreamed about dancing like her one day.

Becca moved aside to allow Jewell a spot at the counter. "Your turn, chickadee."

Jewell was still half-wrapped in her daydream when she ordered, her imagined arms trailing the air gracefully as she twirled on a floodlit stage, the crowd going wild beneath her. The barista cleared his throat politely, and Jewell finally snapped out of it.

"I'll have the White Chocolate Macadamia Nut. Hot, please."

"Whipped cream?" the barista asked.

"Is there any other way?" They all laughed.

As the pair moved to the other end of the counter to wait for their drinks, Jewell said, "Wouldn't it be cool to take lessons from Aniela?"

"I don't know." Becca shrugged. "I mean, I guess. But she's all the way in California."

Still examining Aniela's card, Jewell studied the address. She had grown up and lived on the West Coast her entire life, other than these past sixteen months in Southbridge. But she had never visited Southern California, or anywhere else in the state for that matter.

Their usual round table sat empty, as if it had been awaiting the group's return. Being creatures of habit, the seven took up their usual seats. Nicci at the perceived head, Candi on her left and Sherry on her right. Della Rae between Sherry and Becca. Jewell sat to Becca's right, with Z next to her and an empty seat where Gabby should have been.

Jewell raised her ceramic mug with its eclectic pattern of overlapping vintage license plates. As the cup neared her lips, she inhaled the glorious sweet scent of cream, white chocolate and nuts. It felt like coming home. She admired the coffee shop's collection of mugs, each unique. Half the fun was anticipating in which design her brew would be delivered.

Once settled in their places, the women proceeded to gush over Aniela's performance.

Z used her coffee stirrer to mimic slashing motions. "I think we should dance with swords."

"It's not that kind of sword, Z," Nicci corrected, seeming even more stern with her dark-rimmed glasses and plum lipstick. Her tight brown curls bobbed with each statement. "Plus, she called it a scimitar. I don't think we need to use a gimmick like that to have an impact."

"I don't see why ever not," argued Della Rae in her delicious Southern belle accent. Jewell had grown to love and appreciate Della Rae over the past year. She learned Della Rae hailed from a small Georgian town with a backyard full of majestic magnolias and a front porch swing that she regularly shared with her mama. It was the type of town where, if you didn't attend church on Sunday and pray to Jesus daily, why then you were just a heathen.

"I liked the swords," Becca said. "Excuse me, scimitars." She stuck her tongue out in Nicci's direction. "What does everyone else think?"

"Like, it's alright and everything," Candi said. She must have noticed the man at the next table eyeing her because she struck one of her head-thrown-back poses with her straight blonde hair tousled and her large breast thrust to attention. "But I mean, Maggie never uses them."

"Maggie can do anything she sets her mind to," Z insisted.

"We can always just ask her," Della Rae suggested, then turned away and gnawed her lip. For a moment, Jewell thought she saw tears forming in her eyes. Her jet-black hair was teased big as usual, each strand still perfectly in place but she didn't seem her usual cheerful self.

"You okay, Della Rae?" Jewell asked.

"Why, nothing's wrong, darling. My allergies just have me slap wore out, that's all."

Della Rae wiggled in her chair to sit herself up straight, then folded her napkin into a point and used it to dab daintily at the corners of her eyes.

Jewell let the matter rest. Perhaps Della Rae was telling the truth. If not, it would be wrong to pry in front of everyone. She let the small talk about that night's class distract her, until she spotted a new employee struggling with a large tray full of Rhita's multicolored mugs. As he teetered towards the counter with an already unsteady load, a customer darted out of the bathroom and came crashing into him. The employee put up a good fight, veering this way and that like a cartoon character, but finally the tray crashed down with a shattering sound that made Jewell wince.

Sherry squealed. Becca leapt to her feet, despite no longer working at Rhita's, and rushed over to help. Z followed.

Jewell was about to go too, when she realized Della Rae was sobbing helplessly into her napkin. Jewell scooted into the now empty seat next to her and looked to Candi, Sherry and Nicci for backup. Nicci opened her mouth as if to speak, but nothing came out. She shrugged her shoulders and grimaced. Candi came around the table and knelt down in front of Della Rae.

"What's wrong?" Jewell asked gently, stroking Della Rae's upper arm.

Becca and Z had returned to the table, their faces full of concern, and were moving their chairs into a circle around Della Rae. She pulled her hands away from her face.

"I'm sorry, I don't cry pretty."

"None of us do," Becca said.

"Oh, I might as well get this over with." She let out a deep sigh. "It's Winslow."

The women glanced around at one another. Della Rae's announcement came as no surprise to Jewell, and she figured it didn't to the rest of the group either. There had been subtle indications of 'trouble in paradise' for a while, but they had let Della Rae believe that her facade of enjoying a happy marriage was believable.

"I don't like to burst anyone's bubbles," Della Rae continued. "But this time it's serious."

"This time?" Sherry asked.

"Yes." Della Rae seemed to have calmed. "Remember that Suburban I took on our costume shopping trip and I told you there was a story behind it?"

"Yes."

"Well, let's just say he has a great eye for appeasement gifts. That car came to me the day after I'd found out about some stupid fling he'd had with his new secretary. Honestly, how cliché is that? He couldn't even be creative. And this time it's just as pathetic."

"This time?" Becca asked.

"What did he do?" Z joined in.

"I guess Winslow Young, Esquire, has not one ounce of originality in his body." Her tone was the embodiment of an eye roll. "He's gone and taken up with a classmate of ours from college. And guess where they found each other?"

"Facebook?" Nicci offered.

"You got it, sister."

"Oh Della Rae, I'm so sorry," Jewell said. "Maybe this one will pass too."

"I don't think so. It feels different."

"What can we do?" Becca asked, now rubbing Della Rae's other arm.

"Just what you've been doing. Be my friends."

"Easy peasy," Sherry said.

"What are you going to do about that mansion of yours?" Nicci asked.

"Nicci!" Becca reprimanded, her long-full brown hair swinging with her head snap.

"Why, I'm going to keep living there, that's what. He may be a lawyer, but I've been entertaining his colleagues and their wives for years. Guess who they love more?"

"Good for you," Z said.

"Yeah, you go, girl," Candi encouraged.

"What are you going to do rattling around in that huge house by yourself?" Nicci pushed.

"Well, the kids will be coming home in between semesters, and then when they get married and have their own families, there'll be plenty of space when they visit. I like the house, I like the neighborhood, and I don't see why I should move when he's the one who's been philandering. I'm not going anywhere." She paused. "Except the gym. I'm going to start going to the gym. It's time to get some of this baby weight off now that the twins are in college!" They all laughed and shifted around to their original seats.

"I know one thing," Becca said. "You're not going through any of this alone."

"I second that," said Jewell. She was distracted by the unfortunate cup-smasher, who had reappeared after disposing of the broken crockery.

"Sorry to change the subject…"

"Please, I've shared enough!" Della Rae encouraged.

With all eyes turned to her, Jewell felt her face grow warm. The question forming in her mind seemed so stupid now.

"Have any of you been experiencing things…crashing lately? It seems to be happening to me a lot. Especially when the situation is already tense, or at particularly crucial moments."

Sherry tilted her head thoughtfully. "Maybe? Why?"

"Yeah, why?" Z asked.

"Well, for one example, at the lab," Jewell continued. "Lacey and I were distracting each other with idle chit chat and nearly made a major mistake in our measurements. A tray full of glass beakers crashed to the floor and shocked us into attention. After we'd cleaned up and returned to the work, we noticed the mistake we'd been making and avoided losing weeks' worth of research."

"So what?" Nicci asked. "Maybe the tray was on the edge of the counter and someone walked by."

"That's the thing. We were the only ones in the lab, and the tray had been in the middle of the counter. Lacey and I didn't know what to make of it."

"What are you trying to say?" Nicci asked.

"You know what?" Sherry interrupted. "A shelf in my kitchen gave way and my entire collection of wine glasses slid out and smashed. I lost every single one of them. There was broken glass everywhere…"

"Do do do do, do do do do," Z chimed in with a suspenseful tune.

"I'm listening," Becca said with her eyes narrowed. "What does it *mean?*" she whispered.

Della Rae shook her head as if coming out of a trance. "Winslow's Rolex!"

"What?"

"Yeah, I was in the master bathroom putting my face on, when I thought I heard a thudding sound. I went to the bedroom, and his dresser caddy was upside down on the floor. Everything had spilled out, and the glass on his Rolex was broken. I had it repaired for him, of course, but I never thought 'til now how odd it was that it fell in the first place." The women shared glances. "Oh no," Della Rae said, her eyes wide. "It was right before…before I found out…about you know what. And now, those mugs." They looked at the floor by the counter still shiny from where the young man had mopped the finer shards away. "Maybe it's a warning?"

"Sounds ominous," Becca said.

"But like, warnings from where?" Candi asked.

"From Clara Tessa Berg," Jewell suggested. A little over a year ago, they had summoned the great dancer's spirit in a seance. "Maybe this is her way of looking out for us."

Nicci threw her arms in the air. "Here we go again."

"Wait," Z said. "Seana did tell us that Clara would watch over us."

"Well, let's keep each other updated," Becca said.

"I'm like, actually scared now," Candi said with her fist pressed to her mouth, already biting her nails.

"Well, you all have fun with your crazy talk," Nicci said, pushing herself up from the table. "Some of us have careers and practical matters to get back to."

"I guess I should wrap things up too. I have to be at work early tomorrow," Jewell said.

"Yeah, right." Becca nudged her with an elbow. "It doesn't have anything to do with a certain cowboy waiting for you at home, does it?"

"No, smarty." Jewell flung her hair back with a toss of her head. "He's meeting me outside to walk me home." The pair giggled.

"I really wish we'd made time to practice over the break," Becca said.

"Me too. How's your new romance by the way?"

"Great. I think this one might stick."

"Awesome," Jewell said, trying to sound sincere. Becca thought each one was *the one*, and they always broke her heart.

The group was breaking up now, each, in turn, hugging Della Rae and telling her to call if she needed anything.

Duty done, Jewell rushed outside to Kage.

"Get a room," Becca called, smirking as she watched them embrace.

"Jealous?" Jewell asked.

"Of course." Becca headed back to her car, which was parked by the studio. "Text me later."

Jewell and Kage strolled home hand in hand.

The couple had been spending most of their evenings and nights together. Little by little, Kage had hauled a sizable portion of his belongings to her house, to the point that she wondered if he had anything left at his own home. It had started with a toothbrush, then other toiletries had crept in, until what seemed like the majority of his clothes were hanging proudly in her closet. Not that Jewell minded. In fact, she could have been caught on occasion running her fingers down those tight jeans as they hung neatly on their hangers. She also smiled each time she passed the spare cowboy boots propped in the corner of her bedroom.

Jewell awoke early the next morning. *Aniela's website,* she thought. She glanced at her bedside clock. There was plenty of time before she had to leave, so she slid out of bed and lightly touched her feet to the floor to avoid waking Kage. Romeo's head sprang up as she did so, and she placed a finger over her mouth as if he understood the gesture.

Jewell and her lovable black standard poodle padded to the kitchen.

She fed Romeo two scoops of his meat-and-vegetable kibble, remembering when she first saw him as a fluffy little ball of black curls. He had been three-months old when she heard of his owners moving abroad and seeking a home for their precious pup. He'd been her perfect companion from that day on.

Next, she made herself coffee from the French press the way Becca had shown her. She congratulated herself on taking less sugar and cream these days thanks to brewing a quality cup of coffee.

She made her way to the desk in the living room and set her cup beside the computer, then opened the curtains to the back patio. The sun was casting a pink hue across the room, promising another beautiful summer day in Southbridge, FL.

She seated herself in front of the computer and raised her fingers to type the desired search terms. Without warning, memories came flooding back to her. The apartment back in Washington where she had spent all those lonely nights surfing the internet, as she was preparing to do now. Dreaming of a different life rather than living one had been her way back then, but her fantasies of escape had come to a screeching halt when she moved to Southbridge. She now lived in her dream home. She genuinely loved the people, work and play that made up her daily life. She planned to spend the rest of her life in this quaint and ancient Floridian town.

So why this sudden, fiery curiosity over Aniela and her studio? Could it mean that she was somehow unhappy, and didn't even realize it? She heard Kage shift in the bed and pictured his sleeping face, the muscles running down his exposed back. How could she possibly be unhappy?

It wasn't unhappiness driving her, she knew that. It was something else, something she couldn't quite put her finger on. That same uncanny feeling of *knowing* tingled under her skin, like back at Rhita's yesterday when the cups had smashed. She didn't have the words for what she was feeling, but sometimes even scientists have to accept that not everything can be explained.

She typed the URL listed on Aniela's business card. The screen filled with a photo of Aniela, standing poised with a candelabra balanced on her head. The flames from the candles glowed with real fire, illuminating her milky complexion and crystal blue eyes.

Jewell clicked the "About" tab and read. "Aniela Boch, owner of the Wild Rose Studio, Rosemore Heights, California." She perused the class schedule, noting that Aniela offered blocks of private lessons as well as group classes. A click of the "Hire a Bellydancer" button conveyed Aniela's availability for parties, corporate events and restaurants.

Finally, Jewell clicked on the "Gallery" tab and flipped through photos of Aniela's past performances. In some of the photos she used swords as props, in others the candelabra from the home page. She seemed to have mastery over a whole arsenal of talents: she danced with finger symbols, silk veils, tambourines and, to Jewell's surprise, canes.

Jewell drooled over Aniela's costumes in their vast array of colors. The panel skirt of an emerald green costume showcased her legs with slits cut to the top of both thighs. Green and ruby gems decorated the bedlah. A white costume hugged Aniela's hips with a belt encrusted in large, clear crystals and dangling beads. But Jewell's favorite, she decided, was a skirt painted to look like iridescent peacock-feathers that blazed like blue-green fire or the throat of a hummingbird. What appeared to be real peacock feathers jutted from the matching bedlah and a single, rich-purple broach bridged the center between them.

Jewell noticed a group photo. The title read: "Spring Hafla." In the photo, there among the costumed women, were two male bellydancers. Jewell felt a little embarrassed that she had never even thought about men bellydancing, and so ensued another internet search. *Although currently bellydance is predominantly a female art form, in the past this was not so. For example, in Egypt and Turkey men dominated in the ritual of dance and were permitted to perform for other males, which women often were not. Slowly, in Western society, males have returned to bellydance, but are considerably outnumbered by females.*

She delved further into the pages on Aniela's site, which boasted details about Southern California. With each scroll, Jewell's old feelings of wanderlust began to swell further, like waves when high tide floods the shore. Her pulse was pumping and her mind raced with thoughts of the unknown, of fresh adventure and discovery.

"Wine Country," she read aloud. "Experience the time of your life in our valley tucked far enough away to exude the charm of a small town, yet close enough to the city to provide you with a vibrant nightlife. Take guided tours through our fruitful wineries, bask on a sunny beach, or stroll through downtown enjoying our unique shops and eateries."

Jewell jolted in her seat as Kage touched her shoulder.

"What are you doing, babe? I woke up and you weren't there."

Jewell turned to see him pouting.

"I woke up early. I wanted to look something up."

"Cool. Need more coffee?"

"Yes, please." She almost added, "if you're buying," but thought better of it. After all, that was Josh's line. Kage picked up Jewell's cup from the desk and walked to the French press on the counter.

"Do I need to make anything for your mother's picnic this weekend?"

Kage raised his eyebrows. "You're kidding, right? You've seen the spread Mom and Nona come up with."

"Yeah, I just thought I'd be polite. Plus, there's my culinary expertise." She chuckled. "Well, I better get ready for work."

"Yeah, me too," Kage joked. He was already dressed in his daily work outfit of cowboy hat, T-shirt, tight jeans and boots. Jewell caught herself as her gaze lingered for what she thought might be too long on the tight creases of his pants.

Kage had been leaving Jewell's house each morning to work on the family farm. He told her his father had fussed at first about how late

Kage had been arriving, but that he liked Jewell so he let it go.

It was a bright day. No clouds to be seen, so Jewell drove to the hospital research center in the Beetle with the convertible top down, her blonde locks flying. For the most part, she enjoyed being back to the basics of science. Her management position back at Oliver & Timpleton had buried her in mounds of paperwork and taken her away from true research, so she had enthusiastically hung her hopes and dreams on this new project for the time being.

Although, if she were completely honest with herself, the fulfillment she had sought wasn't materializing yet. The noble gesture of taking this lower position had been, in part, an attempt to get closer to finding a cure for addiction. Now the whole process seemed so daunting, it left her feeling a bit hopeless. No cure seemed even remotely near.

At least her friendship with Lacey, a fellow researcher, was growing. Theirs was a healthy friendship, bearing no resemblance to the negativity she had encountered with Erin back at the Washington lab.

Jewell and Lacey didn't spend much time together outside of work, other than the occasional shopping excursion. Lacey was a makeup master, willing to share her magic with Jewell whenever she asked. She had Lacey to thank for her new smokey-eyed look that drove Kage crazy.

The two coworkers occasionally met up at lunchtime and talked about their relationships and hobbies, a far cry from the catty lunches with Erin. Jewell's entire life had taken a positive trajectory after recovering from Josh's death and Nathanael's blackmailing. She had learned to foster close relationships by opening up to others and sharing more of herself.

Jewell was barely settled into her office that morning before Lacey's head popped into the doorframe.

"Hey, how about lunch today?"

"Sure. In or out?"

"In. I'm still sifting through emails. You?"

"Same here." Jewell made a motion like she was wrapping a noose around her neck and pulling it.

Lacey chuckled. "Meet you here at noon?"

"Okay," Jewell answered. "See you later."

"You should have seen how she moved with the swords balanced on her head." Jewell was eagerly recounting Aniela's dance to Lacey as they ate in the hospital cafeteria. "Then she dropped to her knees and snatched the swords as they were falling! I don't know how that woman has kept all her fingers."

"I've never seen anything like that," Lacey said.

"I can't get it out of my head. This morning, I even woke up early with my mind full of it. I've spent hours already exploring Southern California online. That's where she's based. Just reading about it gives me itchy feet, there's so much to do out there."

"There is. My whole family went on a Wine Country tour from Oregon to Southern California. You should do the tour." She paused, her sandwich almost touching her lips. "Wait a minute." She laid the sandwich back on her plate. "You're not thinking of moving out there, are you?"

"Gosh no, I love it here. But maybe a trip. I've been to Oregon, but never California."

"I think you should go. There's great hiking. Lots of outdoor stuff to do. And of course, the wine. Why don't you go with Kage?"

"That's an idea. How long was your trip?"

"Two weeks."

"Perfect."

Jewell's mind was made up. She was also going to seize the opportunity for a couple private lessons with Aniela while she was out there.

Jewell found it difficult to concentrate for the rest of the day. Her escalating boredom was intensified by the fantasy of a trip shifting to a more practical form in her head. She could already taste the freedom and adventure. She told herself to focus. The purpose of the Bernstein & Beck Center for Addiction was to find a cure for alcohol and drug addiction. She had always longed to work towards a goal like this. To cure all substance abuses, especially in young mothers. If she worked hard enough, perhaps she would be one of the few people in the whole world to break the curse that caused people like her own mother to abandon their children.

She carried few memories of her mother with her. She remembered her dark hair and her smile. She remembered the feeling of being loved. She had asked a psychiatric professor from one of her required courses why, with an IQ of 160 and a photographic memory, she retained so few memories of her mother. Jewell had been around three years of age when her mother left, surely she ought to have a more detailed recollection of her. The professor told her that trauma can affect memory formation deeply, and theorized that the pain caused by her mother leaving had made her instinctively repress memories of that time, even the good ones.

Anything she knew about her mother, Lydia, had come from others. She had heard little about her father and remembered even less. Once she had begun to open up and share the facts of her past with people, her friends asked why she had never searched for her mother. She certainly had the means. She told them she had no desire to locate a woman who could walk out on her own three-year-old daughter and six-year-old son. Besides, if her mother truly drank the way the stories were told, she may have passed away years ago.

Two

Chapter 2

J ewell rummaged through every pastel and floral article of clothing strewn across her bed. She had ransacked her closet earlier searching for the perfect summer-picnic ensemble. Kage had left earlier that Sunday to help his family prepare the farm for his mother's event. Matriarch Liz was well known for her standards when it came to such festivities.

Jewell propped her cell phone on a pillow so she could watch her favorite videos as she dressed for the occasion ahead. Sure, her daydreams about California were now bordering on obsession, but she couldn't help herself. She filled her spare time with watching tours through Wine Country and discovering new bellydance instructors from other regions.

Officially, the area known as Wine Country covered several states, but the Southern California region resonated with Jewell far above the rest. She viewed countless videos about Aniela's location, which held a whopping population of 65,000. Perhaps it was the depiction of the small town's community feel and historical value that had hooked

Jewell, or the never ending array of activities and festivals that seemed to be offered. Whatever the reason, her thoughts dwelled on canvassing the area and learning some of Aniela's bellydance specialties.

"I'm not ready yet," she yelled as Kage's spare key twisted and opened the front door.

"No problem. Take your time." She heard the click of Kage's footsteps coming towards the bedroom, and turned to see him leaning in the doorway. "Whoa, I think you should go like that."

Jewell was standing in her panties and bra, her long blonde ringlets dangling to her waist. She continued to marvel over the sleek muscles she had developed over her otherwise slender body, thanks to the dancing and negotiating the cobblestone streets downtown.

"Ha, ha. Very funny."

She pulled on blue jean cut-off shorts and a pink-and-white floral blouse. She topped it off by tying a white scarf around her neck to pick up the white in the floral print. Now she just had to find her white sunglasses.

"Perfect," Kage said, still staring.

She snatched a light blue printed scarf and knelt next to Romeo. He stuck his snout next to her ear and sniffed, the tickle making her giggle with goosebumps. She tied the scarf around his curly black neck.

"Now it's perfect."

A trail of cars streamed the drive towards the main house as Kage's father, brother and uncle directed the drivers to designated spots in the field.

"Wow, your mom really does go big."

"Told you," Kage answered, resting his arm on the open window of his truck. "She invites about half the town."

"Only half?"

Mimicking the motions of airport ground control, Kage's brother,Hayden, was attempting to direct Kage to park his truck in the field with the rest of the guests.

Kage leaned out of the trunk window. "Very funny, you should've been a comedian."

He spun his truck tires, kicking up dust before his brother could fling a comeback. Then he turned into the family parking area in front of the house.

Once they had parked, Kage took Jewell's hand as they navigated the route through the house towards the backyard, Romeo trailing behind to sniff at every opportunity. Liz was standing at the kitchen counter with her mother-in-law, filling trays with food.

"I got it, Mom," Kage said as he picked up a tray holding various chips and dips. He kissed her on the cheek, then spun on his heels to kiss his grandmother.

"Don't drop anything," his grandmother snapped.

"Hi," Jewell said, with a girlish wave to Liz and Kage's Nona.

"Hi, dear," Liz said. "We'll catch up when things settle down."

The lawn was bursting with strangers. Jewell's newly honed confidence in social settings applied to small groups, nothing on this scale.

"Should I have brought Romeo's leash?" she asked anxiously.

"Nah, let him run."

Jewell kept watch for Becca, who had texted earlier that she was coming. She indicated she'd be bringing her new beau, Max, or Mac. Something like that.

"Jewell, this is my second-grade teacher, Mrs. Randolf," Kage said.

You've got to be frigging kidding me, ran through her mind, but instead, she said, "It's nice to meet you."

Then Kage proceeded to introduce her to an entire constellation from his past. Previous football coaches, teammates, and fellow boy scouts, to name a few. Jewell found it difficult to relate to Kage's life where his family surrounds itself with people they have known since birth. The concept was foreign to Jewell who never stayed in touch with any of her teachers, classmates or foster families, not even the Thompsons who were so good to her.

Jewell panicked under the intensity of the introductions, but she managed to respond calmly each time. "It's nice to meet you too."

She breathed a sigh of relief when she saw Becca arriving with a man she didn't recognize. Her friend had even brought her standard poodles Genevieve and Perci along, who were clearly growing by the day. Romeo caught scent of them and dashed over. The three dogs romped joyfully through the yard. Genevieve and Perci could hold their own now with Romeo. Perci's bark had become deep, and Genevieve's white coat was brighter than ripened cotton.

"Hey," Jewell said as she rushed over to Becca and her new boyfriend. "You have no idea how happy I am to see you."

"Jewell, this is Max."

Max, that's right, Jewell thought.

"I've heard a lot about you, Jewell."

"Same here."

She tried to study his six-foot-plus frame without being too obvious. He had combed-back, dishwater-blonde hair which contrasted interestingly with his dark stubble. Not Becca's usual type. He looked intelligent, well educated. Maybe it was the dark glasses. Or his clothes: he was wearing shorts with a belt and a short-sleeved, buttoned shirt that had been sharply pressed. *What did Becca say he did for a living?* Jewell didn't mean to only half-listen to Becca's ramblings about her boyfriends, but after a while they had all blended and jumbled in her mind.

25

The three of them made their way towards Kage, who had been assigned grill duty next to his grandfather until his father was finished arranging the parking.

"Sorry, I've forgotten some of the things Becca's told me," Jewell confessed to Max. "What do you do again?"

"I'm an analyst with J&S Marketing."

"Wow, that sounds interesting."

"Only to a scientist," he quipped. They all laughed.

Becca pulled a bottle from her oversized bag. "I brought wine." She checked around. "Is it allowed?"

"Of course, there's also a beer cooler over by the stairs." Jewell gestured in the relevant direction.

They reached the grill, where Jewell introduced Max to Kage and his grandfather. The joy was clear on Becca's face as the men exchanged pleasantries.

When Kage was relieved of his grilling duties, the two couples found a vacant table under one of the trees. Jewell was quick to fill water bowls for Romeo, Perci and Genevieve. The sun had become scorching.

"I only have plastic cups for the wine," Becca confessed.

"That's fine with me," Jewell said.

"How about a beer for you, Max?" Kage offered.

"Yes, please."

"I'll be right back."

There was a pleasant breeze under the trees despite the Florida heat. Jewell inhaled deeply and released the breath, purging any thoughts other than being in the moment, right there, right then. She sipped Becca's wine and dreamed of this beautiful snapshot of life being something that would carry on throughout the rest of her life. Her and Kage there on the farm, Becca and her beau, and their pets.

She watched her best friend as she entertained the group. Becca was an exceptionally beautiful young woman with thick brown hair that she had a habit of twisting into precarious buns only to free her locks again so they could swing with her every move. And Becca was always on the move. Jewell had been so strongly drawn to her when they first met and figured it had something to do with just how different they were. Becca possessed a child-like spirit Jewell had always longed to experience herself.

The hours passed pleasantly. Food, drink and conversations were interrupted by the occasional game of cornhole and badminton. However, Jewell's inquisitive mind could not help but eventually drift back to Aniela's business card. Taking time out from one of the games, she pulled it from her backpack while Kage, Max and Becca continued to play. Surely Kage would enjoy traveling through Wine Country and find ways to amuse himself while Jewell took a few private lessons from Aniela. Maybe Becca and Max could go with them, show all their dogs some amazing new scenery to run in.

Her thoughts began to escalate, as they often did. A couple of lessons from Aniela hardly seemed enough. What about a month there, or even a few months? Aniela knew so much that Jewell wanted to learn. Not to think of all the other instructors throughout the country, who no doubt would have further specialties of their own. Those years holed up in Washington had prevented her from traveling even within her own country. A tour, that's what she needed. A tour through the country. Then maybe her spirit would be satisfied for a while.

With adrenaline pumping, she slid her phone from the pocket of her backpack and entered a search for bellydance instructors in the U.S.

Kage returned to the table with a smile. "What are you looking at there?"

"Oh, nothing." She slid her phone back into her bag.

"I really like Max," Jewell said as she hugged Becca goodbye.

"Me too." Becca winked.

Jewell helped with the cleanup as quickly as possible so she and Kage could get back to her place.

"How's your job going, honey?" Liz asked.

"Oh, it's fine. Nothing exciting."

"Why don't you stop by one weekend? We'll have coffee or lunch while the guys are out in the field."

"Okay. That sounds nice."

Once the farmhouse was back in order, Kage and Jewell said their goodbyes.

When they finally made it to her house, she threw her things onto the kitchen island and made a beeline for her computer.

"Aren't you coming to bed?" Kage asked.

"No, not yet. You go ahead."

"Do we need to walk Romeo?"

"I will, don't worry. I just need to get a little research done."

He came up behind her desk chair and wrapped his arms around her. "I'll watch TV in the bedroom then. Let me know when you're ready and I'll walk with you."

"Okay," she said, watching the screen load in front of her.

With Kage in the other room, she entered a fresh search for bellydance instructors in the U.S. Maybe she could spend two months with each instructor, taking private lessons. That should allow enough time both to learn their specialty and explore the local towns. Her stomach fluttered and her skin tingled. She lost herself in virtual tours and bellydance videos for hours, but by the end she had plotted a solid course for her first two stops.

The first was Southern California, obviously, to learn the skills of props and restaurant dancing from Aniela. She sent Aniela an email enquiring after her available dates for two months of private lessons.

28

She also asked about accommodations in the area.

The choice for her second stop became obvious when she was unable to move past the location's description. Jaded Springs. A town nestled deep in the Blue Ridge Mountains of North Carolina. The pictures alone were breathtaking, not to mention the further descriptions of how the town was known for its architectural legacy and how art galleries dominated the scene. The area itself was intriguing enough, but the residents were perhaps the biggest draw of all, hippies lost in a new age.

She stumbled upon an instructor of Tribal Fusion Style. The style was apparently a combination of both tribal and fusion with the tribal portion consisting of group improvisation and the fusion portion consisting of choreographed performances. The costumes in the instructor's pictures were imaginative and unusual, spanning a wide variety of styles and colors from a little dark and mysterious with a circus-like vibe to a sleek and sexy cabaret fashion. Jewell liked the sounds of the tribal improv style where a troupe of dancers all share the same dance vocabulary of moves and how they rely upon one another to influence the course of the performance. A leader provides cues for each move and the flow remains interesting as the roles of leader and follower switch from dancer to dancer throughout the performance.

Jewell clicked on one of the provided videos showcasing the tribal improvisation. She sat back, hypnotized by the synchronized movements. She marveled over the heavily jeweled dancers in their clunky bracelets and necklaces moving as one. Their full skirts flared with each twist, reminding Jewell of vibrant spinning tops.

All this new information swirled in her head, causing her to scheme. If she stayed in Southern California for two months, Jaded Springs for another two, that would place her back in Southbridge before the holiday season. Then she could choose two more locations to set out for in January.

Bubbling with enthusiasm, she rushed to the bedroom to fill Kage in on her plans and take Romeo out for his nightly walk. Her bounding came to a halt when she found Kage sound asleep, Romeo also dozing in his bed. She turned to tiptoe out when she heard Kage stir.

"Hey. What time is it?"

"I don't know." She looked at the bedside clock, which read 12:30 A.M. "Oh gosh, I didn't know I was at it for that long."

"Yeah, I couldn't keep my eyes open anymore." He rolled onto his back and stretched. "What were you doing?"

She plopped onto the bed and angled her pillows so she could sit next to him. She launched into her plan with such enthusiasm that there was little attention to spare for watching Kage's reaction.

When she finished, he got out of bed and stepped a leg into his jeans.

Her heart sank at his action. Most of all, she was confused. "What are you doing? Where are you going?"

"Home." He finished dressing.

"Why?"

"I can't believe you have to ask. If you're not staying here, then I don't have a girlfriend."

"But I'll be back in four months after this first part of the trip."

"I don't care. The point is, you're leaving. Apparently, I'm not enough for you."

"Look, I was trapped in that same small town my entire life. Last year was the first time I finally got a taste of freedom, a chance to explore somewhere new. Can't you understand how freeing that was? I finally got to know myself a bit. My interests, my desires. Don't you think we have the right to have more adventures while we're still young? It's not like we've got—" She stopped herself just short of saying *children*. That was something she hadn't even let herself contemplate.

"I've lived in the same town my entire life too," Kage snapped. "I don't feel trapped. I have everything I need right here, and I thought you and Romeo were a big part of it."

She was having difficulty processing Kage's anger. "We are. And I have no intention of—"

He was already filling his gym bag with clothes and other belongings.

"You can come with me," she stammered, tears forming in her eyes. "I was hoping you would want to. Or you can meet up with me along the way. And if you don't, or can't, I'll still be back before Christmas."

"I told you, I don't do long distance. I told you that on our first date."

"But it wouldn't be a long-distance relationship. I live here. I'm just taking a trip."

"Yeah, quite the trip. It's not like you're going away for a long weekend. And whatever made you think I could go with you? I have responsibilities here. So do you. What about your job?"

Jewell's heart sank with the reality of what her plan was going to cost. It's not like Bernstein & Beck would give her a sabbatical after barely a year of working there. "I'll need to quit."

"Do you hear how crazy you're sounding? I thought you were a genius." Kage zipped his gym bag shut and headed for the front door.

She followed behind him, unable to hold back the tears. Romeo followed close behind, his brow pinched with concern.

"I'm sorry if I've upset you. But can't you try to understand that this is something I need to do? That it's not about you or this town not being enough, it's about something much bigger than that."

Kage turned around sharply. "Do you wanna know what I think?"

"What?"

"I think you're running away from your past. I think you need to forgive yourself and everyone else in your past, once and for all. Then you can start living a real life."

"This is a real life. Exploring other places and having new experiences is living. Not staring at the same four walls."

His expression was hard to read in the shadow of the doorway, but

31

the arc of his shoulders relaxed. His voice sounded hollow. "Goodbye, Jewell. I want you to be happy, really. But you'll never find peace running away like this." He turned to leave. "I'll have Hayden stop by for the rest of my stuff."

She followed him to the door. "Why are you being like this? I make one suggestion and you throw down the towel on our whole relationship?"

He flung his bag into the truck and climbed in without another word.

Jewell held onto the doorway as she watched him drive away. The same doorway he had one day, not so long ago, nervously peeled the paint from while working up the nerve to kiss her.

The desire to contact Becca overwhelmed her, but she was afraid of waking her friend, particularly when she seemed so happy right now. She consoled herself with a plan to call her early the next morning. She had to get to bed. There was no point being even more tired for work. Maybe Kage was right. Maybe she was crazy. She told herself she would re-evaluate the plan in the morning.

A heaviness came over her as she lay awake, contemplating the possibility of giving up on her travel dreams.

After a sleepless night, Jewell plodded to the kitchen for coffee. She brewed it in her old pot this time, for the excuse of adding sugar and cream. She hadn't been keeping fresh creamer on hand, so she reached for the backup of pre-packaged flavored creamers. She didn't want to think about how those creamers somehow stayed safe for consumption stored in cabinets for ages. It defied all scientific logic.

While the coffee brewed, she texted Becca.

You up?

Yep. What's up? You don't usually text this early.
Kage broke up with me last night.
OMG, what? I'm coming over. Right now.

Becca arrived while Jewell was dressing for work. "I came as fast as I could." She was breathing hard. "Will you be late for work?"

"I'm not sure it matters," Jewell said despondently. "I'm going to hand in my resignation today. I'll work—"

"What are you talking about?"

"I'll work a little longer if they ask me to." Jewell felt detached from her body. "Let's sit down."

Jewell made Becca a matching coffee and they went out to the back patio like in the old days. It dawned on Jewell how they had drifted apart over the break from class, what with her wrapped up in Kage and Becca with her string of romances, landing on Max. She had missed their talks.

She laid out her entire plan to Becca and explained Kage's reaction. Becca sat quietly, allowing Jewell to run through her plan in detail, occasionally leaning in closer and nodding.

When Jewell finished, she braced herself for Becca's reaction.

"I'm proud of you," Becca said, shocking Jewell. "I admire you for knowing what you want. Gosh, you're so brave. So many people don't go after what they want and end up regretting it on their deathbed."

Jewell jumped to her feet and hugged Becca fiercely, tears suddenly spilling out of her eyes onto Becca's wavy brown hair. "Thanks for being so supportive. Kage was so convinced I was crazy it was hard not to believe him. I figured everyone else would feel the same."

"I've known Kage pretty much all of my life. He's a country boy.

He has his way of thinking and it doesn't include exploring anywhere further than his own barn and fields. There's nothing wrong with it, but you're different. Give him some time to process. I have a feeling he'll be here for you when you return. "

Jewell was back in her chair, listening intently as she sipped her coffee. She smiled at Becca, feeling calmer thanks to her encouraging words. "When did you get so wise?"

"Actually, there's something I've been wanting to tell you. I know how it feels, being afraid someone will think your dreams are crazy." She cleared her throat. "I want to go to college and train to be a psychologist."

"Ah, Becca that's fabulous. You're such a caring, warm person. I'm sure your patients will love you."

"Really? It's a long way from being a barista and working in the campus bookstore, although…that's where I got the idea. Students my age tell me it's not so hard to go back."

"You'll be great," Jewell assured her. "College is a whole different ball game if you study something that inspires you."

"Plus, if I stay on at the bookstore," Becca continued, "I'll get a discount on tuition and be able to scout out the used books as soon as they come in."

"I'm so happy for you." Jewell jumped up to hug her again.

"You know what?" Jewell said. "You should come with me for the first stop on the trip. That way you can get a last bit of fun in before your classes start."

"I know, but I have to stay on at the bookstore. Plus, I like how things are going with Max."

Jewell tried not to let her shoulders slump.

"Besides, this is your adventure," Becca insisted. "I'm so excited for you."

"I guess I'd better get over to the hospital to drop the bomb."

On her way out the door, she plucked up the courage to text Kage.

I hate how we left things. Let's at least sit down and discuss it calmly. You mean too much to me for it to be over just like that.

Jewell filled Lacey in on her plans.

"I can't believe you're leaving," Lacey said with a pout. "You just got here."

"I know, but we can stay in touch. I'll let you know how I'm doing."

"You'd better be posting every second of every day. I've got to live vicariously through you now."

"I'll post across every platform I can think of. You'll be sick of me in no time."

"How did our 'boss of the year' take it?"

"She wasn't as upset as I thought she'd be."

"Good. You don't need the money anyway. Live your life. I sure would. Oh, and the stuff too juicy to post online, send it to me privately." Lacey winked.

For the first time ever, Jewell left a place of employment with more than one box. Here, she had settled in and decorated her space. It made leaving bitter-sweet, but she was looking forward, not back.

On Wednesday night, the class buzzed from Jewell's news.

"How exciting. I'm so jealous," Della Rae said.

"Why?" Nicci snorted. "You're free to travel too." Then Jewell overheard Nicci whisper to Candi, "I've never met such an irresponsible bunch of people."

"No, I can't galavant about," Della Rae said. "Not with the twins coming home."

"Aren't they in college?" Nicci asked.

"They still need their mama. Why, I still need my mama."

"Tell us about your plans," Z said eagerly.

"Y'all need to do that over coffee," Maggie chimed in. "Let's get started." She walked next to Jewell, leaned in and said, "Good for you."

"I don't see why we're celebrating," Nicci grumbled. "We're going to be down to seven. Eight was a nice even number."

"It's not forever," Jewell tried to reassure her. "I'm coming back."

"Enough." Maggie clicked the remote to start the music. "Let's warm up, then go grab your veils."

Jewell was almost sad she would be leaving the group for a while, especially now that they were moving on to silk veils, the sensuous fabrics after which Maggie had named her studio. She had sent a group email during the first week of their break, instructing them each to purchase and bring a silk veil with them when the new sessions began. There were useful links as well, detailing suitable retailers and ideal dimensions. They hadn't gotten around to veil work last week because of Aniela's visit.

After their usual warm-ups to drum rhythms, Maggie instructed them to grab their veils and face the mirror.

"Get into a straight line now," Maggie nudged them. "What on God's green earth is that?"

"What?" Z asked. "It's my veil."

"But what's that on it?"

"It's Steampunk. Hand screen-printed. Look, it's got feathers, gears, oh and masks." Z held up the veil's repeat designs proudly. Jewell suppressed a giggle, hoping her friend would stop before Maggie unleashed her full wrath on her. "See, the gears match my tattoo.

One gear is Miranda, and this intersecting one is me."

"As I was saying," Maggie continued with the air of a frustrated elementary school teacher. "Wait, was I saying anything yet?" She inspected their lineup. "Now, to start with, get used to running your veil through your hands, especially your fingers." They experimented with the veils. Shaking them out and whipping them through their hands. "Feel the lightness, and how it flows when you raise it over your head. Let it flow down naturally. That's why—" Maggie stopped, distracted by Della Rae struggling to untangle her veil from her big hair. "As I was saying, that's why I wanted you to get silk. For the flow. Della Rae, I'll be showing y'all how to exaggerate your arm movements so that you can sweep it over your head like so." She drew her own veil over her head in a single, graceful movement, making the ripple look like water. "Think about it, many dancers have headdresses on and they can dance with a veil. It comes with time. Nothing to worry about tonight."

"So, what I want you to do now is take the corners of the short ends and bring the veil behind you." Maggie demonstrated. "Now wrap it around your shoulders like a cape." She waited as they all copied her. "Very good. Now arrange the veil so the ends are even on both sides, then straighten your arms parallel to your body. Now, with your hands at your sides, reach for the lowest point of the veil that you can naturally touch. Place the silk between your middle and index fingers, and secure the hold with your thumb. It takes practice to get your fingers flexible. That's it. Now open your arms parallel to the floor, like you're going to fly. Great start."

The class continued with basic overhead moves and arm swirls. Maggie showed them how to hold the veil above their heads while spinning, then at waist level, providing a distinctly different effect. Jewell loved the feel of working with the silk and hated the moment class came to an end.

An excited buzz carried through the group as they walked to Rhita's. Gabby called Kevin to plead her argument for staying out with the women. He conceded, but added a warning that he couldn't make any promises about the shape the kids would have him in when she returned.

As usual, Candi walked with Nicci at the front. She turned back with a dramatic expression on her face. "Jewell, don't spill one detail, like, not one. Not until we get to Rhita's," Candi pleaded.

Jewell smiled. "I promise."

They gathered around their table and the focus turned fiercely to Jewell.

"Okay, now spill the goods," Z demanded.

Jewell filled them in on her plans. Candi held her gaze throughout, elbows on the table and face propped on her fists, like a child intent on soaking up every last detail of a fireside story.

"I'm going to visit you," Becca said.

"I would love that," Jewell said.

"I mean it. Mom and I looked up flights last night. I have a short break from the bookstore scheduled before my classes start."

"I'd like to visit you on one of your stops too," Della Rae said.

"I so wish I could come visit," Candi chimed in. "I mean, I'll never get to do anything like that or whatever." She and Tom had been together for about as long as Jewell and Kage. Jewell wondered whether Tom was equally unadventurous as her boy— She caught her thoughts just in time. Ex-boyfriend.

"Let us know when you get to Jaded Springs," Z said. "Miranda and I could be with you in about an eight-hour drive."

"Aw, I hope you all come," Jewell said. "I am going to miss every one of you so much."

"Hey," Candi announced. "Pics or it didn't happen."

"You'll be so busy, you won't even think of us," Gabby said. "When are you leaving?"

"Sunday. And, you're wrong. I'll think of you all every day. Candi, I promise to post daily."

"You better," Gabby said. "That's the only life I'm going to have for a while."

"Yeah," Candi instructed, "like post your meals, what you're wearing, your struggles, what Romeo is doing. Oh, and it's, like, mandatory for you to do a video recap of like your whole day each night."

"I don't know about that, Candi," Jewell hesitated.

"OMG, like, do it on your pillow," Candi continued. "You know, you can spread your hair out all over the bed. I can show you how to use the best video filters right now, if you'd like." She was already scrambling to pull her phone from her bag.

"We'll see," Jewell said, politely waving away the offer for now.

"Wait," Della Rae said. "Do you mean your leaving this Sunday?"

"Yes."

"Lordy, I was planning a bon voyage party for you. Guess I'll need to move it up to Friday." Della Rae chuckled. "You're still going to be here Friday, aren't you?"

"Yes, I'll be here Friday."

Becca whimpered.

"Alright everyone, 8 P.M. at my house, Friday. I'll text Maggie."

Jewell left Rhita's with Becca at her side.

"Did you ever hear back from Kage?"

Jewell frowned. "No, not a word."

"Are you alright? I know you're not exactly used to sleeping alone these days."

"No, I'm not. But I have Romeo. That's more than most people."

"Good old Romeo, you can definitely count on him. Speaking of him, will he be able to make all your trips with you? If not, I'm happy to have him while you travel." Becca put her hands together for a tiny clap. "Genevieve and Perci would love it."

Jewell laughed. "Sorry, Becca. You know I'd never go anywhere without him. I'll make whatever adjustments are necessary to ensure he can come with me. Even if it means missing out on some places."

"Yeah, I figured as much. It would've been fun though." Becca became thoughtful. "You know, I could talk to Kage for you."

"No, I want him to come around on his own, or not at all."

"I can tell you one thing. When Hope decided to go to New York to further her career, he cut her out of his life so fast it was like a guillotine coming down. But he's different with you. His reaction might have been harsh, but I think he'll soften in time."

Jewell straightened her shoulders. "Maybe I don't want to wait for him to come around, as if I need to earn his permission or trust or whatever. If he's so bent out of shape over a trip, one that I said from the start would be temporary and finite, maybe he's not the one for me."

That Friday, Jewell picked up Becca and drove to the party Della Rae had arranged in her honor.

Della Rae thrust open her gargantuan front doors with a pitcher in hand, proudly announcing that, *this time*, the pitcher wasn't full of sweet tea.

"Margaritas, my darlings. Everyone is out back by the pool. Car keys or fobs, please." Della Rae held out a basket rattling with other keys and fobs. Jewell worked the car key off her ring and deposited it as commanded.

"I hired a limo to take y'all home and then turn around and pick y'all back up tomorrow at 11 A.M. Gives me an excuse to make brunch for everyone too. You can retrieve your cars in the morning, or you're most welcome to stay here tonight." She swept her arm around the twenty-by-thirty marble foyer. Jewell gazed up the expansive staircase leading to probably countless bedrooms.

Jewell and Becca followed Della Rae outside, where she poured them generous margaritas in cocktail glasses with long twisting stems and, of course, salt powdered around the rims. It seemed they were the last to arrive, even Gabby beat them there.

It took a while for Jewell to soak up the elaborate setting Della Rae had arranged. Festive beach music blasted, floods of bright pastel balloons floated about and pink swan-shaped floaters drifted serenely on the pool. Streamers in colors matching the balloons hung from chains of lights and wafted in the soft breeze. The tables, draped in pink-and-white checkered cloths, held pineapples at each place setting, and inflatable pool rings, designed to look like giant donuts, hung on the back of each chair. On the center table, a tall cake dripping in pastel icing sat in pride of place.

"My goodness," Jewell breathed. "Della Rae, thank you so much."

"My pleasure," Della Rae purred. "Why for me, this is like sliding off a greasy log backward."

"Are you all set for your adventure of a lifetime?" Maggie asked Jewell as she sat down on one of the pool recliners.

"I am. I'm packed and, I don't know… a little anxious?"

"I'll bet," Maggie said. "I've visited Aniela myself. Her classes are tough, and you'll be her sole focus in the private lessons. Make sure you attend some of her dance gigs as well. She's impressive."

"Thanks."

"Of course. But you know what above all?" Maggie asked.

"What?"

"Have fun. Cheers." Maggie clinked her glass to Jewell's.

The others yelled around them and lifted their own glasses. "Cheers!" A tear formed in the corner of Jewell's eye.

"Wait," Z said. "In honor of Clara Tessa Berg, our eternal spiritual patron, we should also toast in Dutch. Repeat after me, and make sure you look each other in the eye. Proost!"

They all giggled and rotated from one friend to another as the Dutch cheers drifted upward into the darkening sky.

As the night progressed, the margaritas went down and the music went up. It was a feat that no one's enthusiastic dancing had landed them in the pool yet. Jewell had thought the generous snacks Della Rae had set throughout the patio would constitute the food for the evening, until waiters from San Sebastian's began carrying out covered trays of assorted salads, tapas and desserts.

As the group's energy began to wane, they sat down in pairs around the beautifully set tables. Jewell selected a seat next to Candi, taking advantage of a rare opportunity for a one-on-one with her. Candi told her how happy she was with Tom, although she was as surprised as everyone else about it. She admitted Tom was far from her typical type, but she was more content with him than she ever dreamed possible.

Later the group took to dancing again. Z and Sherry were the last two dancing, until Z stumbled onto a chair. "I'm out."

Sherry slurred at her. "Not yet. You can't quit now. QUITTER. All you sons-a-bitches. Quitters." She staggered erratically as she pointed around the patio, sloshing the drink in her hand. No one had noticed how much she'd been drinking until now. It gave Jewell a tight discomfort in her stomach, seeing her friend lose control like that. She rose to make sure Sherry didn't hurt herself, but Z was already on it.

Z approached Sherry, telling her to come sit down with her. Sherry flung her arm away from Z's reach, toppling backwards from the momentum and hitting her head on the patio. Gasps and screams collided with the music as everyone rushed to help her up. Della Rae fetched ice for the back of her head. Sherry was coherent, but far too intoxicated to be left on her own.

"Maybe we should take her to the hospital," Becca suggested.

"I'm not going to any damn hospital," Sherry protested.

"We'll handle it," Z said. "Miranda and I will take her home and stay with her 'til tomorrow."

Once the drama settled, Jewell asked for the limo to be summoned. She was surprisingly relieved to be back at her own front door. She fiddled with the key, then let the door swing open. An envelope on the floor caught her attention. It appeared to have been slid under the door.

Romeo nudged her for his nightly walk as she bent to pick it up.

"Hold on, Romeo. Let me see what this is."

She flicked on the light and tore open the envelope.

Jewell, I also hate how things ended. I know I've kept myself scarce, but that's the only way I can handle this. If I see you in person, I'll cave in, which will do no one any good. We want two different things. I don't blame you for wanting to venture out, but it's not something I want or need. I'm better suited with a girl who loves her home and is content to be with her friends and family. I wish you the best and I hope you wish me the same. No hard feelings, Kage.

"Ha, no hard feelings. Wanna bet? Come on Romeo, let's go."

Three

Chapter 3

J ewell secured Romeo in his car carrier in the back seat and then threw her suitcases in the trunk. She drove off, watching the little yellow house, the one she had become so accustomed to calling home, get smaller and smaller in her rear-view mirror. She couldn't bear to lose the house, so she had decided to keep up the rental payments and have the property manager check on it regularly. A contractor would maintain the lawn.

She pulled into the Steals' circular drive. Becca opened the garage door and Jewell drove Iris in. Becca had insisted on giving the Beetle bug a name, and together they had landed on "Iris," while sitting on the back patio admiring the flourishing blooms. A few weeks later, Becca had bought magnetic decals of purple Irises for the doors. They made Jewell smile at Becca's eccentricity every time she saw them.

She tossed Becca the keys. "Thanks for keeping Iris here. I'll feel better knowing she's not exposed at the airport or in front of the house for eight months straight."

"Think nothing of it," Lynn said, stepping out through the front door.

She helped Jewell and Becca transfer the luggage into the trunk of the Lincoln.

"Mom and I will stay with you until you go through security," Becca said.

"I appreciate it." Jewell wrapped her arms around her friend.

"Don't be making me cry now," Lynn said as she got in on the hug.

Jewell transferred Romeo's carrier to the back seat and guided him into it, then climbed in on the other side. Lynn was poised to drive the one-hour trip to the airport and Becca sat in the passenger seat. She passed Becca the card Kage had left for her and watched her read it.

"Jeez, he's standing firm, isn't he?"

Jewell nodded her head.

"What's that?" Lynn asked.

"Go ahead," Jewell said to Becca, who then read it aloud to Lynn.

"Oh my," Lynn said. "Well, I'm sure he'll come around when you get back. Or he may even reach out to you while you're gone. It's amazing what time and distance can do to the heart."

"Why does everyone think I'm dying to have him back? Sure, he's kind, and attentive, and fun, and probably the best looking guy I'm ever going to meet. But he's not flexible, not unless things go absolutely according to his way of thinking, and he can't put himself into someone else's shoes. I'm not sure if I want to be with someone like that."

"Good point," Becca said, widening her eyes at Lynn.

Her mother changed the subject. "Do you think you'll go back to Bernstein & Beck when you're home again?"

"I don't know yet. I need to think about what I want to do with the rest of my life. The sky's the limit I suppose."

Jewell's long flight finally landed in San Diego in the late afternoon. She rented a VW Beetle for her two-month stay in California, choosing a happy-looking yellow model she hoped would match her mood throughout the trip. Becca had also given her smiling faces and peace sign decals to slap on it for good luck.

The route from San Diego to Rosemore Heights, the sleepy beach town where Aniela lived, was only a little over an hour's drive away. The time flew as Jewell soaked up the surrounding beauty as she drove. The sky was crystal blue, and palm trees lined the four-lane highway.

With the car's top down, her hair blew and the sun prickled her skin pleasantly. She found herself experiencing déjà vu as she drew in a deep, cleansing breath and reached through Romeo's carrier to sink her fingers into his black curls.

"Another adventure, Romeo. Hopefully even better than our last."

The four lanes narrowed into a two-lane country road. As she neared the beach, Jewell was reminded of how rocky and hilly the West Coast was compared to the South East Coast she had just left. She followed the GPS commands and read the approaching sign. "Welcome to Rosemore Heights." Her navigation system led her directly to Aniela's home, where the dancer was already sitting at a cafe-style table in her front yard. Her fire-colored hair shone bright in the sunlight.

Aniela rose to greet her as the car pulled up. "Welcome to your home away from home, Jewell. We're going to have a grand time together."

"Thanks. I'm so excited."

"Aw, look at your Romeo." Aniela petted him, setting his tail into a fierce wag. He barked with excitement at his new surroundings. "Well, I heard that. Come on, I'll show you where you're staying. Can I carry something?"

Jewell gratefully handed her the backpack and wheeled the over-stuffed suitcases behind her. Aniela led her from the sidewalk around to a small outbuilding behind the main house. It was constructed from aged bricks, with vines of ivy climbing its front adding an aura of enchantment.

"My grandma used this as an art studio. I converted it into a guest apartment when my classes started taking off. It has everything you'll need: dishes, linens, etc. My internet signal reaches out here, so you can stay as connected, or not, as you want. I'll give you the password in a minute."

Jewell smiled to herself. She didn't really need the password. After all, she had hacked into a research department's system to cover up taking experimental drugs for Josh. Hacking into a domestic wireless network would prove no challenge.

"Do you want to go out for dinner?" Aniela asked. "If not, I have some food in the fridge until you can get out to shop for yourself."

"It was a long trip, but you know what? If you're up to going out, I'd love to do that. Just let me get Romeo settled and freshen myself up."

"Okay, meet me out front in say…thirty minutes?"

Jewell selected one of her favorite sun dresses, it was mint green and flared at the bottom. After taking Romeo for a brief stroll so he wouldn't feel so cooped up while she was out, she got him settled in and went out to meet Aniela at the Beetle. Aniela was admiring the decals from Becca which Jewell had already slapped onto the rental back at the airport, one on the fender and one on the passenger door. Jewell took out her cell phone, shook her head to tousle her curls, then asked, "Selfie?"

Aniela moved in next to her, sporting khaki shorts and a crop top the exact blue of her eyes. "Say cheese," Jewell instructed and pressed the button a few times for good measure. "Want me to tag you?"

"Please."

Aniela slipped into the Beetle and gave Jewell directions to their destination. The building sat right in the heart of downtown. Large windows greeted them, gleaming with what remained of the evening sunlight.

"This is one of my favorite places downtown," Aniela explained. "They only serve fresh, locally sourced food."

"Sounds good," said Jewell, reading the sign above the door. "The Baked Beehive?"

"Yeah, funny name," Aniela agreed. "Everyone just calls it the Beehive. Tell you the truth, breakfast is probably their best meal offering. You should try it while you're here."

The inside of the restaurant had a white-and-black color scheme which gave it a crisp, modern feel. Jewell marveled at the beauty of the patrons and staff. She had always heard California housed a disproportionate share of the country's most beautiful people, but it was different witnessing it in person. Maybe it was all the healthy food and fresh ocean air.

The two women slid into an open booth.

"What do you usually order?" Jewell asked.

"Well, everything is healthy. Believe it or not, they actually have their own beehives out back, so I suggest you try one of their honey dishes."

Jewell scanned the menu, boasting items such as Mind your Beeswax Cake, a Bee-happy Martini and Queen Bee Shrimp. The time-zone change had left Jewell with a meager appetite, so she settled for the Bee-utiful spring salad.

The women enjoyed their meal while discussing the educational plan Aniela had devised for Jewell. If all went well, it could even culminate in a little performance together at Aniela's regular restaurant gig at the Acropolis. Aniela intended to teach her lots of traveling steps, since restaurant dancing involved roving between and around tables.

She promised to teach her how to flirt through her dance and how to interact seamlessly with the diners. Once she had grasped the basics, Aniela could then teach her how to use various props, such as the scimitars she had used back at Maggie's studio.

Jewell admitted that it had, in part, been those mesmerizing swords which had inspired this impulsive journey of hers. Aniela was delighted, and explained that she would also pick up where Maggie had left off on silk veil instruction, including double veils. The plan was ambitious, and Aniela cautioned Jewell that it would require a lot of dedication on her part to accomplish the goals they were setting. That would be no problem, Jewell assured her. The adrenaline was already surging through her. The tiredness her trip had brought was gone, as she looked forward with anticipation to what the next two months would bring.

With the meal over, Jewell and Aniela strolled down to the shore only a few blocks away. Jewell was familiar with the Pacific Ocean in Washington, where it was rockier and the water much colder. Here, palm trees lined the beach and she could see further across the waves. The ocean water gushed warm over her bare feet. For a moment, she was transported back to the stroll she had shared with Kage on the Atlantic shore.

When they returned to Aniela's complex, her host gave Jewell a tour of the main house. It was old by the area's standards. Built in the 1970s, Aniela specified. Some of Jewell's unspoken questions were solved when Aniela explained how her grandparents had gifted her the home and property when they opted for a maintenance-free lifestyle in a senior community.

The house had three stories, bursting with character and an artful flair. A wooden staircase curved to the upper floors, with a gold-printed red carpet padding the steps. The scent of essential oils infused the entire house. There were three bedrooms on the second floor, and finally Aniela's studio in the third-floor loft. The studio was empty except for a sound system in one corner. Floor-to-ceiling mirrors covered the wall directly ahead as they stepped inside, and an oversized window ran along the left wall. In contrast to Maggie's cozy but highly embellished studio, the atmosphere in this one felt clear and crisp.

Aniela saved the first floor for last. At the base of the stairs, a formal sitting room spread out to the right, and a living room with soft-looking furniture and a stone fireplace welcomed them to the left. This led on into Aniela's office, in which sat a desk with three monitors to the one computer.

"Do you work for the FBI?" Jewell joked.

"Nothing that fancy, I'm afraid. I'm an account executive, part-time at least, until I can pay my way with just the dancing. At least I get to work from home. But as you can imagine, there's a lot of number crunching, so it's easier to have different screens up."

The office had a door which opened out onto the yard between the main house and the tiny art house where Jewell would be staying. The office also connected to Aniela's modest kitchen.

"Do you want something to drink?"

"No, I think I'll head over and settle in for the night, if that's alright?"

"Sure. Let me get you some snacks though, and a bottle of wine."

"Well, okay, I don't want to hurt your feelings." Jewell joked.

Aniela showed Jewell out through the door. "If you ever need me during the day, just come tap on this door."

"Sounds great. Goodnight."

Despite her exhaustion, Jewell was too excited to sleep just yet, so she decided to explore her new accommodations that would serve as her home for the next two months. Exposed bricks made up the interior walls, some of which still had the ghost of faded paint on them and others that were completely raw. Casual and inviting furniture added to the artsy feel of the house. The front door opened straight into the living room with an open-floor plan with a kitchen hosting a breakfast bar for seating. The bedroom and bathroom were sectioned off in the back of the house. The bedroom had a second door leading out the back of the building. Her exploration of the interior complete, Jewell swung open the rear door and flicked the exterior light switch.

The sight stole her breath. It was as if she had opened a door onto an enchanted forest. Globe-shaped lights hung from chains strung between the trees, dangling amidst the wispy branches as if they were one. Ahead of her, a brook ran between this little patch of paradise and the dense trees on the other side. A wide, sandy patch served as a rustic patio furnished with a raw wooden table and tree-trunk chairs. Jewell immediately conjured a picture of herself sipping wine and reading next to the fire pit, listening to the gently flowing water.

She took Romeo on a well-deserved walk around the area, and then fell satisfied into bed. The nearly full-moon cast a slim beam through the open window carrying a tree-scented breeze that lulled her to sleep.

The next morning, Jewell awoke to Romeo whining. She remembered taking him out before bed, so she couldn't understand his distress. She climbed out of bed only to catch his gaze fixed on the bedroom window. Outside, she spotted the cutest calico cat curled into a ball on the windowsill. This furry visitor seemed completely unmoved by

Romeo's protests.

"Who's this?" Jewell asked. The cat responded to Jewell's voice by standing up, hunching its back for a big stretch and then jumping down to the screened door with a couple of meows. "Well, what's your name?" The cat meowed again. " Romeo, sit." He obeyed, but kept an intent watch on the calico. Jewell opened the door to pick the cat up and held it out to check the gender. "So you're a girl. I'll have to ask Aniela about you." She fetched a pan of water and set it outside the back door, along with the mysterious cat.

Jewell's stomach growled. "The Beehive! Come on, Romeo."

She stopped at Aniela's office door on her way to the car. Aniela opened it, pointing apologetically at the headset she was wearing, mouthing, "Conference call."

Jewell mouthed, "Sorry."

After a brief exchange which Jewell did her best not to listen to, Aniela clicked a button and said, "I'm muted. They're droning on. What's up?" She patted the curls on Romeo's head.

"There's a calico cat at the house."

"Oh yeah, he roams around here."

"She's a female cat," Jewell said. "She doesn't belong to anyone?"

"No, belongs to the neighborhood. Hmm, here I always thought it was a boy. I never really checked. Comes and goes whenever it feels like it."

"She looks healthy."

"I'm sure. She probably eats better than I do."

"I was thinking about going to the Beehive for breakfast. Want to come?"

"I wish. There's nothing better than honey with breakfast. You can take Romeo in with you, you know." She clicked her button again to unmute herself and waved.

Jewell and Romeo headed for the car.

The next few days were filled with intense lessons and practice. Aniela's regime was grueling. The private nature of the sessions meant that her keen focus was thrust upon Jewell alone. Aniela circled her as she executed new moves or stood behind her analyzing the intricate placing of each step. Often, she would stop her and zone in on minute sections of movement, instructing Jewell to repeat them over and over until she had mastered them to Aniela's standards. Her muscles ached as badly as in those first weeks with Maggie.

However, the promise of taking her favorite dance form to the next level, along with the anticipated privilege of performing side by side with Aniela, spurred Jewell on. When she wasn't with her teacher, the space between the foot of her bed and the mirrored closet served as her practice studio back in the guest house. Jewell was fully aware that the only way she would be dancing with Aniela in the restaurant would be to deliver an absolutely polished performance.

When she wasn't putting in the hours dancing, Jewell enjoyed the daily rhythm she was establishing in Rosemore Heights. She made a habit of parking downtown and walking the streets, shopping and exploring with Romeo. Every morning, she sat in the same booth at the Beehive with Romeo at her feet. She ordered the same steaming hot biscuit, split it open to add the butter that melted so quickly it oozed from the sides and out onto her plate. Then she used the dipper to trickle fresh honey, watching the sweet golden effusion flood her biscuit.

Jewell struck up a friendship with the nineteen-year-old waitress Rikki, who served her section of the restaurant. Rikki was a bubbly girl, an aspiring actress, but then again, who wasn't in that town? She may have been just shy of twenty, but she looked about fifteen with her tiny, barely developed body exhibiting zero percent body fat. Jewell never saw her without a wide smile, showing off her bright-white teeth. She had smooth, tanned skin and light brown hair in a casual, jaw-length cut. "Cute" would have been an accurate adjective for her.

Jewell noticed a woman who also had breakfast daily at the Beehive. This woman in keeping with Jewell's habit also sat in the same booth every day. It happened to be the one in front of her and Romeo. Jewell guessed the woman was in her late forties. A very attractive woman with her warm dark eyes and a friendly smile, which made Jewell believe she was possibly a kind person. She had shiny dark hair and wore the same hoop earrings every day. Her clothing was simple and casual, but classy.

After a few days, Jewell couldn't stand the suspense any longer.

"Who is that?" she asked Rikki, nodding towards the woman who was currently gazing out the window.

"I have no idea. She just started coming lately."

"Strange." They both eyed her a moment longer, but the woman didn't stir. "Are you surfing today?" Jewell asked.

"For sure. I get off at noon."

"Great, Romeo and I will come watch."

"Why don't you surf with me?"

"Me? I'd break my neck. Also, I'm working hard with Aniela so I might be able to dance with her at the Acropolis one night."

"Let me know when you do. I want to come watch. I'm not old enough to drink yet, but I can come for dinner, and I'll bring my friends."

"Perfect."

Jewell grinned at the thought of Rikki being under the legal drinking age. She forgot just how young she was.

Later that day, Jewell ventured to the beach and saw Rikki just finish riding a wave. When Jewell motioned to her, she picked up her surfboard and ran over to her and Romeo.

"Hey, Romeo." Rikki petted him with her dripping hands.

"Don't get a chill." Jewell picked up Rikki's towel and handed it to her. "I recognized your spot from the Marilyn Monroe towel."

Rikki laughed. "I know, I'm pretty predictable." Rikki had spoken countless times of how much she admired Marilyn Monroe and aspired to be like her. Jewell surmised for Rikki to fulfill that particular dream, breast and hip implants would be required.

Rikki was drying her hair with the towel. "Weirdorama. Don't look now, but there's that woman from the restaurant."

Jewell turned as subtly as she could. There indeed was the woman, standing on the pier and staring past them out to sea, with her right hand shielding her eyes from the bright sun. Her long straight black hair swirled dramatically in the breeze.

A few nights a week, Aniela hosted parties in the sandy area behind Jewell's house. She would always run the plan past Jewell first, but Jewell was happy to have the company and enjoyed meeting Aniela's other students and fellow performers.

One by one, she had now met almost all of the dancers from the group photo on Aniela's website. One of the two male dancers had moved on, but Andrea, the tall, slender one, had stayed, and was also dancing regularly at the Acropolis. Jewell learned that he was originally from Paris, which explained the sexy accent that rolled off his tongue like sweet music.

Jewell had identified that he seemed to have two distinct looks, and it was impossible to decide which she preferred. He frequently arranged his dark hair back into a sleek style, gleaming with shining, spotless perfection. This was part of the polished, sophisticated version of himself, and went well with his meticulously shaped chinstrap beard and tanned skin. To Jewell, this was his sexy side, but then there was also his boyish look, another je ne sais quoi. For this, he would wear unassuming jeans and let his hair fall loose and natural. He was so cute she wanted to ruffle his hair whenever he showed up like this.

That evening, after a plea from Becca for: 'some pics to make me jealous,' Jewell asked Andrea to pose for her. He embraced the task with the spirit of a true performer. He was wearing a pair of stone-washed jeans torn at the left knee and right upper thigh, and a light denim button-up shirt. Grinning mischievously as Jewell focused the camera on her phone, he unbuttoned his shirt to reveal the rock-hard six-pack he had acquired from all his undulating bellydance moves. He lifted his left foot onto a rock, placed both hands on his left hip and threw his head back for the camera, loosening his hair. He was enjoying himself, and Jewell could only giggle and shake her head as she snapped away in rapid succession. He moved about, changing poses as deftly as a professional model.

Feeling herself begin to flush, Jewell thanked him and sent the best snaps to Becca.

A text reply followed immediately.

Whoa, I'm on my way.

Ha, ha. You stay where you are.

The next morning, the calico cat came weaving in and out between Jewell's legs as she sat outside sipping her coffee.

"You need a name," Jewell decided, lifting the kitty onto her lap. Romeo moved closer.

"I know!" Jewell exclaimed, picking up her cell phone as she snapped a picture of the cat. She posted it on social media with the caption, "Help me name this cute kitty."

Multiple notifications began sounding. The first, of course, was Becca.

You got a cat?!? How about Cali?

She's not mine. Just while I'm here.

Jewell smiled at all the responses coming in. She'd wait until the suggestions ceased and then make a decision, or narrow it down to a handful and have her friends vote.

"You'll get a name soon," she said to the cat. Romeo moved even closer and whined, laying his head on Jewell's knee. "You're still my best boy." She sank her fingers in his puffy curls.

That evening, Jewell climbed the winding wooden stairs of Aniela's home towards the studio on the third floor, when she heard Aniela announce, "Let the fun begin." A buzz of excited female voices rang out, engulfing the entire house.

Jewell entered the studio to see rows of Aniela's costumes hanging on racks she must have rolled in earlier. Deep, bold tones ranging from marigold to emerald to mulberry glistened with complementary gems. The sight was a smorgasbord for the eyes. The early evening sun shined through the wall of windows to her left, illuminating the room like a film set.

Jewell had visited Aniela earlier in the day for a quick lunch, during which her host had explained how she refreshes her inventory of costumes every three months. The designer she uses comes over to present the new season's wardrobe, and sells her outgoing pieces at a discount. A seamstress also attends the quarterly costume event to provide an honest opinion on adjustment and fitting options.

Jewell dove into the sea of lavish materials and sparkles alongside Aniela's other visitors, giggling like a schoolgirl. She opted for the peacock blue-green outfit she had been admiring on Aniela's website, although she wouldn't fill it out as well as her shapelier host. The tailor assured her she could manipulate it to fit.

The shopping adventure was fun enough, but Jewell was preoccupied with the planned evening ahead. Aniela, her regular students and Jewell intended to visit the Acropolis for dinner and entertainment that night. Aniela frequently danced at the Mediterranean restaurant, but Monday was always her night off.

Jewell practically skipped back down the tree-lined walk to the ivy-covered house, her new find streaming behind her like a peacock kite. She hung the costume on a hook outside the closet. This way, it would be the first sight when she opened her eyes each morning.

She fed the cat and snatched the opportunity to fuss over her. Dinnertime was the one time of day she could count on seeing her capricious new pet.

"Hey, let's see if you have a name yet." Jewell fetched her cell phone, sat cross-legged on the bed and scrolled down to her post. "Whoa, look at all the responses. The last reply was yesterday, so I'll assume everyone's had their say." She realized she was now having the kind of one-sided conversation she often held with Romeo with her new furry friend. She read the suggestions aloud to see which one might fit: "Tempest, Gem, Luna, Sophie, Prissy, Misty, Cali, Belle, Juliette, Jasmin, Rascal, Journee', Gypsy, Tabby, Rachel Raccoon, Maple, Molly, Cookie,

Ellie, Ella, Otter Girl, Gracie, Miss Grace, Elsie, Cindy, Mary, Callie, Rosy, Ruby, Buttercup, Butter Bean, Abbey, Poshie, Sabo, Tabitha, Mystery, Velour, Delilah, Jewel, Cinnamon, Amira, Layla, Blossom, Nikia Myriah Petit, Persia, Scarlet, Mitsi, Kai, Tess, Samantha (Sam), Rahab, Lucy, Callie, Bekah, Penelope, Miss Kitty, Catalina, Tasha, Beall Frost, Grizzaeblla, Precious, Priscilla, Cairo, Harem, Salem, Josie, Sheba, Simba, Challi, Cierra, Omi, Maya, Fifi, Wanderlust, Rings, Soft Kitty, Shimmer, Ralph, Spot, Ruby and Summer."

"Hmmm." She tapped her finger against her lips. "I'm thinking Maya or Luna."

The cat looked at her with curious eyes.

"I'll mull it over. Come on, Romeo. Time for your walk."

As she walked beside Romeo, Jewell found herself dwelling on what to wear that evening. Her mood was calling for a dress, but she wasn't sure she had one suitable.

Once they were home, she quickly fed Romeo and swiped through her closet to the few dresses she had brought with her. One caught her attention, a new gold-toned bodycon with the tag still attached. Now she just had to create her signature smoky eyes and position her hair in a teased side ponytail.

Shortly after, she was knocking on Aniela's door.

"Whoa." Her host made a fanning motion with her hand. "You're smokin'."

Jewell blushed. "Is it too much?"

"No, it's perfect."

Jewell indicated the skin underneath the sequined edge of her dress. "My legs are so pale though."

"Hey, protecting your skin is trés chic these days."

They rode to the restaurant in Aniela's car with two other students in the back and plans to meet the rest there. Jewell seized the opportunity to firm up a name for her wandering cat.

"I like Maya," one said. "Vertical figure-eight hips down. And, ooh, how they show off our waists."

"Speak for yourself, skinny," another student shot back.

"Why not Luna? It's almost a full moon."

"Maybe," Jewell said. "What do you think, Aniela? You'll be the one calling it when I leave."

"I like them both." Aniela paused. "But then again, as a bellydancer, I have to choose Maya. It's always been one of my favorite moves."

"Let it be declared, then. 'Maya' is to be kitty's name," Jewell announced theatrically. She swiped her phone screen and posted the announcement, thanking everyone for their suggestions.

The aroma of garlic sautéing in olive oil blasted them as they entered the restaurant. The familiar scent triggered memories of San Sebastian's in Southbridge and also of Josh's cooking. Jewell suddenly missed her Florida friends intensely. And Josh.

They followed the hostess to a half-circle corner booth with a view of the entire restaurant and bar. Jewell scooted around the cushy leather bench until those filling in from the other side began to reach her. Aniela sat down on her right, and behind her came another of the students, Jossie. Jewell enjoyed the company of the other dancers but somehow felt no overwhelming desire to become close to them. Her stay was only going to be temporary and she had her own posse back home.

Burgundy wallpaper hung on the walls, trimmed with gold. The place had the same exotic grandeur of the old theater where Jewell had once worked and watched old classics with Josh through their high school years. This restaurant, with its dark-wood floors and old-fashioned walls, seemed to hold the spirits of all the dancers who had passed through before.

The table sat full of friends, food, and fine wine, yet Jewell kept watch for the dancers. Her eager eye, surveyed; expecting, anticipating. She felt her pulse quicken. He was up next.

As sultry music filled the room, Andrea sashayed into the dining area in triple step, his hips leading, left then right. The tempo increased and he glided in and out, between the tables. His dark hair hidden by a coin scarf. Jewell found her eyes bobbing with the gold fringe belt adorning his black harem pants. The cropped black choli vest with swirls of golden threads highlighted his washboard abs.

She admired the intricate tattoos encircling his ripped upper arms. Her pulse raced faster. Andrea danced skillfully, precisely, with a smoothness like gliding on ice. Drumbeats interjected the taxim and he hit each accent with sharp hip pops and drops.

Women began to beckon him to their tables for the privilege of tucking their paper bills into his belt. Jewell watched, intrigued, as he performed traveling spins to a table of men. One coyly stuffed a bill into Andrea's belt. Andrea smiled and winked at the tipper, then shimmied his shoulders towards the men. Jewell quickly turned to Aniela to gauge her response, but she hadn't even witnessed the act. She was clearly engrossed in conversation with Jossie.

The performance over, Andrea glided out of the dining area only to return moments later in a black cover-up gown. He motioned for Jewell to slide away from Aniela, then climbed over Jossie and plopped himself almost comically between Jewell and Aniela.

"You're such an amazing dancer," Jewell exclaimed, then worried her flushed cheeks were showing.

"Thank you," he breathed, his Parisian accent stronger than ever now that he was worn out. The heat was still practically pulsing from his body.

Jewell handed the waiter her cell phone and asked him to take a picture of the group, which she immediately posted on social media. She was keeping up her posts partly as promised to her Southbridge friends, but also as a kind of digital scrapbook for herself. She had to admit grudgingly that Kage's lack of response to her updates was bothering her. Perhaps these latest snaps of her sitting beside a sweaty, gorgeous man would finally tip him into action.

The wine flowed festively, and further dancers graced the floor. Andrea leaned in close to Jewell and asked if she would be interested in going out to dinner with him. Just the two of them.

She could hardly wait to text Becca on the ride home.

Hi Becca. Remember the male bellydancer I've been talking about and sent you a pic of?

Andrea, right? How could I forget...

We saw him dance tonight. He's unbelievable!

Aw, man. I wish I was there. I've never even been to a restaurant with bellydancers.

And guess what?

What?

We're going to dinner together tomorrow night. I think he could become a great friend!

Friend, huh?

No, seriously. I get the feeling I'm probably not his type...

Oh, as in...

Yeah.

Darn. It's always the best ones.

I'll update you again soon.

By the way, I signed up for my classes.

Amazing! You excited?

I am. Got to go now, sorry. Some of us suckers have to work in the morning. TTYL.

Andrea insisted on picking Jewell up. Then again, she hadn't put up much of a fight. When she opened the door for him, he stood before her holding a single red rose.

"Oh, how sweet," she said. "Come in while I put it in some water."

"You look lovely," he said.

"Is this okay for where we're going?" She indicated her animal-print mini skirt, low-cut red blouse and strappy red heels.

"Perfect," he said, keeping his gaze on her while bending to scratch Romeo behind the ears.

"Warning, he'll be yours for life now." They laughed. "By the way, where are we going?"

"It's a secret, my dear, but I promise you're in for a treat. Does Italian suit your taste?"

"Oh, yeah. I love Italian."

"Then let us proceed," he said grandly, crooking his arm to make a perfect space for her hand.

The food at Andrea's chosen restaurant was heavenly, and they both heartily overindulged on pasta, red sauce and wine. Afterwards, they decided to go walk some of it off.

The echo of the ocean swept through the buildings of downtown Rosemore Heights, more alluring to Jewell than any of the town's other endearing features. They gravitated towards the beach and sat on the pier, watching the sun set.

It was nice, Jewell thought, relaxing with a man without the next step looming over their heads. As they sat, dangling their legs from the pier, Andrea told her about his childhood. How most of his family, except for one younger brother, remained in Paris. How he visited his home city at least twice a year.

"Paris is on my bucket list," Jewell confessed. "I've never been."

"Then I insist you come with me sometime. I can show you the city's best-kept secrets."

She even felt brave enough to share pieces of her own childhood with him. These days she told the truth about it. No more lies. She told him how she had been raised in foster homes and separated from her brother. She no longer lied about her mother either. She called it like it was. The fabricated story she used to give people sounded prettier, saying her mother had died when she was little. But her mother had abandoned them, that was the truth of it. It had been Lydia's choice, and Jewell wasn't going to feel ashamed about it like it had been her own crime anymore.

Andrea drove them back to Aniela's and walked with Jewell back to the tiny art house.

"Want to come in?" she asked.

"Sure."

They took a seat on the comfy sofa with Romeo at Jewell's feet and Maya preening on the top of the backrest. She seemed to be getting used to her new name, and she was spending more time indoors these days too. Jewell had never had a cat, so Maya's ways were still a mystery to her, especially her independence. But Jewell drew extra comfort from her quiet presence.

Jewell was enjoying Andrea's company, but the wine was making her eyes grow heavy. For a moment, she rested her head against the back of the sofa and closed her eyes.

Suddenly, she felt Andrea's lips on hers and jumped away. She drew her knees to her chest, her feet on the sofa now as she pushed herself away from him. "What do you think you're doing?"

"Wow. I can honestly say I've never had that reaction before."

"I-I thought you were gay."

"Gay! Whatever gave you that idea?" He paused briefly. "Wait. You're not one of those narrow-minded people who think that, if a man bellydances, he's gay?"

"No, not at all. It's just that…when you were dancing at the restaurant, that guy stuck the tip in your belt and you…winked at him and then shimmied. I thought you were flirting with him."

"Honey, I'll wink at anyone who stuffs a twenty in my belt." He grinned. "No, I'm just kidding. It's part of the performance. You'll learn that when it's your turn up there."

Jewell was relieved now that she hadn't mentioned the other items causing her suspicion, such as his impeccable style and never mentioning any girlfriends. How narrow minded would that have sounded?

"Oh, gosh, I'm so sorry. Maybe I *am* one of those horrible people," Jewell said.

"I don't believe that." He reached his hand out to her. "Can we start over? Hi, I'm Andrea, a straight male bellydancer and I'm very attracted to you."

She laughed and took his hand, feeling her muscles soften. She slid back to her original position next to him.

"Well," Jewell said. "Under these new circumstances, I should tell you that, until very recently, I was dating someone back in Southbridge. We broke up right before I came here, so I don't know if I'm quite over him yet."

Andrea gently stroked her arm. "If you have to ask yourself that question, then trust me, you're not over him. We can just be friends, if you like. But if you catch me staring at you, it isn't because I want to wear your clothes or swap recipes. It's because I want you."

"Now who's stereotyping?" She laughed and threw a sofa pillow at him.

She leaned her head on his firm shoulder. "Well, this is awkward. Thank you for understanding."

"I should go." He kissed her cheek. "I don't want to get too comfortable here."

She watched him walk away down the path, feeling almost sad. Her first thought was Becca so she reached for her phone and tapped the keys.

Well, he's not gay.

Really?! How did you find out?

I kinda figured it out when his lips were on mine.

Whaaaaaaaaaaat??!

Ha ha.

Oh man, all the good stuff happens when I'm not there. How was it? Tell me everything.

I stopped him.

Why? I thought you liked him.

I do. He's nice and fun to be around, and he does make me...feel things. But there's also Kage...

Kage Who? You mean the guy who BROKE UP WITH YOU?

That doesn't mean I'm over it.

Girl, you need to move on. Want me to teach you how? Becca style!

Four

Chapter 4

⬥⬥⬥

The next morning, Jewell and Romeo visited the Beehive as usual. Still feeling embarrassed about her blunder with Andrea, she confided in Rikki.

"How did you leave things?" Rikki asked.

"He let me off the hook."

The sound of breaking glass behind the counter distracted them.

"Watch the juice glasses," the manager called out to the dishwasher.

Rikki shook her head. "I think we had a lucky escape there. He's a bit flighty, if you know what I mean."

Jewell remembered the theory she and her friends had been forming back in Southbridge. Now this crashing of glass. She wondered what Clara was trying to warn her about. Could it really mean something?

She finished breakfast and headed for the door. Just then, the mystery woman, the stranger in the booth in front of them, reached out to Romeo.

"You're such a good boy, Romeo," the stranger said as she petted him, then cupped his face with her hands. His tail swished wildly.

This woman had clearly been eavesdropping on her conversations, and Jewell didn't care for it. She acknowledged the woman with a nod, then nudged Romeo towards the door.

They were on the sidewalk, halfway to the corner when she heard the woman call out behind her.

"Jewell."

This didn't make sense. How did the woman know her name? Slowly, she turned to face the stranger.

"Yes?"

"Jewell." The woman was cautiously approaching her. "I'm…Lydia."

"Lydia?" Heat rose up her throat as her mind wrapped itself around the name. *It couldn't be.*

"I'm your mother."

The woman reached out to her, but Jewell spun on her heels and ran towards her car.

"Get away from me!"

"Jewell, please, listen to me. I've been looking for you for over a year now. I've come all this way just to talk to you."

Jewell stopped again, but only turned partially this time. She spoke over her shoulder, just loud enough for her voice to carry the short distance. "You're a little late, aren't you? About 25 years too late." Jewell resumed her hurried trek to her car. She just had to make it around the corner. The woman's voice trailed behind her.

"I know. I'm sorry. I only got sober eighteen months ago. I scraped together every penny I had to hire a private detective. I thought I'd found you, but then you moved again."

Jewell reached the end of the sidewalk and rounded the corner, waves of nausea pulsed through her stomach. Her eyes darted around, looking for a safe place. A trashcan. She sprinted over, clutching her spasming stomach, and promptly brought up her biscuits and honey. She heaved and retched until nothing but acid and resentment remained. The woman, Lydia, her mother, whoever the hell this stranger claimed to be, ran up to her already pulling paper tissues out of her bag to offer. Jewell snatched them from her then gave the woman such a look it caused her to retreat without another word.

The drive back to Aniela's seemed to take forever. Her hands were shaking against the steering wheel and it was hard to stay focused on the road in front of her. Once home, she escaped to the sandy area in the back, made herself a sweet tea to sip and listened to the stream babble until her thoughts and heart stopped racing. Romeo and Maya came to sit next to her, and she was grateful for their soothing company. She had to pull herself together, Aniela would be hosting a party later that day, and Jewell didn't want to seem distracted in front of her fellow dancers. She decided to take a nap and start again refreshed.

Somewhere in the late afternoon, Aniela and Andrea arrived. They came into view as they rounded the side of the house, sharing the weight of a large cooler between them. Aniela had a bag of snacks draped over her free shoulder. Jewell grabbed the straps of the bag and eased it from Aniela's arm.

"Thanks, Jewell."

Jewell helped set up for the party. With Andrea, she brought out the long folding table Aniela stored in the guest house closet. They draped a white tablecloth over it and set out plates of cheeses, breads and crackers. She contemplated telling Aniela and Andrea about her encounter with Lydia, but quickly thought better of it. Sharing it with them now would interfere with her more pressing goal of shoving the incident to the back of her mind while focusing on wearing her party-face. She was determined to make this a fun and distracting night. Then she would call Becca in the morning to ventilate.

With the outdoor space set for the party, Andrea wrapped his arms around Jewell and gave her a squeeze. It caused a little tenderness in her unsettled belly, but otherwise felt good, an assurance that the awkwardness of last night was forgiven. She, Andrea, and Aniela positioned themselves in chairs under the sweeping leaves. They were pleasantly ahead of schedule. Water splashed rhythmically against the rocks in the brook . The early evening sun beat down warm on her thighs. Romeo lay next to her, but Maya was out of sight, probably somewhere sulking about all the commotion.

When Andrea suggested they reward themselves with a little wine, Jewell hesitated at first. She hadn't had anything other than water and tea since her earlier upset, and wasn't sure about the golden liquid now being offered. Cautiously, she lifted the glass to her lips. The first swallow was a little rough, but after a few sips, she soon found herself feeling better.

The drinks continued to flow as the guests arrived. Traditional Egyptian music replaced the sounds of the brook, reverberating through the trees. With each glass of wine, Jewell could extinguish a little more of the day's memories from her thoughts. The music was speaking to her, and she danced here and there through the sandy area, adorning herself with a hip scarf. A few others joined in with their own clanking scarves. She still hadn't eaten, and the wine was making her feel like shooting stars and meteor showers were zipping all around her body.

"Jewell, maybe you should eat something," Andrea offered.

"No, I'm fine. I feel goooood." She performed a spin for emphasis.

The full moon cut the night, casting a haunting feel over the party. Jewell was drinking straight from the bottle now, carrying it by the neck. Feeling inspired by the sight above her, she climbed onto one of the tree-trunk stools, emptied the bottle in a final chug, wiped her mouth with the back of her hand then threw back her head triumphantly and howled up at the bright moon. Others joined in her moment of wildness, until their chorus carried through the night air, all the way to the lunar-lit sky.

The last thing Jewell remembered was Andrea flinging her over his shoulder and carrying her to bed.

The next morning, Jewell felt sunlight on her cheek. She eased her eyes open. The light seeping through the window burned, so she closed them again. *Coffee,* was her only thought. *Coffee will help.* She forced her eyes open again, ramming the heel of her palm against the pain throbbing in her forehead. Mustering enough courage to place her feet on the floor, she stood up. The world was spinning, sending fresh waves of nausea through her stomach.

She hobbled into the kitchen directly to the coffee pot, where she managed to take herself through the necessary steps to start brewing. Sugar and cream would be required this morning.

There came a knock at the door.

"Come in," she called weakly.

It was Aniela.

"I think I drank too much last night," Jewell confessed.

"No shit. You look like hell. I brought Bloody Marys. You know, 'hair of the dog.'"

The mention of alcohol made Jewell bend deeply at the waist. "Please, no. I feel so sick."

Aniela bent to look at Jewell. "Oh sweetie. You've got it bad. Let me see you." Jewell straightened with Aniela's assistance, still pressing tight against her lower abdomen and bracing herself against the kitchen bar with her free hand. Aniela placed her hand against Jewell's forehead. "Let's get you dressed and in the car."

"Why? I'm just hung over."

"No, sweetie, you're burning up. Hangovers don't cause belly ache and fever. You know better, you're a scientist. We're going to the hospital."

Jewell lay in the backseat of Aniela's car, flickering in and out of consciousness. She resurfaced in the exam room of the emergency department. Somehow, Andrea was there too. A nurse was hooking a bag of fluids to a pole attached to Jewell's cart. A doctor of some sort was firing questions at her that some automated part of her brain was able to answer. He recorded her information on a clipboard.

Her awareness pricked up when a team of surgical staff in scrubs and caps entered the room and asked Jewell for her full name and date of birth. One of them placed his foot on the break of the cart to release it. He addressed Aniela and Andrea.

"Go to the surgical waiting area. You can use that code to keep track of her progress on the monitor," he indicated a card in Aniela's hand.

Aniela leaned down and kissed her forehead, the area left bare by the surgical cap.

"You're going to be fine."

Andrea asked what in the world was going on. Jewell was relieved because she had been wanting to ask, but her words were thick and heavy in her mouth.

One of the staff in scrubs answered, "She's got a hot appendix. It needs to come out."

The doctor who had been firing questions was injecting something into Jewell's IV. "Something to relax you."

Andrea touched her hand as the team wheeled her out of the room. "We'll be right here," he said.

Jewell lay, stunned and helpless, as they wheeled her into a corridor.

An unbefitting smile sneaked to her face as she felt the smooth ripple of peace from the drug he must have injected, now coursing through her veins.

She heard the buzz of voices as she watched the ceiling tiles pass overhead. The cart stopped and she felt herself being lifted.

We need to get you on the surgical table.

"Ouch!" The same pain shot through her.

A mask was placed over her nose.

"Jewell, I need you to count backwards from 100."

Her lips had barely formed the first syllable.

A massive field spanned her entire view. The sky was a crystal-blue backdrop. The grass in the expansive field was a green so pure she had never laid eyes on anything like it before. A group of people populated her view in the distance. Their shapes rose and fell, traveling in a circle, like in a game of Ring Around the Rosie. They were wearing daisy chains in their hair. Their hands were locked together, and they were laughing joyfully, passing loving glances at one another. She had never seen such happy people. It was a mixture of men and women, young and old. Although, none of them really looked old. Their smooth skin glowed and their smiles were radiant. The women's hair flowed like the silk veils she now danced with in an array of yellows, browns, reds, whites and blacks. Up and down, up and down, bouncing away.

And then she saw him, among the group. Josh. His complexion was perfect. He was beautiful, and his relaxed smile flickered in the bright sunshine. She couldn't recall ever seeing him so happy, not even the first time they had made love.

"Josh," she called, raising her hand to wave.

He broke away from the others.

"Jewell?"

His tone was concerned. He moved towards her and was suddenly so close with scarcely any effort, it was as if he had traveled on a conveyor belt.

Her most forceful squinting couldn't shield her eyes from the brightness.

"What are you doing here now? I wasn't expecting you yet. Are you sure this is right?"

"I don't know what's going on," she said. "You look so good." She reached to touch him.

"Blondie," he said, "listen." She stared at his hands now gently holding her wrists.

"Listen to them," he continued. "They're calling to you. You need to listen to them." Josh began to fade and she desperately lunged for him, longing to hold him.

Sounds from the operating room. Blip. The clinking of metal instruments. Blip.

"She's coming back," a male voice said.

"Her heart rate's down to 92, doctor."

"Temp's down to 100.8."

"Good. Ross, give another 120 of Dantrolene. Katrina, add more ice packs and check the cooling blanket."

She sensed she had been moved to another area.

"Jewell, what's your pain level on a scale of zero to ten? Zero being no pain and ten being the worst you've ever felt."

"Um, maybe a two?"

"Good. I'll hold off on your dose for now. You're starting to wake up, so no sudden movements please. Let your body adjust."

She felt a warm soft hand holding hers and the feel of her hair being brushed from her face. It felt nice. She smiled.

"You scared us to death," a woman's voice said.

Jewell struggled to place the voice, but was too groggy to think.

"What happened?" She couldn't quite open her eyes yet.

"Malignant hyperthermia. It caused you to have a dangerous reaction to the anesthesia," the woman said.

"Really? That's hereditary." Jewell remembered studying the condition.

"That's what the surgeon said. I couldn't think of anyone in our family who ever had it."

Jewell's eyes shot open. Lydia was sitting next to her, holding her hand. "He also said it's often fatal. Thank God your friend had the instinct to bring you here when she did."

Jewell pulled her hand out of her mother's, but couldn't pull together the emotional or physical fortitude to protest further.

"Did your detective tell you I was here?"

"No. When you and Romeo didn't show up at the Beehive this morning, Rikki and I got worried. She had one of Aniela's flyers with her and told me that's who you were likely to be with, so she called her. I came straight here when she told me what had happened."

A wave of vertigo came over Jewell, she suddenly had a compelling need to talk about her still-fresh experience. "I was in a field, and Josh was there. It felt like…heaven. It was so peaceful. He looked so happy, for the first time…" She swallowed hard through her delirium. "Do you think he's happy?" She began sobbing, desperate to hear his voice again, telling her that it was alright, that the pain was over.

"I'm sure he is, honey," Lydia said and stroked her hand. "Is Josh a friend?"

"He's…he was my boyfriend. Since ninth grade. Didn't your detective person tell you that?"

"And Josh died?"

"Yes, a little over a year ago." Jewell's brain was beginning to focus again. "How come your PI didn't know?"

"He kept losing track of you. Until recently. I didn't have a lot of funds. I guess I got a sub-par detective. Tell me about Josh. That was a long time to be with someone."

Jewell ran her tongue around her dry mouth. She already regretted sharing what she had, exposing herself like this. She put it down to the surgery and the drugs. "We helped each other, a lot. But in the end, I couldn't save him. He had a heart condition and died soon after I moved to Florida. He was alone, and I'm still struggling to…to forgive myself for that. I guess I just want to believe that he's in heaven. That he's getting a second chance to be happy. That would bring me so much comfort."

"Well, whatever you saw, I believe he was sending you a message. I truly do." Jewell looked at her mother, her face was unnervingly kind right now. She slowly raised a hand and ran her fingers through Jewell's hair again. "I'm sure of it."

"Thank you," Jewell said, and meant it. She lay her head down and dozed again, not fighting the woman's touch. She didn't have the strength in her current state and, besides, she had to admit it felt good.

Jewell fidgeted in her wheelchair, dressed and ready to go home with her two friends and Lydia beside her, while a nurse recited the discharge instructions. "You really ought to wear a medic alert bracelet as well. If you ever need emergency surgery again and no one is with you to tell the staff, you could end up in serious trouble."

"Thank you, I'll look into it."

"In fact, the whole family needs to give this history in medical interviews. And, your mother can make sure you get a bracelet," the nurse said.

"She's not that kind of mother," slipped out of Jewell's mouth.

Lydia dropped her gaze to the floor and the nurse glanced awkwardly between them. She continued with her instructions.

"You were lucky. They were able to perform your surgery through laparoscopy. They didn't have to make a huge incision, so you only have four butterfly tapes." She provided instructions on the care of the bandage strips, along with signs and symptoms of infection to watch out for. She instructed Jewell to take it easy for at least two weeks until her follow-up appointment with the surgeon.

"What about dancing?" Jewell asked. "I have classes booked."

"Sorry. Absolutely no dancing."

"That's okay," Aniela said. "Your health is top priority right now."

Andrea started pushing the wheelchair towards the exit.

"How long have you been here?" Jewell asked him.

"I got here right before your surgery. Don't you remember?"

"Maybe. I don't know. My memory is a little fuzzy. Weren't you working?"

"I was, but making sure you were okay was a little more important than work."

"Thank you, I appreciate it. What about you, Aniela?"

"I can catch up, don't worry. That's the beauty and the curse of working from home, it's always there. Let's concern ourselves with you first, eh?"

Andrea helped Jewell into his sedan, since it wasn't as low to the ground as Aniela's car. Lydia stepped quietly into the back and Aniela drove behind them.

When they arrived at Aniela's, Andrea held onto Jewell's arm as she eased herself out of the car.

"Do you want to sleep in my house?" Aniela offered. "The guest beds are all made up."

"That's very kind, but I think I'd rather stay where I am."

"You shouldn't be alone though," Aniela insisted.

Jewell grudgingly accepted that her friend was right. She closed her eyes, trying not to lean too much on Andrea. She couldn't believe she was going to say this. "Well, maybe…Lydia will stay with me for one night." Jewell shot a glance at her mother, making sure she understood the time limit being imposed.

Lydia's concerned frown turned to surprise, and her posture straightened. "Of course. Of course, I will."

"How did you get to the hospital, Lydia?" Andrea asked. "Is your car still there?"

"No. Jewell's friend from the restaurant, Rikki, dropped me off. I should update her actually."

"That reminds me," Aniela said. "I took the liberty of texting Becca from your phone and let her know what happened. She knows you're okay now."

"Oh, thanks," Jewell said as Aniela handed her the cell phone. She noted a slew of message alerts. She would trawl through them after she'd rested.

They settled her on the sofa in the art house and Romeo came bounding over.

"No, Romeo." Aniela grabbed his collar and eased him slowly towards Jewell. "Your mommy's a bit delicate right now. You've got to be gentle."

"Why don't I go out and get some groceries?" Andrea offered.

"Good idea," Aniela agreed.

Jewell reached gingerly to feel the comfort of Romeo's tight curls running through her fingers.

"I'll go make you a snack," Lydia said. She sorted through the cabinets. "How about some soup and crackers?"

"Sure," Jewell said. She wasn't ready to add a thank you yet. "Can you see a cat anywhere?"

Lydia searched the house, then looked out back. "Sorry, no."

Hours passed. Lydia sat in the chair next to the sofa and Jewell dozed off and on. During one of her waking moments, Lydia told her that Aniela and Andrea were hanging out in the sandy area in the back. In another, Lydia asked her if she knew where Nathanael was.

"I don't know where he is, and I don't care."

Lydia looked puzzled. She stood up from the chair and went to the kitchen to clean up. Jewell tried to fight the next wave of sleep but felt herself drift off again.

There was a knock at the door. Lydia opened it.

"Hi. Is this—"

"Becca," Jewell croaked, sitting up on the sofa. "What are you doing here?"

Becca dropped her bag and rushed over to Jewell. "Am I allowed to hug you?"

"Of course. Just gently, please."

Romeo barked and leapt onto the sofa next to Becca. Jewell groaned and clutched her wounds.

"Oh no, Romeo, you have to be careful," Lydia said, guiding Romeo off the sofa. "Sorry, Jewell. Are you okay?"

"I'm fine," Jewell answered through gritted teeth.

"I'm Becca." Her friend stood up, extending her hand.

"Oh yeah," Jewell remembered. "I was going to call you this morning. This," she gestured towards her mother, "is Lydia."

Hand still outstretched, Becca turned to Jewell with a puzzled expression.

"Yes, as in my mother," Jewell said.

"Oh my," Becca said, quickly giving her best smile. "It's so nice to meet you."

Lydia took her hand briefly, then let it go and stepped away. "Well, I'll let you two catch up. I'll go out back with Aniela and Andrea. Come on, Romeo."

"Wait," Becca said. "Andrea is outside? I'll be right back." She dashed past Lydia. Romeo ran behind her.

"I'll stay 'til you return then," Lydia called to Becca. She sat down on the sofa next to Jewell. "Do you still want me to stay? I guess Becca will be here now."

"It's fine, you can stay. If you want. I'd rather sleep on the sofa anyway. I can prop myself up more easily out here. You and Becca can sleep in the bed, or one of you can go sleep in the main house."

Jewell couldn't understand why, but she was actually finding herself not wanting her mother to leave. Not just yet. She reasoned it must be because she was still feeling vulnerable from the anesthetic and the near-death experience.

Becca returned and Lydia traded places to go join Aniela and Andrea.

"Yowza! You said Andrea was cute. He's downright gorgeous. The pics didn't do him justice. And, hey, if you don't want him..."

"Geesh, you've only been here fifteen minutes."

Becca laughed and Jewell braced her arms around her abdomen. "Oh no, don't make me laugh."

"Sorry. By the way." Becca nudged Jewell gently with her shoulder. "I'm still dating Max."

"Nice. So, you'd better behave then." Jewell wagged her finger teasingly at Becca.

Becca looked over her shoulder and dropped her voice to a whisper. "So, what the heck? That's your mom?"

"My mother," Jewell corrected. "I know, right. Isn't it wild? Honestly, I planned to call you this morning, but then this little thing happened." She pointed to her aching abdomen. "At first I just thought it was a terrible hangover. I got...well, pretty drunk last night. I think Andrea ended up carrying me to bed."

"Oh-la-la." Becca waggled her eyebrows.

"No, not like that. Wait." Jewell tried to recall a single detail after her howl-at-the-moon performance. "I don't *think* it was like that."

"If you say so."

"Hey, do you want to hear the story about Lydia, or not?'"

"Absolutely."

"Remember I told you about that mystery woman at the Beehive? Who was there every morning in the booth in front of me?"

"Yeah."

"Well, yesterday she stopped Romeo to pet him. Called him by name! Then, on our way to the car, she called after me. It was her, all along. Said she had a PI locate me!"

"Wow."

"Oh yeah. She said she's been sober for…gosh, I can't remember for how long now. I think the anesthesia messed with my brain."

"Yeah, it does that, and the pain medicine. Plus, Jewell…" Becca lowered her tone and took Jewell's hands in hers. "…Aniela was texting me, and things turned really serious during your surgery."

"I know. I think I nearly checked out at one point. I think…I think I visited heaven."

"What?" Becca jolted back, shock and concern in her eyes.

"I really think so, it felt so real. And I saw…Josh."

"You did?" Becca leaned her upper body towards Jewell and stared intently.

"He was in this big field with some other people. They were all happy and laughing. He was so beautiful and relaxed. But it was absolutely him, I have no doubt. He spoke to me."

"Wow."

"Of course, there is a scientific explanation," Jewell said.

"Like what?"

"Basically, the lack of oxygen to the brain causes cell death, which leads to hallucinations. But you know what?"

"What?"

"I don't care about the logic of it. I know how that moment made me feel. I really believe I saw heaven, just for that brief minute. And if that's true, then I know Josh is safe, and happy at last. I was more at peace in that moment than I've ever been in my whole entire life. Maybe that's why it stopped bothering me so much that Lydia was there when I woke up, and is sticking around now. Maybe it's rewired me somehow. Does that sound crazy?"

"No, not at all. It seems almost normal for people to have spiritual experiences from things like this."

"I still don't know anything about her though. Why she left. What she's been doing all this time."

"Do you want to know?"

"Oh, I don't know. I feel like my whole sense of reality has shifted. Maybe I'll feel different once I'm off the meds. Right now, I don't mind if she's around."

"Well, that's a start." Becca looped her arm through Jewell's. "This doesn't hurt, does it?"

"Don't worry. Contrary to popular belief around here, I am not actually a china doll."

Becca chuckled, and then a thought passed across her face.

"Did you…see Clara, when you were…well, you know?"

"No. I never thought about that. Maybe she's at a different level. Who knows?"

"Was that thunder?" Becca asked, turning suddenly.

"I didn't hear anything. Just one more thing."

"What?"

"When Kage broke up with me, he said I needed to get over my past or I could never move on."

This time, she heard it. A loud crack of thunder. In seconds, Aniela, Lydia, and Andrea bolted into the house, followed by an already soaked

Romeo scampering in behind them.

"Where's Maya?" Jewell asked.

"Oh, cats are resourceful," Aniela said. "I'm sure she's fine."

Becca jumped to her feet, "Where's your towels?"

Lydia grabbed a couple towels and the pair began to dry Romeo who was shaking his body fiercely distributing splashes of water everywhere.

"Eep, Romeo, stop!" Becca exclaimed, leaning her upper body away as she covered him with a towel.

"I'll make us some dinner," Andrea announced.

"And he cooks!" Becca called theatrically, still performing her duty.

"What're we having?' Jewell asked, her stomach suddenly rumbling with hunger pangs.

"Ratatouille and crepes."

"Yum," Aniela said.

"What a treat," Lydia echoed.

"Fancy," Becca sang, with a wink to Jewell.

Large raindrops were pelting the tin roof like a machine gun while the succulent fragrance of sautéing vegetables began to fill the room. The house had never felt cozier until right at that moment.

Aniela passed wine glasses to the women in the living area as they watched Andrea in the kitchen.

"Sorry, Jewell," Aniela said, withdrawing a wine-filled glass as Jewell shook her head and held her belly. "Oh, you're right, I've just remembered." She came back with a glass of sweet tea. "You'll have to use your imagination."

"That's okay. Trust me, after last night I am good with no wine for a while."

Andrea glanced up from his pan for a moment but didn't say anything.

"Actually, none for me either," Lydia said, stopping the glass traveling towards her.

"Oh, sorry, Lydia. I wasn't thinking."

"It's alright. Luckily, I have no desire to drink anymore. I just wish I could turn back time."

"But you can't," Jewell snapped without thinking, feeling bad as soon as she caught the pained look on her mother's face.

Andrea's dinner was predictably fabulous, and Jewell savored every bite. As soon as she set her fork down on her empty plate though, her eyes grew heavy and she had to retreat to the sofa.

With the kitchen cleaned up thanks to Andrea and Lydia; and Romeo walked and fed for the night thanks to Aniela and Becca, they sat in the living area for a short period.

"Okay," Lydia said, noticing Jewell's fatigue. "Let's clear out of Jewell's sleeping space. Becca, where do you want to sleep?"

"To be honest, I'd rather stay here, close to Jewell. I don't mind sharing a bed with you, if that's okay?"

"That's perfect," Lydia said.

"Right, I'm calling it a night," Aniela said and kissed Jewell on the top of her head.

"Let's get set up in the bedroom," Lydia said to Becca.

Andrea sat down next to Jewell on the sofa.

"Hey, maybe I was out of it," Jewell said, "but I could have sworn I heard you and Lydia speaking French with one another as you cleaned the kitchen."

"Is that so?"

"Yeah, I'm a little out of it. Um, thanks for last night," she said. "For carrying me back."

"You're welcome. I feel just awful about your appendix. I flung you over my shoulder like some caveman. I had no idea you had something wrong."

"Neither did I. I thought I was just upset about…" She stopped, unsure whether her mother would be able to hear her. "Besides, you probably did me a favor if you moved things along. I'm glad to have it over with."

"Okay, I feel a bit better now." He blew out his cheeks in relief. "So what's this with your mother appearing?"

Jewell kept her voice as low as possible. "Turns out she was the mystery woman at the Beehive."

"Yes, she was telling us about that when we were in the waiting room. She said she's been searching for you."

Jewell was itching to get the most uncomfortable part of this conversation out of the way. "Just so I know…when you were tucking me into bed last night, um, we didn't…you know…do anything, did we?"

Andrea snorted. "First, you think I'm gay. Then you think I take advantage of compromised women."

Jewell rolled her head back in embarrassment. "Oh gosh. Remind me to keep my mouth shut around you, forever. Just bring me some duct tape next time you come visit."

Andrea opened his mouth, clearly to make a rude joke. Jewell caught his look and fought against the urge to laugh.

"Relax," he said. "Last night, the only thing I could hear you saying was, 'I love you, Kage. I love you, Kage.'"

"No! I didn't."

"Yes, you did," Andrea sang. "Now, goodnight, my love. I'll check on you tomorrow."

After he had left, Jewell lay drifting off to sleep when she felt the presence of someone close by. She opened her eyes to see Becca and Lydia hovering over her.

"Here's some bottled water," Lydia said, setting it next to her. "Do you need another pain pill?"

"I don't think so. I feel okay."

"Call if you need anything," Becca said. "We'll be right here in the next room."

Five

Chapter 5

The next morning, Jewell awoke to the clanking of dishes from the kitchen. She swung her legs around to sit herself up.

"Be careful," Lydia said, leaving the kitchen area to assist her.

"I've got it," Jewell said.

"How are you feeling?"

"Okay, I think."

"Do you feel up to coffee?"

Jewell paused to assess herself. "Yeah, I think I do."

"I watched you at the Beehive. Cream and sugar, right?"

"How'd you make it?"

"I found your coffee press and made it with that."

"Great. I'll take it black, then."

Lydia delivered her a cup and took a seat in the chair next to the sofa.

They sat in silence. Jewell occasionally glanced at Lydia, and they smiled a quick smile at one another.

Becca stumbled into the living room, rubbing the sleep from her eyes. "What's up?"

"You are. Finally," Jewell said.

Lydia stood up."Well, I'm going to take my shower now if that's okay with you?"

"Fine," Jewell said.

As Lydia walked towards the bedroom, she called back. "Becca, there's coffee for you as well."

"OMG, I could hug you."

With Lydia out of the room, Jewell reached for Becca, making wide sweeping motions with her arms. "Come here."

"What?"

"Come here," she indicated a spot next to her.

Becca sat down on the opposite end of the sofa.

"No, over here." Jewell motioned her closer.

Becca scooted over towards Jewell, upon which she immediately took both of Becca's hands into her own. "I can't do this. I think the drugs, the surgery, the whole thing with seeing Josh and heaven, all that has worn off. Now I'm pissed at Lydia again."

"You're what?"

"She left me. Twenty-five years ago. And now, all of a sudden, she shows up and wants to just pick up where we left off?! How dare she! I worked so hard to—"

Becca pulled Jewell closer. "Listen to me. She's your mother. That has to count for something." They sat in silence for a few moments. Then Becca continued. "I had a friend once, a great friend." She looked pointedly at Jewell. "I found out that she'd been keeping a huge secret from me, one of monumental proportions. It really hurt when I found out. And then, one by one, even more of her secrets began to spill out. I nearly walked out on the friendship."

"I know, I was there," Jewell said, remembering that painful time.

"But then Kage, of all people, convinced me to stay and hear you out."

Jewell felt like she'd been struck with electricity. "Yeah?"

"Well, I thank God every day that I did. There would be a huge hole in my life now if I had listened to my instinct to flee. All I'm saying is, this might be your only chance to listen to what your mom has to say. I'm not saying forgive her right away or become best pals or anything like that. Just don't be hasty. Don't close a door you might regret later."

Jewell leaned her head against Becca's shoulder. "I can't get over her walking out on me the way she did. I was a toddler, for God's sake. And now she's taken all these years to show up, when I've found a way not to want her anymore." She sat back and stared at Becca, as if she could somehow pluck the answers out of her. "Where's she been all this time? What is she really after that 's made her come track me down now?"

"The answers may come." Becca was clearly trying to sound reassuring. "They may not. Just do me a favor, give it time."

Jewell exhaled, studying Becca's face, then scrunched her lips to the right. "Okay, I'll try. Will you stay with me though?"

Becca gave her hands a warm squeeze. "Every step of the way."

Over the next few days, Jewell, Lydia and Becca enjoyed a quiet, restful time knocking around the house. In the mornings Jewell and Lydia sat at the kitchen bar, drinking coffee and sharing mostly superficial aspects of their lives. Becca tended to sleep in, so Lydia would make the coffee and wait for Becca to lumber into the kitchen before cooking breakfast. Rikki complained jokingly to Jewell that she was missing the tips.

Jewell asked Lydia if she had a lease somewhere in Rosemore Heights.

Andrea had driven her to get the rest of her belongings the day after Jewell's surgery.

"No. I was just renting a room by the week."

"What about a car?"

"I had no need. The room was in a house downtown. I was happy walking everywhere."

As Jewell recovered from the surgery, she observed Lydia while trying not to be obvious about it. Lydia was a tall and slender woman who Jewell calculated would be around 47 years of age. She seemed to be a stoic woman, who carried herself with the grace and pride of a woman of much greater wealth. Although, Jewell recalled her saying she didn't have the funds for a high-end PI. Her voice was low and breathy, delivered with a slow, methodical cadence. She reminded Jewell of the sex symbols in the 1950s movies she and Josh used to watch. Jewell's curiosity began to grow, wondering where Lydia had been all these years, and what she'd been doing. But she wasn't prepared to start that conversation yet.

On one particular morning, Lydia entered the kitchen carrying what looked like a photo album under her arm.

"What's that?" Jewell asked.

"It's a scrapbook, all the way back to my high school days," Lydia answered. "The picture quality wasn't as good, so they're fading a little, but you can still make out what's important. Do you want to see?"

Jewell hesitated. "I guess."

They opened the album out on the kitchen island. The first page displayed photos of teens at a swimming pool. A chain-link fence surrounded the pool.

"Where's that?" Jewell asked, cocking her head.

"Oh, that was a public pool in Port Eastlyn. They've filled it in since then, built commercial buildings on top of it. It was gone by the time you were born."

Jewell examined the beautiful young girl smiling next to a good-looking man. The girl had black hair.

"Is this you?" she asked, pointing at the photo.

"That's me. Many moons ago."

The man in the photo had a broad chest and thick blonde hair, with one prominent curl at the top of his forehead. "Is that…?"

"Yes, that's Jason Caldwell. Your father. We were so in love." Lydia gazed at the photo lovingly. His looks reminded Jewell of the "Sundance Kid" from one of Josh's favorite movies.

Then Jewell noticed Lydia in a photo with another woman. They were wearing similar bikinis and looked almost identical. In fact, the only way Jewell knew which one was Lydia was the slight differences in their swimsuits and the cut of her hair.

"Who's that?"

Lydia's voice was calm. "That's my twin sister, Laura."

"You have a twin sister? I don't remember ever hearing about her."

"Had," Lydia said.

"Oh?"

"Yes. The PI I hired was also searching for Nathanael and Laura. He hasn't had any luck locating Nathanael." She briefly glanced at Jewell, then changed the subject. "But he did bring me closure on Laura. Turns out she died suddenly. A blood clot that went to her brain before anyone could stop it."

"Oh, gosh. I'm sorry."

"She smoked," Lydia continued matter-of-factly. "We all did back then. Only, she was on birth control pills too. It was only a couple years after I…" Lydia shook her head. "She had moved to New England, apparently."

Tears silently began to trickle from her eyes. Jewell retrieved a box of tissues from the other end of the counter.

"That's awful," she said, handing the box to Lydia. "When did you say she died?"

"That's the worst part. It was only a few months after I left. I guess I disappeared a little too well. The news never reached me." She gazed off, speaking almost to the air. "The entire time, I thought you and Nathanael were with her."

"With her?!"

"Yes, I left the two of you with her. She was married to a doctor, she had everything you could possibly need, unlike me. My only comfort in all that time had been the thought that the two of you were living with her, leading a safe, comfortable life. Piano lessons, tutors, private schools, nice unif—."

"But we weren't with her. I never even knew I had an aunt. All I remember are some vague recollections of our first home. Nathanael had to fill in the gaps for me." Jewell was fighting now not to cry herself. But she could feel her chin trembling, and angry tears were threatening to spill from her eyes. "After what you did, we got passed from foster home to foster home. We were separated."

Lydia covered her face with her hands and sobbed. Jewell stared at the counter top, her hands firmly between her thighs, her feet on the base of the bar stool.

Lydia strained to speak. "I swear, I only learned of what happened to you when I started my search." The veins in her neck were bulging. "I feel detestable. I so badly wish I could take it back, all of it."

"You can't," Jewell said. Her voice was as flat as she felt now. She just wanted to go back to the sofa and pull the cover over her head. She watched Lydia's shoulders droop. Jewell tried to sympathize, tried to believe what her mother was saying was true. "What I meant was, what's done is done. None of us have the luxury of changing the past. Don't you think I want a do over with Josh too?"

"I know. I'm sorry." Lydia placed her hand on Jewell's forearm. "Have you seen Nathanael at all in the past years?"

"We met twice a year on each other's birthdays. Sometimes we also ran into each other randomly. It was a small town."

"But you don't know where he is now?"

"No. I told you, I don't."

They resumed flipping through the album. Jewell motioned to stop at the pictures from Jason and Lydia's wedding. Her mother was wearing a plain white gauze dress. It was floor-length and off-the-shoulder. Jason was in a light blue suit. Jewell traced her finger lightly over the picture.

"Oh, that's what we called a leisure suit." Lydia chuckled. "Popular back then, believe it or not."

"I can't believe it," Jewell said, and they both laughed. Jewell studied Lydia's face, searching for similarities. Her hair was as far from Jewell's on the color spectrum as possible. Lydia's skin was a few shades darker too, and her round eyes were the color of midnight. She saw Nathanael's features in her.

"Who's that?" Jewell asked, pointing to a woman standing behind Lydia in the photograph. "Is that your grandmother?"

"No, that's *your* grandmother. She looked old even then."

"Where was she all that time?"

Lydia fidgeted with a loose corner of the book. "Her? Well, she was in really bad shape, truth be told. She couldn't get around very well. I heard about her death sometime later."

"What about our grandfather?"

"He left us."

Jewell had heard about him. She squinted at Lydia with wrinkled brow, trying to comprehend the kind of family she had descended from.

Lydia quickly turned the page. Jewell saw pictures of Lydia and Jason holding a baby, looking far too young themselves. They were sitting on an orange-patterned sofa in a trailer with paneled walls.

"That's Nathanael."

"I figured as much." Jewell's lips instinctively tightened.

Lydia glanced at her. "Let's find you." She flipped through more pages. "There you are. You were such a beautiful baby. You look just like your dad." In the picture, Nathanael was standing next to their father, who was cradling Jewell. Lydia drew in a long breath. "Can you at least tell me why you won't talk about your brother? The PI said he practically dropped off the face of the earth."

"Hmm, I'm not surprised."

"Why? What do you know?" Lydia asked.

"Nothing." Jewell's voice was escalating. "I know nothing about where he is. But, if you're so obsessed with knowing why I won't talk about him, he blackmailed me, okay? I don't know, and I don't care where he is. If you're so desperate to find him, get yourself a better detective!"

Becca wandered into the kitchen, rubbing her eyes. "Hey, what's with the yelling?" Romeo was close behind her, barking.

"Why don't you ask Becca about your precious Nathanael?" Jewell blasted, then stormed through the bedroom to the back sandy area, Romeo following her.

The house was quiet over the next few days. Aniela and Andrea stopped by occasionally. Becca and Jewell hung out in the back area, sipping wine or coffee depending on the time of day, and throwing Romeo's toys for him like old times back in Southbridge. Maya also graced them with her presence from time to time.

One morning over coffee, Jewell told Becca with relief that her follow-up appointment would be the next day. "Hopefully I'll be able to dance again. I need to burn off some of this pent-up frustration."

"Can't you forgive her? I mean, can't you at least see why she'd want to find her son as much as she wanted to find you?"

"No. No, I can't. You know he's a monster."

"I do, in principle. But, all and all, he really didn't hurt me. You do know he had an organized crime ring threatening his life."

"So now you're on his side?"

"No. I'm absolutely on your side. But I think most people would do anything if they had some serious thugs breathing down their necks. His life was in danger."

"He could have come to me and asked me for money. Legitimately. I would've given him whatever he needed."

"I know, but his mind doesn't work like ours. He doesn't trust anyone. He only operates with people who are searching for an angle. Always. That's got to affect your psyche at some point."

"Wow, so you're already a qualified psychologist? I thought you hadn't even started classes yet."

"Okay, I get it. Let's change the subject."

"Well, since you're in psychology mode, do you want to hear what Andrea told me?"

"Oh?" Becca leaned closer on the arm of her wooden chair.

"He said, when he was carrying me to bed, the night before my surgery, I kept repeating, 'I love you, Kage, I love you, Kage.' What the heck does that mean? Do I still want him subconsciously, even when I think I've moved on?"

"Uh-oh," Becca responded.

"Uh-oh what?"

"Kage is, um, he's seeing someone."

"Really? That was fast."

"You almost dated Andrea," Becca chuckled, snapping her mouth shut when Jewell threw her a look. Becca gazed at the table in front of her. "I didn't want to tell you. I thought it would either blow over, or you'd find out when you came back to Southbridge. By then, I figured, you'd be long over him, maybe even have a new love of your own, and it wouldn't matter. I don't know, guess I was trying to protect you."

Jewell stared over at the streaming water. "I appreciate it. I think next time I'd prefer the ugly truth though."

"Do you want to see her?" Becca asked, picking up her phone from the arm of her chair. "She's like a mini you. She's friends with Brook on Instagram."

"No. I don't want to see, that would be too weird. Wait a minute, friends with Brook?"

"Yep, she's...young."

"Wow."

"Okay, maybe you'll want to look later." Becca moved to place her phone back on the arm of her chair, when it pinged. She studied her screen. "Hey, it's Della Rae." Becca appeared to be reading her screen and then gasped, she snapped her head towards Jewell.

"Okay, you're scaring me now. What is it?"

Becca passed the phone to Jewell, who read the text aloud. *Get back here right away. Sherry has been arrested for questioning about the death of Gaylen Spalding.*

"Who's Gaylen Spalding?" Jewell asked.

"I have no idea."

Jewell used Becca's phone to text Della Rae. *Who's Gaylen Spalding?*

Della Rae's response came immediately. *Just hurry back, no time to explain. I don't want to share too much in writing. Our phones could be confiscated. We're meeting at Rhita's tomorrow morning and going over everything. Try to be there at 11 A.M.*

Becca and Jewell stared at one another in disbelief for a few seconds before springing to action.

Jewell darted into the kitchen and found Lydia cuddling Maya. "We have to go back to Southbridge. Right now."

"Why, what's wrong?" Lydia asked, setting Maya on her feet.

"We have to pack."

Lydia remained still.

"Aren't you going to pack?" Jewell shrieked, flinging her arms for emphasis.

"Me?"

"Yes, you, unless you want to stay here by yourself?"

"No, of course not, I want to go. I just thought…" She headed towards the bedroom to gather her things. "Wait, Jewell."

"What?"

"Your doctor's appointment tomorrow. You shouldn't travel without the all-clear."

"Good thinking."

Jewell got out her phone and called the surgeon's office. The nurse on duty asked her a series of questions, then thankfully gave Jewell permission to travel, as long as she promised to schedule a follow-up appointment with her own physician as soon as she arrived in Southbridge.

Relieved, Jewell joined Becca and Lydia's packing furry in the bedroom.

Jewell had scrambled to secure three tickets back to Florida for that evening, and they were stuck with a red-eye flight. Jewell and Lydia had the most luggage to pack, Becca fortunately had only brought a small carry-on. They loaded as much as possible into the rental's trunk and stacked the rest on the back floor. Becca crammed into the back next to Romeo's carrier and held her bag on her lap. Lydia held the cat carrier Aniela had managed to rummage from her shed.

Aniela and Andrea met them at the car. Jewell had prepared an entire speech about why Maya would be better off with her in Southbridge, only to find that pleading her case turned out far simpler than expected.

"She's more your cat than she's ever been anyone else's," Aniela said simply. "And it's time your pooch had a sister." Jewell laughed and gave her a fierce hug.

"I just hate that you never got to dance with me at the restaurant, or complete your classes. Promise you'll come back when things settle down in Florida?"

"I'll try," Jewell answered. "Thank you for everything. You've been a legendary host."

She turned to Andrea. Their eyes locked, and they both grinned at what might have been.

He shrugged. "C'est la vie, ma belle. Your destiny awaits you elsewhere." Then he added, with decidedly less whimsy, "You just might get a visitor in Southbridge someday."

"I would like that."

"Yes, please!" Becca exclaimed.

Jewell rolled her eyes, feeling herself blush. "Hey, wind up your window there."

Six

Chapter 6

A sense of nostalgia infused Jewell as she crested the steps into Rhita's. The rest of the troupe, minus Sherry, were already at their usual round table with drinks. Z sprang from her seat and rushed over to hug Jewell and Becca.

"Hey, Z," Jewell said. "This is Lydia."

"Hi, Lydia," Z said, thrusting her arm around Lydia and pulling her in for a hug.

They approached the table and Jewell provided introductions. "This is Nicci, Candi, Della Rae, and Gabby." Lydia nodded to each in turn. Jewell remained standing. "I can't speak for Becca or Lydia, but I need something warm and sweet before we start talking." Lydia and Becca agreed, and the three of them filed into line.

Jewell recommended her favorite drink to Lydia.

"I love the feel of this place," Lydia said, reading the humorous signs and rustic decor.

"I know, isn't it sweet?" Becca agreed. "I used to work here."

"You said, on the way here. And you described it perfectly."

"Oh yes, that's right."

Jewell smiled when she heard Lydia order a White Chocolate Macadamia Nut.

With coffees in hand, they returned to the table and Jewell motioned for Lydia to take the seat where Sherry usually sat. Becca and Jewell took up their usual places.

Finally settled, Jewell's eyes migrated to Candi's rounded belly. "The rumors are true then. Congratulations."

Candi rubbed the top of her basket-ball belly. "Yeah. I knew before you went away, but we weren't telling anyone yet. I'm going on five months now. This bump basically popped out overnight."

"Congratulations," Lydia echoed.

While the others focused on Lydia and blasted her with questions, Jewell leaned into Becca and whispered, "Omigod, like what happened? I mean like what happened to Candi's speech or whatever? I mean like has pregnancy caused her to speak in full sentences or whatever? I mean, like really."

Becca spit her coffee across the table, then covered her mouth as laughter shook her body. The group turned to them.

"Sorry, we're just a little crazy from sleep deprivation." Jewell dabbed up the mess. "We had an overnight flight."

Becca composed herself, but Lydia was peering at her and Jewell with narrowed eyes.

Jewell mouthed to Lydia, "I'll tell you later."

Nicci clanked her mug with her spoon. "Let's get on with the matter at hand." She nodded to Della Rae. "Go ahead."

"I got a call from Sherry the night before last," Della Rae started. "Friday night, well actually it was Saturday morning by then. She wasn't making much sense, saying she'd been arrested and needed me to come get her. I picked her up and found out she hadn't been arrested, she was being held for questioning about Gaylen Spalding's death."

"Who on earth is Gaylen Spalding?" Jewell asked.

"He's a well-known local rich boy," Gabby explained. "Southbridge high-society. The family is well respected, but he's known for his…partying."

"You sound like *The Seaside Sentinel*," Z joked.

"So what if I do?" Gabby sipped her coffee haughtily.

"That rag is just gossip!"

"Go on, Della Rae," Nicci said, crossing her arms.

"Well, they didn't have enough to hold her. They don't even know if his death was from natural causes or foul play. But she's been instructed not to leave town. There's going to be an autopsy. Y'all need to pray he died of natural causes."

Jewell bit her lip. She knew all about waiting for an autopsy report.

"Tell them the worst part," Nicci urged.

"Apparently, Sherry found him dead *in bed*."

"How?" Jewell asked.

"I think we can all guess how," Gabby said with a mixture of sympathy for her friend and delight in the story.

"She um…apparently woke up next to him."

"Were they dating?" Becca asked with raised eyebrows. "I don't recall her ever talking about dating."

"No," Della Rae answered. "All she remembers is going to Las Fuentes."

"That's that high-class bar about five blocks up," Candi chimed in.

"What else did she tell you?" Nicci urged.

"She said it was early evening and the bar was fairly empty. Then, some cute guy came in and sat on the barstool next to her, and just started chatting her up. She remembers conversing with him, not about what in particular, just that he was easy to talk to. *And* easy on the eyes." Della Rae raised her eyebrows for emphasis. "From what she can recall, at some point they started doing shots. The last thing she remembered was the room starting to spin. Next thing she knew, she woke up in a strange apartment next to this cute guy. She couldn't even remember his name. She thought about slipping out, but then couldn't remember how she'd gotten there. No idea where her car was, nothing. So she decided to wake him. But she couldn't, no matter how hard she shook him. Eventually, she realized he was dead and immediately called 9-1-1. That's all she knows."

"The first thing we need to do, pronto, is get her a top lawyer," Jewell said.

"Already done," Della Rae confirmed. "Montgomery Alex. He's the best in the area. He's meeting me at her house this afternoon. It's going to cost her, calling him out on a Sunday."

"It'll be worth it," Nicci said.

"Where was her car in the end?" Jewell asked.

"What? Oh, I didn't even think to ask. Lordy, I was in such shock," Della Rae said.

"I'm sure," Z said.

"Where's Sherry now?" Becca asked.

"She's a basket case right now," Della Rae said. "I gave her a sedative and she's been sleeping off and on. I'll go back and check on her when we're done."

Jewell looked towards the coffee counter for a notepad and pen. "We need to compile a list of questions for her."

"I'll get you something," Becca said, getting up.

"I have my laptop and tablet, you know." Nicci said. "This isn't 1980."

"I like to write in pen," Jewell said. "It helps me process the information. But thanks."

Nicci shook out her curls. "Suit yourself."

Becca returned with a notepad and pen and handed them to Jewell.

"Why don't we all go to Sherry's this afternoon when the lawyer is there? One of us might think of something no one else does," Nicci said.

"Good idea," Z agreed.

"Then, when he leaves," Nicci continued, "we'll fill in any gaps we can think of. For example, we'll make sure she retraces every single step of that day."

"And ask if she's ever seen the guy before," Gabby added.

"Didn't she say he was a stranger?" Nicci asked.

"Well, she referred to him as 'some cute guy,'" Della Rae said. "But personally, I think any questions are good at this point. We don't have much else to go on."

The group began blurting out questions and Jewell worked hard to keep up with the note taking.

"Did anything out of the ordinary happen that day?"

"Did she see anything unusual in the bar?"

"Was Gaylen alone? Did he enter the bar alone?"

"Can she remember who the bartender was?"

"Did she drive to the bar and where is her car now?"

"Hey, slow down," Jewell said.

"We'll want to go to the station and find out who's assigned to the case," Lydia said. "It's in Sherry's best interest for you to assist him where you can."

"Good thinking," Jewell said.

"Let's go to Las Fuentes and check around the block, see if we can find her car," Jewell suggested.

The group walked to the infamous bar. Candi paired up with Jewell. "How was Southern California?"

"I was having great fun until I had to have emergency surgery."

"Yeah, I heard," Candi said. "That's a bummer. Did you get my card?"

"I did, thanks." Jewell looked over her shoulder. "I liked your 'get well' memes, too, Z. Even if it hurt to laugh."

Z grinned her devilish grin.

They arrived at the bar, only to discover it would be closed until 4 P.M.

"Let's walk around to the outer perimeter to see if her car is there," Nicci suggested.

They spotted it. Della Rae tested the door. "It's locked."

"She must have ridden with Gaylen to his place," Jewell said. "Or maybe they got a taxi together."

"Or even a friend," Gabby added. "In which case, someone else might know something."

"Take a picture," Nicci said. "You never know what she might need. We'll also need to ask the lawyer if we should leave the car here or not."

"I'm kind of surprised it hasn't been tagged in some way," Lydia said. "Surely the police did a license plate search. It's not exactly hard to find."

The group turned to Lydia. She shrugged. "I watch a lot of detective shows."

"Good point," Della Rae said. "Do you still have your notepad, Jewell?"

"Hottest sexatary ever," Becca said jokingly, then quickly recanted. "Oh gosh, Della Rae, sorry. I wasn't thinking."

"No worries, Winslow isn't the first to cheat with his secretary and he won't be the last. Besides, the affair that stuck was with a woman his own age. Go figure."

"Awkward," Z sang, and completed her photography of Sherry's car.

The group met at Sherry's house at 2 P.M. as planned. The lack of sleep was catching up with Jewell. She had dozed on and off during the flight, but not enough to substitute a good night's sleep. The Florida heat wasn't helping either, and the combination had her jonesing for some of Becca's strong brew.

Jewell and Lydia pulled up at the address they had been given. This was the first time Jewell had been to Sherry's house. It was impressive, located between downtown and the beach in a well-established neighborhood. It was the type of home that was overflowing with character and surrounded by lush trees and shrubs. Jewell guessed it was built circa 1950. It was a two-story home with classy gray siding trimmed with white railings and window-panes. It looked like a well-maintained home and Jewell wondered how Sherry possibly afforded it. She had never heard her talk about a job. In fact, she realized how little she really knew about Sherry outside of bellydance.

Sherry opened the door with red and swollen eyes. Jewell hugged her immediately and introduced her to Lydia.

"Some of the others are here already." Sherry sniffed. "We're still waiting for the lawyer. Oh, and Candi and Gabby."

The door opened onto a tastefully decorated living room in coastal style with blues and whites similar to Jewell's rental house, only not quite as whimsical. Sherry led them through to the dining room, where Della Rae, Becca, Nicci and Z were sitting.

"We were wondering who was at the door," Della Rae said.

"My money's on Gabby being last," Becca said with a chuckle.

"How are you, Sherry?" Jewell asked before taking a seat next to Becca.

"I'm trying to hang in there. Della Rae's pill has worn off but I don't want any more. In fact, now is probably a good time to let you all know..." The room fell silent while Sherry took a deep breath.

"I think I need to stop drinking. I might need to go to A.A."

"Oh, Sherry, I'm so happy to hear you say that. Now I don't have to suggest it," Della Rae said, leaping up to hug her. "I'm so proud of you. And we'll be with you every step of the way."

The doorbell rang. "I'll get that," Sherry said.

"I've got five says it's Candi," Z wagered.

"I'll say the lawyer," Becca said.

"Okay, who'll give me three to one if it's Gabby?" Nicci asked.

Jewell scoffed at them. "Look at you all, betting. And, you, putting your money on Gabby."

"Hey, bigger risk, bigger payout."

Sherry returned with a looming figure walking in behind her. It was a man with glorious good looks.

"Ah," Z threw her hands in the air. "Darn it."

"Shit," Nicci snapped.

"Pay up, homies." Becca beckoned with her hands.

Sherry stood in the doorway with a deadpan expression. "This is Montgomery Alex," she said. "My lawyer."

"Your names are backwards," Jewell said.

"So I've been told," he said matter-of-factly.

Shame, Jewell thought. His missing sense of humor just canceled out his perfect looks.

"Let me leave a note on the front door for Candi and Gabby to see themselves in," Sherry said. "I'll be right back."

The women sat, eyes fixed on Mr. Alex as he opened his briefcase and removed a pad and folder. He looked up to see the trance-like focus on him.

He must be used to women staring at him, Jewell thought. She began hoping for an all-female jury. That was, of course, if it came down to a trial, which she prayed it wouldn't.

Sherry returned and drew up a seat next to the lawyer.

"Okay, let's get started," he said. Jewell's gaze followed his oversized hand as it swept through a tuft of his hair. Hair so dark it cast a plum hue. He took a pen from the breast pocket of his black starched suit, which must have been hellish in the steamy Florida afternoon.

"Sherry Ann McKenna?" he asked.

"Yes," Sherry said.

He glanced around at the others. "I'm not accustomed to my clients having a full house when we speak. Is it okay if I talk openly?"

"Yes, they're my friends. More like my family, really."

"What's your age?"

"Thirty-six." She glanced at her friends. She had never divulged her age before now.

"How long have you lived in Southbridge?"

"My entire life. In this house, actually. I inherited it from my parents. I'm an only child."

"Are you employed?"

Everyone leaned in.

"Yes."

"And who is your employer?"

"I'm self-employed. As a personal organizer."

"Can you describe your service?"

"I go to people's homes and organize their closets, their offices, sometimes their kitchen cabinets. Anything they need, really. I arrange their belongings in systems for ease of use and then teach them how to use the system to keep it working. I have a lot of repeat customers."

Jewell shot Becca a 'who knew?' look.

The lawyer peered from his papers to Jewell. She straightened in her chair.

"I picked up your police report. There are no charges against you, nor are you named as a suspect, so everything currently rides on the results of the autopsy report. I must be honest with you. If foul play is suspected, the fact you woke up next to the victim doesn't look good."

Sherry put her head in her hands. Della Rae rubbed her back.

"Please, let me clarify. I will prove you innocent, but it will require rigorous work. And only if Gaylen Spalding's death is determined suspicious. I need you to describe the events of Friday evening, starting with the lead-up to your trip to Las Fuentes. Tell me everything in as much detail as possible." He took his phone from his briefcase, set it on the table and, after receiving confirmation and permission, pressed a button to begin recording.

Sherry wrung her hands. "I have to start by saying that I don't remember everything after a certain point. Some snippets are starting to come back, but after the point we started doing shots, my memory gets a little fuzzy."

"Okay, tell me everything you remember as best you can."

During Sherry's pained narrative, Gabby and Candi crept in with apologetic looks and sat down quietly among the others.

"Well, I don't always go out, but I do drink every night." She looked at her friends. "I mean…I drank every night. I'm quitting. I drank through the week, but felt I should hold it together and take it slow on weeknights. With my business and all. I drank, but not always to the point of passing out. On weekends it was different. I would drink until I blacked out. Typically, I drank at home. It was rare for me to go out." She paused. "I-I'm not used to telling people all of this personal stuff."

"Would you like to speak to me alone?" he asked.

"No." She gazed around the table. "It's fine." She gave a brave smile, then her eyes flicked away. "Where was I?"

"You said it was rare for you to go out," Della Rae offered.

"Yes. But now and then, it got lonely."

"Hence, the night in question?" he led.

"Yes," she continued. "I had already been drinking some."

"I put on makeup and dressed up, something I hardly ever do, but the mood struck me. I had been to Las Fuentes before, once. It's nice. Upscale. I drove there even though I knew I shouldn't have, since I'd already been drinking. Is that going to make it worse?" she asked.

"Two separate things, criminally speaking, but it may hurt character-wise. We won't offer the information. Continue. You're doing well."

Della Rae nodded in encouragement.

"So, I parked in a spot on the outer perimeter—"

"We have to confess." Nicci addressed the lawyer. "We found Sherry's car today. Should we pick it up?"

"Yes, and the sooner the better." Mr. Alex turned to Sherry. "Do you normally park in your garage?"

"Yes."

"Perfect. Park it there," he instructed Nicci. "Continue, Ms. McKenna."

"So, I parked and walked around to the bar."

"What time was this?"

"Probably around 5 P.M. I knew it was early to be going to a bar, but then again, I had already been drinking. It was dimly lit for a classy bar. There were blue and green lights around the bar itself, but otherwise it was pretty dark. Even the window-shades were pulled down."

"How many people were there?"

"There was a couple in one of the booths and three women in another."

"Where did you sit?"

"I sat at the bar. I was the only one at the bar."

"Who was the bartender?"

"A girl named Lizzie. I do remember that. She told me before I got plastered."

"Did you know anyone in the bar at this time? Had you ever seen them before?"

"No, not one person."

"What did you do next?'

"I ordered a Rum Mojito. I was content sipping it and looking around. I was happy to be out among people. I struck up a conversation with Lizzie and learned that she's in her third semester at St. Frances. And that she rides motorcycles. Then, he came in."

"Gaylen Spalding?"

"Yes. Only in this part of my memory, I didn't know his name. I'm sure he told me, but I don't remember it happening. We began flirting. I started drinking faster, because he was fun and extremely good looking. I have only had a few boyfriends in my lifetime, but they weren't what you would call good looking. He was an eleven on a ten-point scale. I'll admit, I was soaking up the attention. We started doing shots. I remember the room starting to spin. I told myself I should stop. And that's the last I remember until…"

"Until?" Mr. Alex asked.

"Until I woke up confused about where I was. I was lying on my right side, and when I opened my eyes, I didn't recognize anything. The room was dark, but a light from an open door showed a dresser with a mirror and a chair with jeans flung over it. My brain was really foggy. I rolled over and could make out there was a man on the other side of the bed. Then I remembered drinking with some guy at the bar and figured it must be him. I thought I'd sneak out of there, only I realized I didn't know how I had gotten there, where I was or where my car was, so I thought I'd better wake him up. Fortunately he was covered so I didn't have to see him naked. It was a king-sized bed and he was a distance from me. I stretched my arm and shook him over the covers, but he didn't move. I shook him harder. Getting nervous, I yelled, "Hey." Nothing. He still didn't move. I thought, wow, someone who gets drunker than me. I jumped up to turn on the lights. That's when I saw that his eyes were open. It freaked me out, so I screamed. I stood there for a minute, just staring at him. His eyes were fixed on the ceiling. He had blue splotches on his skin and his lips looked blue. I felt his neck for a pulse, not really sure what I was doing, but I couldn't feel anything. His skin was cold. I closed his eyelids and called 9-1-1. I tried to figure out what to do. I didn't know whether to wait or not, but I had already given my name and used my cell phone. So, I waited."

"You did the right thing," Della Rae said.

"Yes, you did," the lawyer agreed. "I'm glad you didn't leave without realizing he was dead. That apartment building has a doorman and security. It would have complicated our case further had you snuck out and the body was found later. Do you remember anything else, or have anything else to add?"

"No, that's it. They held me for questioning and then I called Della Rae to pick me up. You know the rest from there."

"Very good. There's no need for concern at this time. We'll await the autopsy report. There were no obvious signs of murder, no apparent trauma to the body, no blood anywhere. I think you'll be fine. I shall follow up with the precinct and update you as any news comes in. You said you are planning to quit drinking?"

"I have quit," Sherry said.

Mr. Alex fished something out of his papers. "Should you choose to seek out a support group such as the A.A., might I suggest you take this sheet with you? Have it signed at each meeting you attend. There should always be someone they call a secretary leading the group. I used to counsel clients with DWIs and this is valuable documentation to have on standby."

After Sherry saw the lawyer out, Jewell watched Lydia touch Sherry lightly on the shoulder and overheard her say she would go to an A.A. meeting with her, if that would help. She confessed to her own problem, and said she'd been planning to get a local schedule anyway.

Jewell volunteered to pick up Sherry's car. Sherry dug through her purse and handed the key to Jewell. Becca left her car at Sherry's and rode downtown with Jewell and Lydia to where Sherry's car was parked. Della Rae stayed with Sherry, and the rest of the gang went home.

"See you Wednesday, Jewell," Gabby called out.

"Wednesday?" Jewell asked.

"Yes, silly. Class!"

"Oh, right, I really am out of routine. See you then!"

Becca drove Sherry's car to her house with Jewell and Lydia following behind. Della Rae was awaiting their arrival, poised to open the garage door. Jewell and Lydia went inside with Becca to say goodbye to Della Rae and Sherry.

Lydia also wanted to firm up their plans for attending the next A.A. meeting together. "I checked the schedule for Southbridge on my phone. We can go first thing tomorrow at 8 A.M., if you'd like. Jewell tells me it's in a huge Catholic church downtown. I can walk and meet you there?"

"Or I can come pick you up," Sherry offered.

"That's okay. I like to walk, especially in the morning."

On the drive home, Jewell said to Lydia, "You know, you can use my car anytime you want. I was also thinking, maybe we should get you your own car while you're here."

"That's sweet of you, but I really don't need one. Like I said, I like to walk." Lydia paused. "To be honest, there's really nowhere I need to go unless you're going too." That comment gave Jewell pause. "Besides," Lydia continued, "I'm trying to ration the little bit I still have saved up. I can't go back to waitressing, it's too hard on this nearly fifty-year-old body."

"Is that what you did for a living?"

"It is."

"Well, you can always use my car if you need it. I don't want you to feel stranded."

"I don't."

Jewell turned the radio on low, selecting a station playing Nineties music. "I like the oldies," she confessed.

"Oldies?" Lydia said with a chuckle. "Now, the Seventies, that's good oldies music."

"The SEVENTIES!" Jewell shot a quick sideways look at Lydia, then shook her head.

"You know, Jewell, after watching Sherry go through all of this, I'm glad nothing like this ever happened to me. It could have. I used to black out. But I'm glad I'm free and over my addiction. Otherwise, I never would have found you."

Jewell clutched the steering wheel tighter and stared at the road ahead.

"Jewell?"

"Yes?"

"Are we ever going to talk about Nathanael?"

"There's nothing to talk about."

"He's my child too, just like you."

"And he's a criminal and a blackmailer. You want to talk about someone who blackmailed his own sister."

"Yes, that's certainly bad." Lydia pushed some of her hair behind her ear to reveal her silver hoop earring. "It's just, I know his heart is like yours, deep down."

"I'm sorry, I just can't envision us ever talking about him."

They arrived home. Lydia retrieved her things from where she had thrown them in the spare room and headed to her bedroom to unpack and settle in. "I really like your house, by the way. It's cute."

"I'm only renting it."

"Nonetheless, you chose a nice place."

Jewell fed Romeo, then escaped to relax on the back patio.

The next morning, Jewell sat at her kitchen island with the *Southbridge Times* spread out over the surface. She watched Lydia walk over to the coffee press and see the empty mug Jewell had set out for her. The corners of Lydia's lips turned up, and it gave Jewell a warm surge all over.

"Good morning," Lydia said cheerfully.

"Good morning. Look at this." Jewell slid the front page towards her mother. The headline read, "Wealthy Playboy Found Dead."

"Oh my."

"The entire town knows now. I suggest we take a proactive approach and try to figure this out before the autopsy results come in," Jewell said.

"Really?"

"Yes. Josh's autopsy results were delayed because of the volume of cases at the time, but I did some exploring of my own. It was never my area of expertise, and I found that, even when volume isn't an issue, it can take weeks for the toxicology reports alone to come back from outside labs."

Jewell sent a group text to the troupe.

Did you see the front page of the newspaper today? Let's meet at Rhita's. I know it's a workday for many, so how about noon for lunch?

Once agreements had come in from the others, she filled Lydia in on the plan.

"Don't forget though," Lydia said. "I'm meeting Sherry for A.A. this morning. Plus, you need to have a doctor check you out for your surgery follow up. You shouldn't dance until you are cleared."

"That's right. Thanks for reminding me. I will. And, thanks for meeting Sherry at A.A."

They continued to review the article.

"See the picture of his fiancée?" Jewell said. "He was engaged." She indicated the picture featuring Chantal Darcey. "I'd say this says a fair amount about the type of woman she is. The snobby type. Look at her puffed-up hair."

"A look like that comes with a high price tag, I'd say," Lydia added.

"And her perfect makeup on her perfect face looks like it would crack if she smiled. She looks like she hasn't eaten in a year. I'd be afraid she'd gnaw my arm off given half a chance."

Still chuckling from their shared pettiness, the women finished up their breakfasts and got themselves ready to tackle the day ahead.

Seven

Chapter 7

The whole troupe made it to Rhita's this time. Lydia had opted to stay home. Gabby came with two of her boys in tow, the other two were at summer camp.

"Sorry." She placed her palm to block her pointing at the boys. "Kevin is at work."

While the group sat around their usual table, Tyler and Tristan made a dinosaur park out of the coffee shop, shouting dinosaur calls and littering tables with their plastic green and gray toys. Some of the women only ordered drinks, while others indulged in the light lunchtime fare Rhita's offered.

Jewell pulled the newspaper from her backpack and laid it out in the middle of the table.

"Sherry has something to share," Della Rae said. "Being sober is already clearing her brain."

Sherry looked up. "I've been getting my memory back. Snippets keep flashing back."

"That's fabulous," Nicci said. "Let's get on with it then. I can't be away from the office too long. I normally don't even leave for lunch."

"Tell us everything," Jewell said, retrieving her notepad and pen. "Just tell us everything you remember. Anything at all."

"Well, I remember getting into his car. The leather seats were so luxurious, I remember thinking I could sleep right then and there. He told me they were made of Italian leather. Then I'm blank until the part where his elevator doors opened into his apartment. Imagine, elevator doors opening directly into your apartment."

"Man, I want an apartment like that," Z said.

"Me too," Candi said, still chewing a bite of her egg croissant dripping with sauce that landed on her protruding belly. "Oops, a shelf." She shrugged with a giggle. Jewell shook her head wondering where the appearance-obsessed Candi disappeared to.

Sherry continued. "Then he asked if I wanted a drink and I said yes. I know, I know." She waved her hands. "I was already so drunk I was blacking out, but I'm an alcoholic. Drinking is what I do. Did. Anyway, he poured himself a fizzy drink and I asked him what it was. He said he has a horrible time with leg cramps in the night so he had created this concoction that prevented the leg cramps. Without it, he'd have to get up to walk off the cramps in the middle of the night."

"It must be quinine," Jewell said.

"That sounds major," Gabby said.

"No, it's in tonic water. He probably mixed tonic water with something more palatable.'"

"Yeah, I tried that stuff by itself once," Candi said. "Nasty."

"Okay, what else do you remember, Sherry?" Jewell directed.

"The next thing I remember, after him handing me a cocktail, was waking up in a strange room. Oh wait, I remember him telling me to call him Len."

"Well that's something." Jewell tapped the pen on her lips while she stared ahead, strategizing. "Here's the plan. We take this extra information to the detective Montgomery Alex said was on the case, Ethan Bowers. He should go to Gaylen's house and confiscate the concoction he told you he used for his leg cramps. This then needs to be tested. They may not have retrieved it from the fridge yet, not realizing how significant it might be. Then Bowers needs to review the security tapes. This is all probably already in the works, but let's make sure."

"Doesn't anyone else get a say in these plans?" Nicci asked.

"Of course. What are you thinking?"

"Nothing else. I think you covered it. Just remember this is teamwork."

"What do you know about teamwork?" Della Rae snipped.

"Chill," Z said. "We're in this together. It's all good."

"Actually, Nicci made a good point," Jewell said. "What do you think, Sherry? This is your life, after all."

"I think it sounds good and I'm all for someone else doing the thinking."

Nicci excused herself and flew out of Rhita's to go back to work. The others stayed, filling Jewell in on the bellydance classes she had missed while she was in California. She told them she had a doctor's appointment scheduled for that afternoon to clear her to dance. Jewell lifted her cup to take another sip of coffee and found it empty. Rhita's was filling up, a line already forming at the counter.

Jewell took the opportunity to grab a spot before the line grew even longer. In front of her was a man a little taller than her. From behind he appeared to be fit, but not overly muscular in a body builder kind of way. She breathed in the enticing scent of his cologne, spicy with a deep woodsy base tone. When he turned to greet her, she froze, caught red-handed in the middle of a deep inhale. Her eyes grew as wide as his smile. She held her breath, paralyzed for a moment.

"Hello," he said. *He's British,* she realized from his accent. "Getting a refill?"

She blew her breath out. "Huh? How'd you know?" She continued to stare at him, then laughed. "Oh, the mug!" She shook it, feeling like a total nerd.

"No, actually I spotted you the moment I walked in," he said. "Over there with your mates."

"Troupe."

"Pardon?"

"They're my bellydance troupe. And friends, or mates, also of course."

"You bellydance?"

"I do."

"Excellent. Hobbies are a must, don't you think?"

"Do you have a hobby?"

His warm smile drew her in as she felt her muscles loosening. It was a robust smile, the kind that caused his eyes to sparkle. She paused to admire their bright green.

"I do have a hobby," he said. "I play the trumpet."

"That's amazing. Taps?"

"Afraid not." He drew back.

"Oh, then Reveille?" She grinned and fought back a giggle, looking towards the floor.

"Ah, I see. You're a bit of a comedian. I play mostly for myself. Jazz. I find the trumpet can fit any mood."

Jewell was pleased he had positioned himself to stand next to her in the line now as to not have his back to her.

"You're right," Jewell agreed. "How about when the trumpet bellows to fit a movie scene? Like when the character is engaged in introspection and the trumpet strings out slow, melancholy notes."

"Or," the man said, "when two lovers are the only ones in a pub, slow dancing as a single trumpet moans a sultry refrain. They're holding one another up, barely swaying."

"Aw." Jewell sighed, her head cocked to the side, forming a picture of the scene.*Darn,* why didn't I think of a romantic one? She was startled back to reality when she noticed the dwindling line left ahead. She didn't want their back-and-forth to end, so she quickly added, "Speaking of sultry trumpet music, um…, what about those, um…, movies from the Fifties where a woman is being seductive and a lone trumpet plays in the background?"

"Oh, yeah," he continued. "Did you see the black and white one where the woman has split personalities, and every time the naughty one takes over, you knew because of the trumpet tunes? Well, naughty by those days' standards anyway."

They laughed.

Tristan passed in front of them and flicked his dinosaur into Jewell's mug.

"Grrrraaawr," Jewell called to him as he flew on to his next destination.

"Do you watch a lot of movies?" he asked, seeming to ignore the line progressing ahead of them.

"I used to. In another life." Jewell saw the customer in front of them move to the side. "So, who's your favorite trumpet player?" She asked in a rush.

"Next," the barista called.

Darn her.

The man motioned for Jewell to order ahead of him, but progressed alongside of her still chatting.

"Miles, of course."

"Next," the barista increased her volume.

Jewell ordered then slid to the side to await her specialty brew, still a little stunned by the commonality of his favorite trumpet player, Miles Davis' name, and her family name.

Her heart sank as their conversation halted. He then ordered in turn, all the while watching Jewell from the corner of his eye. She wished the girl behind the counter would speed up entering his order so he could scoot next to her while they awaited their drinks.

He caught her glancing over, and they shared a smile. The barista was called away from the register before taking his payment. He shrugged towards Jewell and she gazed, melting over his casually tousled dark hair and dark facial stubble. There was an ease to him. His dark-framed glasses amplified those vibrant green eyes.

"Ah, thanks," he said as the barista took his payment and handed him his order. Jewell figured he ordered an already brewed coffee.

Then she realized it was in a to-go cup. *Darn* again.

"You're not staying?" she asked, nodding towards his to-go cup.

"Sadly not. My son is home with the nanny." He reached into the breast pocket of his burgundy plaid button-up. "I'm Christian. Here's my card. Give me a ring and we can get another coffee? Anywhere you like."

They stood face to face. She studied him, oblivious to the card she now held in her hand.

He tapped his to-go cup and cleared his throat.

"Oh, my goodness!" She shook out of her trance. "I'm Jewell. Jewell Caldwell."

"Okay, Jewell Caldwell, I have to go, but I hope to hear from you soon."

Jewell retrieved her refill and glided back to the table, reading the card. She hadn't noticed until she looked up that every face at the round table was now turned to her.

"Who's he?" Becca was the first to ask.

"Yeah, who *is* he?" Candi sang.

She read the card aloud. "Christian Harrington, Professor of Science, St. Francis University."

"Wow, what did he say about you being a scientist too?" Gabby asked.

"I bet y'all had lots to talk about."

"He doesn't know I'm a scientist. I only just discovered he is from this." She held up the card. "But we had lots to talk about anyway." She stared off into the distance, unable to focus on anything else. She couldn't recall talking with such spontaneity to anyone, ever.

"Well, when are you seeing him again?" Della Rae interrupted her daydreaming.

"The ball is in my court."

"Then this weekend," Z insisted.

"No, not a weekend for a coffee date," Jewell said. "He specifically said to call him sometime for 'coffee.' Besides, he said he has a son. Don't people with kids do things with them on the weekend?"

"That's a good point," Della Rae said.

"He has a son? How do you feel about that?" Z asked.

The whole group leaned in with the same interest they had the first night Jewell met them, when they had asked her if she was married.

"I haven't thought about it. I've only known him, what, ten minutes?"

"Uh-huh." Della Rae gave a quick eye roll. "I'm not buying your indifference."

"I'm with Della Rae, you're full of it," Becca said. "A lot can happen in ten minutes."

"I guess I think it's sweet that he takes care of his son. Wait, what if there's a wife too?"

"I don't think he would've given you his card and asked you to call him for coffee if there was a wife," Candi said.

"How old is his son?" Gabby asked.

"He didn't say. I guess there's a lot I need to learn about him."

"Just take it slow," Della Rae said.

That afternoon, Della Rae, Jewell and Lydia went to the police station and asked for Detective Ethan Bowers. The thirty-something man came charging towards the women like a bull. His sudden appearance and aggressive approach reminded Jewell of the way lightning comes out of nowhere and strikes before anyone knows what hit them.

Della Rae nudged Jewell. "He's got some kinda burr in his saddle."

He reached them in record time and blasted out, "Yeah? What is it?"

"Can we talk to you about the Spalding case?"

"Shoot." His sharp tone matched his scowl.

"Here?" Jewell asked.

He glanced around the station lobby. "Oh, alright. Come into my office."

They followed him in, and he plopped into the faux-leather swivel chair behind his desk. The three women sat themselves on chairs lining the side of his desk.

"So, who are you and what's this case to you?"

"We're friends of Sherry McKenna. And—"

"Right, the one who killed him."

Della Rae gasped. Lydia looked to Della Rae and Jewell with raised eyebrows.

Jewell felt her blood course hot. "She did no such thing!"

"Well who do you think spent the night with him? Maybe you'd better talk to your friend."

"We have talked to her," Jewell corrected him.

Lydia shot her a sideways glance shaking her head in warning. "Jewell, maybe we should just read our suggestions from the notepad. The ones we discussed."

"Fine." She flipped open her notepad. "First, there is…" Jewell stared at her notes. "You know what? I brought the wrong notepad. We'll come back when we have the right one."

"No need. If I need anything from a bunch of her party friends, I'll come find you. In the meantime, mind your own business."

They exited his office and the police station in silence. When they reached the sidewalk, Della Rae asked, "What was that all about? You had the right notepad."

"Let's just go to the car," Jewell said.

When they arrived at the Beetle, Lydia sat in the front passenger seat and Della Rae climbed into the back. Jewell reached from the driver's seat and tossed the notebook onto the back seat next to Della Rae.

"Did you see how convinced he was that Sherry is guilty?" she asked.

"It sure seemed like it," Della Rae answered.

"That's why I stopped you from defending Sherry," Lydia explained. "I think the less we say to him, the better. He's way out of line accusing her like that. The autopsy report isn't even back yet. He must be breaking all sorts of protocols."

"I agree, but who is going to listen to us?" Jewell said. "When I looked at my first suggestion on the notepad about testing the leg cramp mixture, I just froze. I could just picture him tampering with it or getting rid of it altogether. Plus, I'm sure he already has the security tapes. No need to suggest that."

"What would make him so sure that Sherry killed Gaylen?" Della Rae asked.

"Maybe it makes his job easier?" Lydia suggested. "He wouldn't have to look for other suspects."

"That's pretty wretched if that's the case," Jewell said.

"I agree," said Lydia. "But stranger things have happened. Or maybe he has another motive for pinning this on Sherry."

"Like what?" Jewell drummed her fingers on the steering wheel as she watched people coming in and out of the police station.

"Maybe we have two cases on our hands," Lydia said quietly.

"You know what this means?" Jewell said. "We need to start building a case to save Sherry. We can't just sit back and wait for the autopsy report, and we obviously can't wait for Detective Bowers to take action."

"Dang, and all I wanted to do was bellydance and throw elaborate parties," Della Rae said.

"Let's rally the gang. Can you hand me my cell phone out of my backpack?"

The women had coordinated a meeting at Della Rae's for that evening. On the drive over, Jewell discussed Christian with Lydia.

"He had this way about him. Yes, he was cute, but in a sweet and gentle way. Have you ever known anyone who has an immediately calming effect on you, yet you're so full of things you want to say to him you can't get it all out?"

"Yes, I have known someone like that," Lydia said, patting Jewell's hand on the gearshift.

The gang was all at Della Rae's, except for Z, who had made prior plans with Miranda; Gabby, who had to feed her kids dinner; and Nicci, who complained about having to work late due to taking a lunch break at Rhita's.

They arranged their chairs into a circle near the pool. Jewell filled the rest in on how Detective Bowers had acted and his accusatory attitude.

Sherry gasped. "I think I'm going to be sick."

"I'll bring some more sweet tea," Della Rae said, heading back inside.

"We discussed taking matters into our own hands," Jewell continued. "I don't think we can trust Detective Bowers."

"I agree one hundred percent," Becca said.

"I can double that," Sherry said.

"Candi," Jewell began. "We need to get into that apartment, and who better to charm the doorman than you? Plus, you could easily pass as his fiancé's sister."

"What? Look at me, I'm a whale."

"You're not a whale," Becca said. "You only have a little baby bump and you can wear one of those loose summer dresses. Now let's see you strike one of your famous poses."

Candi stood up, thrusting her nose up to the sky. Becca giggled. Candi strode a path on Della Rae's patio, pivoting like a model on a catwalk. She stopped with her hand on her hip and sucked her cheeks in, causing her lips to scrunch. They all laughed.

"I guess I do still have it. Okay, I'll do it. But I have to tell Tom, and he might protest." She rubbed her hand on her belly.

"Look at you, having a grown-up relationship and everything," Della Rae joked, re-entering the group with her sweet tea.

"Supposing Candi can get us in," Jewell continued. "I'll need a sample of the drink he used for his leg cramps. I'll bring some specimen jars with us. I already called Lacey and she'll get me into the lab. I just told her I had a follow-up experiment to conduct. I hate lying, but we've got to look at the greater good."

"I appreciate this so much," Sherry said. "I was relieved after talking with Mr. Alex yesterday, but now, with the detective's attitude, I'm scared again."

"You're shivering," Della Rae noticed. "I'll get you a blanket."

Becca wrapped her arms around Sherry and they sat in silence for a few moments. Della Rae returned with the blanket and she and Becca secured it around her.

"We hated having to tell you," Della Rae said. "But it's better if you're prepared for the fight."

Jewell continued. "Someone also has to talk to the bartender who served you that night. I don't think it should be you, Sherry."

"No, I think Sherry should lay low, like Mr. Alex recommended," Della Rae agreed. "Except for the A.A. meetings. I heard it went well this morning?"

Lydia smiled at Sherry.

"It went very well," Sherry said. "And I got this twenty-four-hour coin." She pulled a shiny silver token from her pocket. Congratulations rang across the patio.

"Jewell, why don't you and I go to the bar?" Becca suggested. "We'll blend in like regular patrons, we just need to act like we're asking questions out of general curiosity. I bet we won't be the only ones."

"Well, I think this gives us enough to work on for a little while," Jewell said.

"I can't tell you how much this means to me," Sherry said, then began to cry. "I don't know what I'd do without y'all."

"We told you we'd be here every step of the way," Della Rae reminded her.

"Becca, when do you want to go to Las Fuentes?" Jewell asked.

"No time like the present."

"Wait a minute." Jewell held up her hand. "Sherry, didn't you say the bartender's name was Lizzie?"

"Yes, that part I remembered because it was before the shots."

"We need to make sure it's her shift when we go."

"She should be on tonight. She told me her only night off was Sunday."

"Perfect," Jewell said. "Lydia, how about I drop you off and then Becca and I go to the bar?"

"That's fine with me," Lydia said. "But I want you to be careful."

Della Rae turned to Lydia. "You can also stay here and I'll drive you home later."

"Whatever you want to do," Jewell echoed.

"Okay, I'll stay here with Della Rae then."

"Candi, you need to let us know what Tom says about you helping us out," Becca said, and they all broke up for their respective assignments.

As they walked towards their cars, Becca turned to Jewell.

"Should we maybe change into something that looks more like we're going out on the town?"

"Nah, it's not like we're going clubbing," Jewell said.

"But it's an upscale bar."

"True." Jewell stopped and turned to Becca. "Hmm. Maybe." She paused. "Although, it is summer, in a vacation town. I don't think shorts will be that out of place."

"Okay then. Meet you at your house in a few," Becca said.

They parked their cars in front of Jewell's house and walked the short distance to Las Fuentes. It was a little after 7 P.M., so the bar wasn't exactly hopping. The place had a new-car smell to it which Jewell found odd given the age of the building. Then again, the inside had clearly been remodeled from top to bottom with what appeared to be high-end materials. Jewell imagined it held little resemblance to its original design. The gray and white color scheme at least seemed classy in the ambient lighting. There were about twenty patrons scattered throughout, some on bar stools and some in booths.

Jewell and Becca's choice for seating required no contemplation. They went directly to the bar and sat at two of the empty stools.

The bartender laid a drink napkin in front of each of them. "Hey, ladies, what can I get you?"

"I'll have a Pinot Grigio," Jewell requested.

"Californian or Italian?"

"Oh, Californian. I'm just back from visiting there."

"Sweet. And you?" The bartender turned her focus to Becca.

"I haven't had a cocktail in ages. What's your best?"

Jewell snapped her head in Becca's direction. Becca shrugged.

"I make a mean Cosmopolitan. Just to warn you, we only carry top-shelf liquor though, so the drinks aren't cheap."

"That's fine," Becca said, glancing around the bar. "Maybe after my first one, I'll find a cute guy to buy me the rest."

"Becca, that's sexist. We can buy our own drinks."

The three of them laughed.

"By the way, I'm Jewell. And this, as you probably heard, is Becca."

"I'm Lizzie."

Jewell tapped Becca's foot with her own.

When Lizzie delivered their drinks, Jewell leaned over the bar towards her. "I'm sure you get this all the time now, but did you know Gaylen Spalding? The newspaper article said he was last seen here before he died."

"I saw the girl he drank with that night. And left with. My money's on her killing him." Jewell struggled to keep her body relaxed as her stomach tightened. Lizzie's matter-of-factness was cold. She just stood there, polishing glasses like she was discussing the weather. "He was young and healthy, far too young for natural causes in my opinion. I guess we'll know soon enough."

"Yes, how awful," Becca took over before Jewell could burst out with anything. "So, did you know him?"

"Yeah, he came here a good bit. I get to know the ones who sit at the bar. He was a real player," Lizzie's tone turned flippant. "Left with someone different every night of the week. Rarely the weekends though. That's when he saw his fiance. A weekend-only relationship. Her idea from what I know. It was rare for him to take a night off from his prowl, but sometimes he would hang out with his guy friends. I know darn well his fiancé couldn't be dumb enough not to know about the other women. I mean, she's blonde, but no one can be that stupid." Lizzie paused, glancing at Jewell. "Oh, sorry. I didn't mean—"

"I'm used to it," Jewell said. "But having an IQ of 160 does soften the blow of blonde jokes." She gave Lizzie a tight-lipped smile and tilted her head. "So, the girl who was with him that night, do you know her?"

"No, that was the first time I ever saw her. A real drinker though."

"Gosh, were they drunk?" Becca asked.

"Hell yeah. Doing shots like hell hounds. But she was downing them way quicker than he was."

"Really?" Becca encouraged her.

"I told him not to drive at one point, but he was a stubborn guy. Excuse me, ladies, I've got to go check on my tables. The cocktail waitress doesn't get here until 8 P.M." She scanned Becca and Jewell's glasses. "You okay for now?"

"I'm good."

"Me too."

Jewell picked up her phone from the bar and typed a group message. *We got some answers. Can we all meet before everyone goes to work tomorrow? Say 7 A.M. at Rhita's?*

The group text responses came flooding in.

Della Rae's answer came in first. *I'll be there with bells on.*

Sherry was more reluctant. *I think I need to keep a low profile. Come fill me in after?*

Della Rae responded, promising she would fill Sherry in.

Nicci texted she could come, but not for long.

Gabby sent her regrets and Z confirmed she would be there.

Candi responded last. *Yes, and Tom says it's okay for me to talk to the doorman. I didn't use the word "seduce".*

When Jewell arrived home from the bar, she found Lydia on the back patio with Romeo and Maya. She slid the patio door open, and Lydia turned to greet her. "Hey, honey. Della Rae just dropped me off. She said you and Becca got some information out of the bar visit."

"Yeah, I need to add you to the group on my phone."

"I can come, too, tomorrow morning. But I need to meet Sherry by 8 A.M. for the A.A. meeting. Want some sweet tea?"

"I can get it."

"No, you sit. Let me take care of you for a minute."

"You've been cooking, that's enough."

"Jewell, it will never be enough." Lydia stood up and laid her hand on her daughter's shoulder. "Let me get you some tea." She tilted her head mischievously. "Unless you prefer wine?"

"No, tea is perfect."

They sat together and watched the sunset while Jewell filled her mother in on the information they obtained from the bartender. At one point, Lydia slapped her leg to squash a mosquito.

"What's going to A.A. like?" Jewell asked.

"Do you want to come? You can go with me to one of the open meetings, if you like."

"Maybe. What made you get sober all of a sudden?"

"I got cancer."

Jewell gasped. "Cancer? What type? Is it gone?"

"Cervical. And, yes, thank God, it is gone. They told me it isn't hereditary, so you aren't at any higher risk than the next woman. It's probably because I was a bit self-destructive after…" She paused. "After I left Port Eastlyn. I went through some dark times and didn't have the best judgment. Promiscuity led to HPV, that increased my risk of cervical cancer."

"So, you had to get sober to undergo the chemo?"

"No, plenty of people are instructed to get sober before cancer treatment but don't. It was more of a wakeup call. With alcoholism, it's not a choice to drink or not. You *have* to drink, until some kind of transformation happens, usually of the spirit. From the first day I left Port Eastlyn in 1993, I always told myself I would find you, Nathanael, and Laura again one day. But I couldn't sober up for long enough to do anything constructive." Lydia looked out over the yard. "You always think there will be plenty of time. Somehow, in my mind, you all stayed the same age as when I left. I thought I would breeze in to find you exactly the way I saw you last. I know that's crazy."

"It's probably normal," Jewell said.

"But then the cancer brought my mortality into focus. That's when I knew I had to do something. So, I finally got sober, went through my treatment, and then launched out to find you."

"How are you now? You said it's all gone."

"Yes, the cancer is completely gone. I had a hysterectomy and chemo. I just need regular check-ups. And as far as the drinking is concerned, I don't miss it. Not at all. A.A. helps, and now helping Sherry also keeps me focused on my own sobriety and program."

Jewell wondered what had made Lydia reach for alcohol in the first place. Perhaps, she thought despondently, there was little other comfort in her life at the time. She plucked up the courage to ask an even harder question.

"What was my dad like?"

"Oh, that's easy." Lydia smiled. "Imagine a man so vivacious and outgoing he always had a friendly smile and a kind word for anyone he greeted, even strangers." She laughed. "He was one of those people who had to talk to everyone. Standing in line at the grocery store, at the movies, waiting to grab a seat on a fairground ride. You get the idea."

"I don't take after him then," Jewell said.

"You do in other ways. Now, imagine that same man is so blessed with an understanding of numbers that he sees formulas in everyday activities. From junior high onward, he talked incessantly about how he was going to MIT on a scholarship, and that he was going to work for NASA." She took a deep breath and blew it out slowly. "This same, incredible man gave up all of his dreams because his high school sweetheart fell pregnant when they were sixteen. He never complained. Not for one minute. We struggled daily, financially, but the rest of our lives were good. The parts that mattered. We had each other, and then two babies. Our families thought we had lost our minds when we had you as well, but you were exactly what we wanted."

"It sounds like things were…good," Jewell said hesitantly. "I wish I could remember."

"Those days were good, until they weren't."

"After the accident?"

"I guess I wasn't prepared to carry on without him."

"Where have you been living all these years?"

"Now, that's definitely a conversation for another time." Lydia began to stand up, suddenly looking weary. "I'm getting pretty tired, how about you?"

Jewell agreed and gathered up their cups, deciding to let her mother have her peace now that she had shared so much tonight.

Eight

Chapter 8

Jewell and Lydia met the rest of the group, minus Sherry and Gabby, at Rhita's as planned.

Nicci scrunched her nose at a group sitting at their usual round table. "We'll need to pull two together."

Strategizing to sit away from the crowd so they could talk freely, Z and Becca pulled together two tables in the front corner of the coffee shop. They set their belongings on the tabletops and got back in line with the others.

"Hey, I was wondering," Becca began. "Is Maggie getting updates on Sherry's status? We have class tomorrow."

"I've been keeping her up-to-date," Della Rae said.

"So have I," Nicci seconded.

"Well then, I guess she's covered," Z said.

Once everyone was seated with their respective brew, Jewell filled them in on what they had gathered from the barmaid Lizzie.

"I got a mind to go set her straight," Della Rae said. "Ha! Accusing Sherry of killing that rich brat."

"We can't do that," Jewell said. "We didn't let on that we even knew Sherry."

"Oh, I know you're right, Jewell. Still, it just makes me so mad."

"But did you hear what good information we got?"

"What are you talking about?" Nicci asked.

"If he was the player Lizzie said he was, with a different booty call almost every weeknight, then maybe his snooty fiancé, who couldn't be bothered to see him during the week, got wind of his carrying on and did him in."

"But how? And why didn't she ever see him over the week?"

"My Granny once worked for an extremely wealthy family," Candi chipped in. "And according to her, people like that live totally different lives than the rest of us schmucks. Like, they have really strange lifestyles. I could see this fiancé being too caught up in her society life, or whatever, to see him more often than on weekends. She probably thought she was slumming it going to his million-dollar penthouse."

"I can imagine," Nicci agreed. "So, how could she have killed him if she wasn't even in town?"

"She probably had access to his apartment, plus she was there every weekend," Jewell said.

"But still, how would she have killed him? How will they even propose Sherry killed him? If the report is accurate, there was no overt trauma or blood."

"Poison," Jewell said. A collective gasp. "I'm convinced the toxicology report will tell us that. But before it does, I need to get a hold of whatever he drank that night and test it. Maybe he kept a premixed batch of his anti-cramp concoction in the apartment and maybe there'll be some left." She flipped the page in her notebook to see the next item.

"What are you writing in there?" Nicci asked. "You really shouldn't be carrying that thing around. What if you lose it?"

"I'll keep track of it," Jewell insisted. "I say Candi goes to the apartment, flirts with the doorman on duty." She looked up at Candi to ensure she was following. "Tell him you're Chantal's sister." Candi perked up. Jewell then searched for tactful words. "We'll need to get you an expensive outfit. Don't worry, I'll pay for it."

"I guess. But what do I do?"

"You tell him you're Chantal's sister—"

"Younger sister," Candi interjected.

"Okay, younger sister. Tell him she sent you to get some of her things from Gaylen's apartment. He's going to protest because it's a crime scene, but I think you have your ways." Jewell winked.

"I don't know, Jewell," Nicci said. "That seems like a stretch. Not all men turn to putty just because a beautiful woman is present."

"Aw, you called me beautiful," Candi said.

"I agree with Nicci," Della Rae said. "I think it'll be a tough sell."

"If they haven't gathered all the evidence yet, there will also be guards manning the door," Lydia added. "Like I said, I watch a lot of Law and Order. But, you know, eventually crime scenes are cleaned up, once all the evidence is extracted. Maybe we could find out if they're still gathering evidence."

"Well, it's a little scary, and I swore I would never do it again," Jewell said, "but I do have excellent hacking skills."

"Jewell, no way," Lydia said.

"I agree with your mother," Della Rae said. "That's too risky. You could end up being the one in jail."

"How do you even know you have excellent skills?" Lydia asked. "Or, do I even want to know?"

"Never mind. The less everyone knows, the better."

"Well, I could probably persuade the doorman to tell me if the crime scene is still active or not," Candi offered. "Or if it's been cleaned. That shouldn't be too hard."

"Good point," Nicci agreed. "It's not like that's particularly confidential information."

"I know!" Z said. "Candi could say she needs to gather Chantal's things for her. Surely she left items in the apartment."

"Should I be scared?" Candi asked.

"Nah," Becca said. "If he lets you into the apartment, you'll be the only one there."

"What if I take someone with me and say they're Chantal's personal assistant?" Candi asked.

"That might work," Jewell said, looking to the ceiling and then back to Candi.

"But who?" Becca asked. "Rich people would have the means to pay a well-educated professional."

All eyes landed on Nicci.

"Oh no, no you don't," Nicci protested.

"Oh, so it's okay for me to take a risk like this," Candi said. "But not you."

Nicci grimaced. "Alright. I'll do it."

"It sounds like we have a plan," Della Rae said.

"Wait, does Nicci need another outfit?" Candi asked.

"No, she's posing as a professional personal assistant." Jewell chuckled. "Now say that ten times fast. But, no, I think Nicci has plenty of professional suits."

"Hey, I know," Becca said. "My mom has that big ol' Lincoln. She could be your chauffeur."

"Okay." Jewell continued to write in the notepad. "So, Candi and Nicci gather the information about the apartment's status. Then, if it's no longer a crime scene and hasn't been cleaned yet, I suggest we pose as the cleaning service."

"Great idea," Lydia said.

"But what if it's still a crime scene?" Della Rae asked. "Or it isn't, but it's already been cleaned?"

"Then we'll have to figure out a plan B," Jewell answered. "But in the meantime, this is our best shot."

That Wednesday, Candi went disguise-shopping with Jewell and Lydia. They settled on a red designer romper that accented Candi's long legs, but with the added advantage of a loose fit around the waist to conceal her baby bump. A silk animal-print kimono Candi discovered floated behind her when she sauntered like she hadn't a care in the world. Gold flats, jewelry and a red leather bag solidified her air of wealth.

Candi eyed herself, turning about in front of the mirror. She did a happy dance and hugged Jewell. "You know, I'm going to return everything to you when we're done. Except for the romper and the shoes. They'll never fit you, so I'll just have to keep them." She giggled.

"Don't be silly. You're going to keep it all. My treat for doing this."

"Now you need to practice your 'beatch,'" Lydia said, then laughed.

"Right." Candi tightened her eyes with an intent focus and turned the corner of her lip slightly up. She practiced what she called an "I couldn't care less" appearance.

"That's it. You've got it," Lydia said.

Then Candi drew out her words in a low tone. "Don't I sound like a Darcey, darling?" They all laughed until Candi pleaded for them to stop due to her not-so-reliable bladder these days.

"Oh, look what I found." Candi turned her phone screen so that Lydia and Jewell could see the blog article displayed: "How to Act Like a Rich Person."

As Jewell and Lydia drove Candi home, Lydia said, "You know I was thinking, instead of Rhita's tonight after your belly dance class, what about meeting at Sherry's? I think she's getting lonely. Maybe we could all go there for coffee. I could bake a cake."

"That sounds good to me," Jewell said.

"Me too," Candi agreed. "I can't seem to get enough to eat these days. I'll text the others."

Jewell had been seeing more of Sherry than the others had lately, since she'd been coming home with Lydia once a week following their A.A. meetings. They had explained to her how Lydia was her sponsor, and that they needed to go over what they called step work. Jewell would give them privacy by going out to the patio or taking a walk downtown with Romeo.

"When someone quits drinking at first," Lydia explained, "they crave the sugar they're missing from the alcohol. That's why the cake might be a nice touch for Sherry."

"Then what's my excuse for craving sugar?" Jewell joked.

Lydia walked to class with Jewell, planning to continue on to shop downtown. She would meet Jewell at the studio after class so they could walk home together, retrieve the cake and the car and then drive to Sherry's.

Jewell entered the studio together with Della Rae and Sherry. The whole troupe was present now, minus Gabby.

"How are you?" Jewell asked.

"Hanging in there," Sherry said. "I couldn't survive without your mother."

Jewell smiled.

Maggie's classes had continued to focus on silk veil moves. Jewell had mastered most of the basics thanks to Aniela's intense teaching. In fact, Jewell was so comfortable with the veil now that she had begun creating her own moves. She had noticed the other students watching her in the mirror, and on one occasion Becca and Z had stopped by her house begging her to practice with them. Jewell derived a new sense of satisfaction from her advancement. The deep connectivity to the music this development had afforded her brought moments of pure joy, just being able to flow with the rhythm without having to stop and think about her next move.

That Wednesday, Maggie introduced them to veil wraps. She explained how entering the stage in various wraps was a great way to add mystique to a performance. She encouraged them to watch videos with veil dancing to explore different wrap options. Sometimes a dancer would be covered from head to toe, she told them, and other times only their costume is covered. Then, typically during a spin, the veil unwraps to reveal the dancer and the beautiful costume.

"And the crowd goes wild," Z said, mimicking applause with her hands cupped.

Gabby rushed in and fell into line with her veil.

"I think y'all will appreciate tonight's wrap," announced Maggie. "It's called the 'ghost wrap.'"

"I like it already," Becca said.

"Me too," Candi said.

This wrap was new to Jewell too, so her advantage was lost. Maggie demonstrated the wrap, making it look simple, but when the class attempted to imitate their teacher, the sight was funnier than any comedy show even Z could cook up.

"Hold the veil behind you, shortest ends to the ceiling and floor. Pull it up so it's about two inches or a little more off the floor. I don't want anyone tripping. Grab the middle edges and tuck them into the front of your belt or pants. Bring the middle edges as close as possible to the center of where your belt will be. Some of you will have more material left over than others." Maggie cleared her throat. "So, if you have a good bit, like Jewell does." Maggie approached Jewell to demonstrate, "take your bottom corners in front and then tuck them into your pant-line to make a drape."

Maggie found it necessary to go from student to student, correcting the positions of their veils. They tried to help one another, making a blunder of the instructions until Maggie had reached them.

"Well, there y'all go now," Maggie said with her hands on her hips. "Okay, here comes the ghost part. The top half that is hanging behind you, find the ends and bring it up and over your face."

Jewell believed this step of the wrap may be even more entertaining than the first. Z's attempts to grab the edges of the veil behind her reminded Jewell of a dog chasing its tail. Candi continually bent forward trying to get the veil over her head, fluffing her hair over her face in the process. Maggie went from student to student, covering their faces with the back upper portion of the veil. Now, only their arms were showing through the wrap.

"Wow," Jewell said. "We do look like ghosts." She could just about see into the mirror through her white veil.

Maggie was also draped in a ghost veil wrap. She turned off the overhead lights, so that only the lamp and window lit the studio. She instructed them to hold their arms to the sides, making wrist circles while performing figure-eight hips horizontally, backward then forward. The light material of the veils swayed like ghosts moving through air.

Maggie clicked on a haunting Egyptian instrumental.

"Whoa," Sherry said.

"This is actually pretty cool," Nicci admitted.

After the class, Lydia stood waiting for them at the top of the steps.

"We're going to walk home and get the car, then meet up at Sherry's," Jewell announced.

"With the cake?" Z asked.

"Yes, gooey coffee cake," Lydia confirmed.

"I'll go home and put the coffee on," Sherry said.

Jewell took Lydia's arm and leaned in to whisper, "Let's take cream and sugar too."

"Check," Lydia said.

When they arrived home and opened the door, the smell of cinnamon blasted Jewell straightaway. It felt so nurturing. She found herself becoming grateful that Lydia had come back into her life.

The ride to Sherry's was filled with the divine and sugary cinnamon scent.

They rang the bell and Sherry opened the door. "We're in the kitchen. Big discussion going on."

Jewell and Lydia looked at one another and followed Sherry to the kitchen, where the others were all gathered around the table. The smell of fresh coffee was everywhere. Nicci and Candi were sitting in the back of the table, Z in the chair at one end, Becca at the far end and Della Rae and Gabby at the front of the table. Jewell was startled to see Nicci had pulled down the top of her shirt, revealing the edge of her breast. It was like walking into a parallel universe where everything was upside down.

Z stood to offer Lydia her chair, but Lydia shook her head and graciously brushed the offer aside with her free hand. Jewell sensed the troupe was in the middle of an intense conversation. Moving closer, she could see the inked image Nicci was revealing. "Is that some type of warrior?"

"Very good, Jewell. It's a warrior princess."

"Far out," Z said.

Becca stood up and leaned on the table for a better view. "Whoa, the shadows and detailing are amazing. And her gaze is so intense."

"I can almost see her blade glistening," Della Rae said.

"So, what's the story?" Sherry asked.

"Have you ever noticed that I know a ton about your childhoods, even Jewell's now, but none of you know anything about mine?" Nicce asked.

"You aren't exactly an open book, Nicci," Della Rae said.

"Have any of you ever gone to bed cold and hungry?" Nicci asked. They all glanced from one to another, shaking their heads. "Well, I have. Plenty. I grew up in Chicago, living in a one-room fifth-floor walk-up with my grandmother and two sisters." Jewell felt certain she could see a tear forming in Nicci's eye. "We had nothing. School was the only thing I looked forward to, and even that was bittersweet. The other kids poked fun at my…let's say lack of fashion. My bed was a collection of whatever blankets my grandmother threw on the floor, with a thin sheet to cover myself with, if I was lucky. And I shared it with my two sisters."

She took a sip of her coffee, and the tear escaped. She threw her head back for composure then continued.

"But there was one particular night. I was lying in bed. My sisters had managed to get to sleep, but hunger pangs and the cold were keeping me awake. Ironically, they became the catalyst for my determination." She paused, looked up to the ceiling and groaned. The room was dead silent. No one moved. Jewell held her breath, waiting for Nicci to continue. "I knew I had to find a way out. But how does an eight-year-old-girl get out of something like that? And then I remembered a teacher telling the class about the power of education. I had no way of knowing if she was telling the truth, but what other options did I have? So, lying there that night, I vowed to myself that I would do nothing, and I mean nothing, but study and work hard until I pulled myself and my family out of that hole and into a life worth living."

She swallowed hard and composed herself back into the Nicci Jewell was accustomed to. "And that is exactly what I did. So, when you're judging me about being a workaholic, and I know you do, just remember where it comes from. I'll never stop. I can never do enough."

One by one, they crowded round to hug her.

"I have always admired you and your strength," Candi said.

"In slightly lighter news, I brought cake!" Lydia announced. Everyone cheered.

"And I have ice cream," Sherry said.

"Okay, enough serious stuff," Z declared. "Back to the tat talk. Who else wants to reveal?"

Candi pulled her long blonde hair to the side and turned to show the back of her neck.

"Ah, pretty," Becca said, craning to view the vining flower.

"Yeah, very pretty," Della Rae agreed.

Lydia and Sherry passed plates full of cake and ice cream.

"This smells so good," Gabby said. "Plus, I never get served like this. Thank you."

Jewell walked around the group with the coffee pot, offering refills.

"Okay," Becca said, standing up. She pulled the top of her pants down to reveal a colorful butterfly on the inside of her right groin.

Next, Gabby attempted to fling her foot up onto the table, but failed and placed her foot on her chair instead. She pulled up the bottom of her yoga pants. A chain tattoo was wrapped around her ankle with two pieces dangling a star and moon.

"See, I've had this all along and y'all never saw it because I always wear pants."

"I love it," Becca said. "I think I need some more tats."

"We all do," Z said. "Now, who else? You silly girls and your hidden tats. You got to be out and proud."

"Jewell?" Nicci asked.

"Nope. Sorry to disappoint."

"Don't you want one?" Becca asked.

"You know what I want?" Jewell said.

"What?" several shot back.

"My bellybutton pierced."

"Oh, me too," Becca chimed in.

"And me," Candi said. "But not right now." She rubbed her baby bump.

"You know, that's one place I don't have pierced," Z said.

"Let's all go together," Sherry said. "We'll make it an event."

"We sure are good at making events out of things," Nicci quipped.

"Just wait for me and Candi though," Della Rae said.

"Wait for you?" Becca asked.

"Yeah, I want to lose my belly weight first, and I'm on my way. I've already lost twelve pounds."

Sherry sat back in her chair and let out a smile, gazing at her friends.

"Thanks so much for coming over, guys. I could almost forget the trouble I'm in."

The next day, the plan spun into action. Outfitted for the task at hand, Candi and Nicci climbed into the back of Lynn's Lincoln to be chauffeured to the condo building. Becca exited from the passenger seat and closed the door. "Good luck," she called to them.

Becca, Lydia and Jewell waited anxiously on the back patio. Romeo whined for them to throw a ball or a disc or anything, but they were preoccupied so he barked at Maya trying to get a rise from her. She ignored his existence as usual so he finally gave up and lay at Jewell's feet.

"Oh, a text from Mom," Becca said, examining her phone. "Candi and Nicci just went in."

Jewell bit down on her knuckle. Lydia crossed her fingers. Other than the rumbling of passing cars, there was silence.

Becca blew through her lips and began laughing. "I just realized I was holding my breath. We can talk, you know."

Jewell's shoulders dropped and Lydia's leg quit shaking.

"When do your classes start, Becca?" Lydia asked.

"The third week in August. I can't wait."

"She'll make a great psychologist," Jewell said.

"I can tell."

"I hope so," Becca said.

"So how are you and Max?" Jewell enquired. "You don't talk about him much."

"Still going strong."

"Hey, I know," Jewell said, heading inside. "Let's open a bottle of wine."

"Good idea, and put on some music," Becca answered.

Jewell returned to the patio with a bottle of red wine and two glasses. She carried out some sweet tea for Lydia.

About thirty minutes later, Becca got another text from Lynn. "She says they're on their way home and all is good."

"What does that mean?" Jewell asked.

"Let me text her, hang on. Oh wait, she wrote back. TTYS."

"Let's wait out front," Jewell said.

"We never sit out front," Lydia said.

"I know, it's not exactly private. But they'll appreciate the gesture."

The previous resident had left brightly colored metal chairs under one of the trees in the front yard. Yellow, blue and green. They were dirty from rain and fallen leaves, so Jewell brought out a rag to wipe them down. Romeo followed the women through, and Maya lifted her head momentarily, then went back to sleep on the table at the back.

"That's one thing I never thought about," Jewell remarked. "Romeo never climbed up on tables."

Becca laughed. "Well, it's a good thing, or you wouldn't have any tables left."

They weren't settled in the front yard for long before Lynn's car pulled up. Becca, Lydia and Jewell stood to greet them.

"Let's all go in the living room," Jewell suggested.

Lynn, Nicci and Candi sat down on the sofa. Lydia took the side chair at Lynn's end, and Becca sat cross-legged in front of them on the floor.

"Want some wine?" Jewell asked.

"I do," Lynn answered.

"I can't," Candi said sadly.

"Me neither," Lydia said. "I'll pour you some tea."

"No, no caffeine either," Candi said.

"I forgot. You young ones can't have anything when you're pregnant these days. Water?"

"Perfect."

"So, spill," Becca demanded.

Jewell supplied Lynn and Nicci with wine and refilled Becca's glass, then sat on the floor next to Becca. Lydia delivered Candi's water.

Lynn glanced at Candi and Nicci, then smiled. "Well, we've still got it."

Candi brushed her fingernails on her kimono in a bragging gesture. "The apartment is no longer a crime scene and it's not been cleaned yet. We introduced Nicci as 'my sister's' assistant and told the doorman on duty she would be arranging a cleaning service for the apartment."

"I told him I would call with the date and time," Nicci added. "And that I expected whoever was on duty to let the service into the condo." She smiled and looked at the others. "Apparently, I sounded very authoritarian."

"I'm sure you did," Becca said.

"Excellent! You're the best!" Jewell said.

Becca slapped a couple of high-fives with Candi, her mother and Nicci.

"Now we need to come up with a fictitious name for a cleaning service," Lydia said.

"Easy peasy," Becca answered and tapped her phone screen. "There's a name generator for businesses. Let's see...businesses, cleaning businesses."

"See if they have an option for crime scene cleaning!" Candi joked.

"Hmm, that just gives me selections for how to start a crime clean-up service."

"Just see what the general business name generator suggests for a cleaning service," Nicci said.

"OMG, this is the first one that popped up. I swear I'm not making this up. 'A Clean Getaway.'"

"That's hysterical," Jewell said. "Do we dare?"

"Yes," Lynn said. "If you're taking all these other chances, why not."

Jewell jumped up to retrieve her notebook. "Okay, we need to figure out a date and time so that Nicci can inform the doorman. Then, do we need uniforms if we're posing as a cleaning service?"

"I think you should wear some type of cover up," Lydia said. "Maybe in a drab color, like brown. Pull your hair back and maybe even wear a hair net or a bandana. And you'll definitely want gloves. Wait, who is going to pose as the cleaners?"

"Well, I have to go to retrieve the sample," Jewell said.

"I'll go too," Becca said.

"That should be enough of us," Jewell said.

"I don't know about you Lydia," Lynn murmured, leaning over the end of the sofa. "But these two are driving me crazy with worry."

"Yes, me too. All this sleuth work is so risky."

"How about we get out and go shopping one day?"

"I think that would be a perfect distraction."

The day of the faux clean up, Jewell opened her front door to find Becca standing before her in the brown jumpsuit they had agreed upon, her long wavy hair wrapped up in a scarf. The sight made Jewell giggle and slap her thighs.

"Go on, laugh away. You look just as hot though." Becca gestured at Jewell's matching outfit. "And not the good kind of hot."

They drove to the condo building, making sure to park around the corner so their brand-free car would be less obvious. They walked to the reception with supplies in hand.

"We're here to clean…" Jewell flipped through the clip-board of fake documents she'd created to appear more official. "Apartment 901. The Gaylen Spalding crime scene?"

"I'll send you up," the doorman said, seeming unfazed. "There's a code to get up, but you won't need it to come back down. Just press 'L' for lobby."

The elevator doors opened directly into the penthouse. The bright blue view of the ocean and sky came blasting in through the-wall-to-wall windows, showcasing between them slick white furniture and a gray shag rug. A classy teak coffee table in the center subtly pulled together the array of light colors.

"Whoa," Becca called.

"No wonder he didn't have any trouble getting women to come home with him."

"It doesn't look like anyone ever lived here."

"We need to focus. Let's get what we need and go."

"I feel so weird going into the…bedroom." Becca scrunched her nose.

"Let's put our gloves on now before we forget. We can't afford to make any mistakes."

The doorway to the kitchen had crime tape blocking it. Jewell pulled it off and crumpled it to take out with the trash. They would have to perform a proper crime scene cleanup, since they were posing as such, and hope that no one actually hired a real service any time soon. There was always the possibility that Gaylen's family would, but they were so private and low-profile compared to the Darceys and Gaylen for that matter, that no traces of them showed on the news or in the newspaper.

At least the apartment was impeccably clean; apart from the finger-printing powder, it wouldn't take much effort to restore the place to a pristine condition.

Jewell opened the fridge and pulled a rag from her pocket to wipe the handle as an extra precaution. She lifted out the specimen containers she had stowed in her cleaning caddy and filled them with all the liquids she could find in the fridge, labeling each in turn. Sherry had told her she remembered Gaylen pouring himself something from a glass pitcher, so she labeled the corresponding specimen "the concoction."

"I got what I needed," Jewell called to Becca.

There was no answer.

Feeling spooked, Jewell stepped through the apartment until she found Becca. Her friend was frozen at the foot of the master bed.

"Someone actually died here," Becca said.

"Yeah, but it's not the worst I've seen."

"Oh gosh, Jewell." Becca turned to look at her. "I wasn't even thinking about what you had to face in Washington. Sorry, I shouldn't be making a big deal out of this."

"No, it's okay. You and I have lived very different lives." Jewell threw her arms around Becca. "To be honest, it's a good thing that this disturbs you. It means you're normal." She let Becca go. "I also got the specimens."

"Jeez, now we have to actually clean," Becca said.

Jewell met Lacey at the lab during off-hours. Jewell and the gang had brainstormed fake reasons for needing use of the lab, but all had fallen short. In the end, Jewell had decided to tell Lacey the truth.

"Thanks for helping me with this," Jewell said.

"Are you kidding? I'm glad to have an excuse to see you. Besides, I don't want to see a murder falsely pinned on your friend. I'll do some more routine work when we're done and make a point of telling the boss, you remember the Maverick, you stopped by to visit. That way there'll be no suspicion."

"Good idea. And how could I forget the Maverick?"

"By the way, she was devastated when she learned you and the cowboy broke up."

"Me too," Jewell said.

"I set up the spectrometer before you arrived so we could get right to it."

"Amazing. Let's get started then." Jewell pulled the mini cooler carrying the specimens from her backpack.

"Now this is what we live for," Lacey said, and the pair smacked their palms together in a double high-five.

"It doesn't get any nerdier than this," Jewell admitted as they donned their coveralls and goggles.

The analysis began and they quickly identified the quinine they had already anticipated. Hours after performing the initial physical property and chemical reaction tests, they sifted through the lab's extensive database of substances to match their results. The key feature that stood out: tropane alkaloids.

They stared at one another and said in unison, "Belladonna."

"So, who would be growing deadly nightshade around here?" Jewell asked.

"I have no idea. Wait, doesn't your ex live and work on a farm? Farmers tend to know one another and keep an eye on what everyone else is doing. Maybe he can help."

"I'm fairly certain it would require a greenhouse to grow Belladonna around here. That already narrows it down."

"That would make sense. It's native to Europe and Asia."

"More detective work then." Jewell sighed. She felt weary now. "I'd better get going." She gave Lacey a tight hug. "I can't thank you enough. Can I buy you dinner?"

"Oh, that's mandatory."

Nine

Chapter 9

Jewell took a deep breath to summon up the courage to text Kage.

Kage, can we meet? I need to talk to you about something.

I guess. What is it?

Can we meet soon? Today? How about Chelsea's?

How about anywhere other than the place we first met?

Oh, right. Sorry. How about you pick.

The Old City Craft Bar. This is pretty short notice, you know.

I know. It's urgent though. 7 P.M.?

I'm having dinner with someone then. How about 6 for a quick drink?

Ouch, she thought. She sighed then continued to type.

Okay, see you at 6, and thank you.

Jewell strode across the outdoor patio of the bar and grill. She passed customers who were joyfully laughing and chatting, longing for the days when she and Kage did the same. Scenes ran through her mind, like the first night they had made love, when Kage, in his haste to get his boots off, had lost his balance hopping across her kitchen floor and gone crashing into the counter. She had laughed so hard it doubled her over. The memory filled her eye with a tear. She shook her head and quickly blinked it back.

Kage wasn't outside, so she swallowed hard against the lump in her throat and turned the knob to enter the craft bar. Kage was already seated, his hat lying on the table in front of him. She noted an inch or so of growth in his brown locks. He must have glimpsed her in his peripheral vision because he turned and stood as soon as she began to approach the table.

"Hey."

"Hey."

They hugged stiffly.

"I ordered you the house white. I hope that's okay."

"You still know me well."

Silence.

Jewell peered awkwardly around the room. She had never been inside here before. The tables and counters were a rich granite, copper brew kettles covered the wall behind the bar and a string of colorful taps lined the top of the bar, designating each type of flavorful draught. She felt Kage's gaze upon her, and their eyes locked when she turned her gaze back toward him.

"You look good," he said.

"So do you." She was sure he could see the imprint of her heart pounding against her chest as her eyes lingered on his.

"I—"

"You're—"

They laughed, and Jewell felt relief as the level of tension dropped ever so slightly.

"You go first," Kage said.

"I forgot what I was going to say."

"How about why you're back so early?"

He was watching her expectantly. She looked down at the table.

"Yes. Have you heard about Sherry?"

"I have."

"That's what I need to see you about. We're, the troupe, I mean, we're trying to solve this case because Detective Bowers isn't doing anything."

"I heard." Without any warning, he reached for her hand from across the table. Jewell froze, watching his fingers about to touch hers—but stop short. He pulled his hand back and placed it on his lap. "I don't think it's safe. If he was murdered, then the person who killed him is on the loose and not going to be happy about you trying to solve the case. I don't like you doing this."

"I can't let Sherry go to prison for something she didn't do."

"Then let the police do their jobs. You have no idea what you might be up against. You know how bad it was when Nathanael was blackmailing you."

"Yes."

"Well this could be worse. Deadly even."

"I understand, but I'll be fine." She took a deep breath. "And I need your help."

Kage's eyes widened. "How?"

"I identified an herb in Gaylen's nightly drink that is poisonous in concentrated amounts, and I need help finding who could have grown it."

"And just how did you come about discovering this herb?"

"Um…we may have posed as a cleaning service and obtained a sample from his condo."

"Jewell! See, you've already gone too far." He glanced around the bar, but no one was paying them any attention. He leaned in closer and lowered his voice. "You know, you can't even use that as evidence in court."

"I know, I don't intend to. I just need it to identify the killer."

"Can you even hear yourself right now?"

"It's the only way. Now can you help me figure out who could have grown something around here or not?"

"What is it?"

"Nightshade. Probably grown in a greenhouse."

Kage thought for a moment, drumming his fingers against his drink. "I know two people who use greenhouses. The Martins and Travis Browdy."

"Where do they live?"

"The Martins go to church with us. Their farm is about five miles from the edge of our land. They mostly have crops, but Mrs. Martin grows medicinal and kitchen herbs in their greenhouse. She's made a side business of it. But I can't picture her over there growing poisonous plants."

Jewell mimicked Kage by leaning forward slightly, unkeen for anyone to overhear and misunderstand what she was about to say. "Deadly nightshade, a.k.a. Belladonna can actually be used medicinally. With the correct dosage, and in the right circumstances, it can help with all sorts of problems, including intestinal disorders and menstrual cramps. Of course, used improperly, it can result in neurotoxicity, and even death."

"You're such a nerd."

"Very funny. Do you suppose I could drive out there and visit them?"

"Sure, there'd be no danger in visiting them. Although I don't see how that's going to help any. They wouldn't harm a fly and I can't see them selling something that could harm anyone."

"She may have sold it for completely the right reason, not realizing that person was going to use it to cause harm. It would be worth at least checking for the plant there."

"Okay then. Just drive past our farm and keep going. Do you remember where the property line ends?"

"Vaguely." He looked disappointed. "Sorry, I'm not accustomed to so much land."

"Once you pass our drive, watch your odometer until you've gone another one and a half miles. You just passed our property line. Then, another eight-tenths of a mile from there, start watching for a sign with the Martins' name on it."

"Thanks. And what about Travis, the other person you mentioned?"

"He's a bit of an odd duck. Maybe I should go with you—" Kage quickly looked away. "Well, I guess I better not…but you ought to take someone with you. Just because his place is kind of isolated."

"Becca has been doing everything with me so far, I can take her."

"A lot of good she'll do. A guy would be better. Are you, um…you dating anyone?"

"Now how could I be dating anyone this quickly? I just got back to town." *I'm not like you,* she thought.

"Right, sorry. Well, at least text someone else when you're leaving and give them a time limit to come look for you if you're not back."

"Kage, you're scaring me."

"You should be scared, running around like this. Again, why don't you just drop this whole thing?"

"I can't do that to Sherry."

"I wish you would've had this much conviction for us."

"I wasn't the one who jack-knifed this relationship and wouldn't wait for me to come back."

"You mean waited for you to come back when you darn well felt like it?"

"No, waited for me to come back when I said I was coming back. You clearly had no faith in me."

"And then what? Wait until January for you to leave again for months on end?"

"Maybe. If I needed to."

"That isn't what I want. I want…" He shook his head, and his voice became low. "I wanted you, but you're not a person for settling. I am."

Jewell took a good sip of her wine to stop herself from blurting something back. She didn't want to fight with Kage. The cool tang of the liquid felt good in her throat. She set the glass down with renewed composure. "I heard you didn't wait very long. My flight probably hadn't landed by the time you were ensconced with someone else."

"I wanted to be ensconced with you."

Kage reached into his pocket for his wallet, laid enough money on the table to cover both drinks and a tip, then stood up and grabbed his hat.

Jewell stood too. "Don't leave like this."

He reached out to draw her in. She could feel him breathing in the scent of her hair. He hugged her tightly and laid his cheek on the top of her head. Jewell hoped that someone would poke her with a pin so that all the love she felt for Kage would gush out and not allow her pride to hide it for one more minute. She didn't dare move, just let him hold her with their deep breaths pressing their bodies further together.

The waitress came to clean up their glasses, shaking them from their trance. Jewell watched longingly as he brushed his hair back and placed his cowboy hat on top of his curls. They went out together, past the patrons on the patio and onto the sidewalk.

"Kage."

"Yes."

"My mother found me."

"What? How did you react?"

"She's here. With me."

"I think that's great. As it should be."

"Oh, you never said where Travis lives," Jewell said.

Her heart warmed at the genuine smile that pushed his cheeks up and creased the corners of his eyes.

"Sorry, I guess I got a little distracted. Travis lives close to the river. Most people own vacation cabins in the area, but he lives there full time. He's a bit different, you know, but he's probably harmless. Anytime I've seen him, he's got a huge smile on. Just drive to the lake and you can ask anyone in the bait shop for directions."

"Thank you."

"And how's my little buddy?" Kage asked. He looked like he missed Romeo as much as he'd missed Jewell.

"He's good. I got him a friend, although they're not exactly friends."

"Oh?"

"Yeah, a calico cat showed up on my windowsill in California. I kept her."

"Really?"

"Yeah, Maya. She's named after a bellydance move."

"I bet she's as beautiful as her owner." He paused. "Well, I better get going. I've got dinner plans."

"So you said."

A hollow space opened up in the middle of Jewell's chest. As she turned and headed back towards Iris, he called to her.

"Be careful."

Kage had been right, there was nothing suspicious about the Martins or their herbs. Jewell and Becca had visited under the guise of Becca needing an herbal remedy for menstrual cramps. Jewell saw no nightshade. When she asked Mrs. Martin about belladonna, the farmer informed her that she specifically grew only benign herbs and would never touch such a potent plant. Jewell asked about other herbalists in the area and Mrs. Martin conveniently suggested Travis.

Equipped with the perfect excuse to visit him, Becca and Jewell made plans to go to the river. The sun was blazing, so Jewell decided on cut-off jean shorts and a sleeveless floral top. She twisted her hair into two pigtails, draping each of them in front. She chuckled when she opened the door to see Becca in jean shorts, a T-shirt, and one thick brunette braid draped down her right side.

"Great minds," Becca said. "Is Romeo coming?"

"No, it's too hot." Jewell petted him and Maya, who had decided to grace Becca with a greeting by weaving in and out of her legs.

The pair rode to the river in the Beetle with the top down, making a stop at Simon's Bait Shop. Parking was casual, a dirt lot with no paint lines. Jewell pulled in near the front steps. There were no other cars.

"Do you think Simon is his first or last name?" Becca asked.

"Not sure, but we're about to find out."

The building was made of untreated wood with a precariously leaning porch. The two women climbed up the steps and opened the screen door with a creak.

"Y'all girls fishin'?" A deep male voice asked.

Peering around, Jewell answered. "No, not us, but we were told you could direct us to Travis Browdy's house."

A man dressed in overalls that barely covered his barrel-round belly slid out from behind a row of shelves. "Oh yeah, you're pert near there." He motioned for Becca and Jewell to follow him back out the creaky door. "Ya see the road up yonder, left around the bend?"

"Yes."

"Take that about a half a mile. Take a right at the black and white cow with the white mark on his forehead, now don't take the turn at the cow without the white mark."

Jewell and Becca shared a wide-eyed look.

"I got ya. Gets 'em every time." He shook his head, pleased with himself. "Nah, I'm just messing with ya. There'll be a fork in the road. Go right and keep on winding around. You're in his driveway by then. It's a long driveway, just keep a following it. You'll start to see his bushes and that stuff he's always growing. Then there's his house and the green house. Can't miss it."

"Thank you," they said, nearly in unison.

"Can we purchase anything to say thanks?" Jewell asked.

"No need. But on your way back through, stop and get yas a coke."

"We will, thank you," Becca said.

They followed the directions. Dust from the dirt road stirred so fiercely that Jewell had to stop and pull Iris's top up. She and Becca coughed as she whirled the air conditioner to life. They came to a fork in the road and veered right as instructed. He had been right, it was a long drive, lined with various bushes and shrubs. The fields beyond the shrubs appeared to be all weeds. Travis apparently owned a good bit of land.

Growing concerned about how isolated the area was becoming, Jewell turned to Becca. "Do you have any cell reception?"

"Not a bar," Becca replied, winding the window down and turning her phone this way and that in an attempt to capture a signal.

"This is creepy," Jewell said.

"Right?" Becca agreed, followed quickly by, "Wait. I see something." Becca pointed to Jewell's left.

They curved around and saw a farmhouse with an expansive greenhouse to the left of it. Jewell sighed and sagged against the seat. She slowed the car as they neared the house.

"Are you sure this is safe?" Becca asked. " I mean, two young women out here, no cell phone reception, no weapons."

"Kage said he was odd, but fine."

"Okay, at least we'll go together if he chops us up into little pieces."

"Becca!"

They gathered their backpacks and walked to the front door of the modest but clean-looking farmhouse. The door was closed. Jewell opened the screen door and knocked on the wooden door. No answer. They glanced around. Several vehicles sat to the right of the house in a make-shift lot, all in questionable states of functionality.

"Should we walk over to the greenhouse?" Becca asked.

"Probably."

As they approached the greenhouse, they heard singing. Jewell recognized the song from one of her foster homes. It was a solemn love song sung by Bette Midler from some movie. The pair glanced at one another, not sure how to proceed and unsure of the proper etiquette for visiting someone in a greenhouse.

Jewell simply rapped on the door. "Hello?"

The singing stopped. "Yes?"

A figure turned abruptly inside the greenhouse, making both women jump.

"Sorry, we don't mean to bother you."

"No bother, come in. Just don't touch anything."

They walked in single file through the rows of plants, Jewell taking the lead with both arms tight to her sides. When they reached the man, he turned out to be young, approximately their age, with wild bushy hair that sprung about as he spoke. Kage was right, he had a boisterous smile. He looked more like he belonged on a beach surfing than in a greenhouse in the middle of nowhere.Jewell felt her muscles sag with relief.

"I'm Travis, but I guess you knew that." He raised a pair of dirty-gloved hands, waving them in lieu of a hand shake.

"I'm Becca."

Jewell couldn't help but notice that Becca was twisting her shoulders back and forth and offering her most girlish grin. She rolled her eyes. "And I'm Jewell."

Travis leaned in towards them, the back of his hand to the corner of his lips, and whispered, "Y'all here for the good stuff? Cause it's out in a special greenhouse." He winked.

Jewell paused for a second, before his meaning became clear. "Oh!" Her eyes widened and her mouth dropped open briefly.

"Oh!" Becca echoed.

"No, no," Jewell said, shaking her head fiercely. "We're not here for *that*. We're here for something for cramps. You know, monthly cramps. We heard you grow a plant for that. The Martins didn't have any and suggested you. I think they called it something like Bella?"

"Hmm," he said, his eyes scanning them up and down. "Belladonna. It's not just for anybody. Taken properly, in controlled doses, it can help, but it's also highly poisonous. Follow me."

He led them through the greenhouse. His nearly six-foot frame blocked their view as they followed him through the aisles. Chills ran through Jewell as she realized they'd potentially tracked down the plant that killed Gaylen. This Travis could be a killer, or at least have supplied a killer.

Set high in the corner of the greenhouse, sunlight streaming in behind it like heraldic rays, was the plant. It was beautiful, with deep purple flowers and dangling berries. Its foliage as bushy as Travis' hair.

"I can cut you a tiny amount to try, but you'll have to come back. Harvesting involves a process and I have to use protective equipment. Although, just between us, I keep a small supply in the house for hangovers and such, you know." He nudged Becca with his elbow. "But one bite of this part here or too much of the harvested stuff and…" He took his index finger and ran it across his throat with a garroting sound.

Jewell glanced at Becca, who was starting to look nervous too. "Thanks for the warning. Out of interest, how many customers do you have for this?"

Travis tilted his head.

"Just curious." She shrugged in what she hoped was a convincing manner. His smile never faltered.

"You know," he said slowly. "It's been years. These days I just keep some stored in the house, but it's mainly for personal use."

"Do you have something milder for her ailment?" Jewell tilted her head to indicate Becca. Becca's mouth fell open as she turned to Jewell, who shrugged.

They walked to the car with a somewhat milder herbal mix in Becca's backpack. Once inside, Becca turned to Jewell.

"Why was I suddenly the one with menstrual cramps? Why does it always have to be me?"

"What does it matter? We got the information we needed. He has the plant. Someone must have gotten it from him, either from his house or the raw plant in the greenhouse."

"Or…he did it!" Becca quickly surveyed all around them.

Jewell shivered, started the car and stirred up dust clouds with her spinning wheels.

Tempted by his earlier suggestion, they stopped at Simon's to purchase drinks.

"They're on the house," he said. "How'd your visit go? Any trouble finding the place?"

"No, you gave great directions. We saw the black and white cow with the white mark on her forehead just fine."

Before they pulled out of the bait shop lot, Jewell sent a text to Lydia assuring her that they were safe and that she would fill her in on the details when they got home. Becca also sent a group text to the troupe.

We have new info. Send times for availability to meet today.

When they arrived at Jewell's house, Lydia flung open the door and rushed to the car. She enveloped Jewell in a warm embrace as soon as she got out. Jewell hesitated at first, but then hugged her back.

"How'd it go? I was scared to death until you messaged me."

Becca and Jewell took turns filling Lydia in while they headed to the living room. Jewell plopped onto the sofa and Becca sat on the floor with Romeo, while Lydia scooped Maya from the end chair and then sat, placing the drowsy cat on her lap.

"Do you think he did it?" Lydia asked.

"We talked about it in the car," Jewell answered. "Travis doesn't seem like the murdering type, but it doesn't mean someone didn't take the herb from his house or greenhouse."

"Fascinating. I wonder who his friends are?"

"I can think of some ways to investigate," Becca said. "We can call Kage, see if he knows who he hangs out with. And stop by Simon's again."

"Good point. I bet he sees everyone who uses that road. Let's put together a list of Travis' friends and connections and investigate them one by one. Also, I think we need to view those security videos from the condo building. Detective Bowers isn't going to do anything."

"How can you get the security footage?" Becca asked.

Jewell couldn't believe she was here again. At least this time she'd be doing it for a nobler cause than just protecting herself. "I can hack into the security system. Candi got a glimpse of the name of the building's security service. That will help me get in. Once I am, we can view the videos, although it's going to be laborious. There'll be hours and hours of normal day-to-day activity to sort through."

"I don't like it, Jewell," Lydia said. "I already have one child in trouble, God knows where. I don't need another."

"No one will know."

"How can you be so sure?"

"You don't want to know. Just trust me. I know I can get away with it."

"Can we at least do something light and fun this weekend as well then? Even if it's just making some nice food here and inviting people over?"

"Oh, can we?" Becca chimed.

"Yeah, that's a good idea," Jewell agreed. "I guess we've been a little consumed with this case lately. I'll put something together. A welcome to Southbridge party for you, Lydia."

"Speaking of together," Becca added. "I'm getting responses in about meeting tonight. Looks like most can get to Rhita's anywhere from 6:30-7:30."

"But we talked about holding future meetings outside of Rhita's. Can you see if they can come here? Say 7:30 P.M."

"That's perfect," Lydia said. "That'll give us time to get dinner and clean up. I'm making shrimp and grits for the three of us."

"Yummy," Becca said enthusiastically.

All eight troupe members, plus Lydia and Lynn, were in attendance at

Jewell's house. The non-public gathering felt safe enough for Sherry to attend. Becca and Jewell told the rest of them about Travis and their plans to examine the security footage.

"And, by the way, I told Lydia I would put something together for her," Jewell added. "A party welcoming her to town. How about we do it this weekend?"

"I love it," Z said. "Count me and Miranda in."

"Have it at my place," Della Rae offered. "I'll take care of everything. You know how I like to plan."

"Are you sure?" Jewell asked.

"Yes, that's a lot to ask of you," Lydia agreed.

"I'm sure. But maybe let's not make it this weekend if Jewell has so much hacking to do. Let's get Sherry clear of these charges first, then I'm going to host the biggest bash this side of Florida has ever seen."

Ten

Chapter 10

Becca and Jewell made a beeline for the computer after everyone had left.

"I don't want to know anything," Lydia said, setting herself up on the island. "If you need me, I'll be here with my scrapbooking."

Romeo padded over to Jewell's side as she logged in.

"Okay, work your magic," Becca said.

Jewell struck down feverishly on the keys.

After some time, Becca wandered over to the island for a break. Jewell half listened as Becca asked Lydia what she was working on.

"I'm scrapbooking my arrival in Southern California after my PI picked up on Jewell's presence there, then when I finally got to meet Jewell, then our days at Aniela's, and now our time, so far, back here."

Becca stayed behind at the island, presumably watching Lydia work on her project.

Jewell plugged away stretching her skills until a breakthrough. She shouted, "I'm in!"

Romeo barked as Becca and Lydia rushed over to the computer.

169

Jewell was already scrolling through the security footage.

"We can jump ahead in time so that we're starting at the beginning of June. This will give us an idea of patterns so we can catch anything unusual around the time of his death in August."

The only footage Jewell could locate in the system came from two cameras. They had already scoped these out on their visit to the condo building. One, the most useful for their purposes, was positioned on the entry wall to capture residents and guests coming through the lobby as they entered and exited. It also had a full view of the elevator. The other was on the outside of the building's entrance. Jewell scrolled through the video clips from the indoor camera. She knew this would be a time-consuming job. She fast-forwarded as rapidly as she could while still retaining the ability to recognize scenes.

"There he is," Becca called, pointing at the screen.

Jewell paused the tape. Gaylen was by himself.

"The timestamp is set automatically," Jewell said. "So we should be able to trust its accuracy. Plus, if you check the clock on the wall, you can see it's in sync. So here it's morning." The scene showed the sun coming through the lobby windows. Jewell continued to scroll.

Next, they saw Gaylen, Chantal and the doorman-on-duty together on the screen. Jewell stopped the footage again. Gaylen was chatting to Chantal while she was looking straight ahead. It was now a Friday evening early in June. The camera caught his profile as the doorman wheeled over a small suitcase and summoned the elevator. All three stood in front of the elevator doors, Gaylen continuing to talk at both the doorman and Chantal. She was displaying as much interest towards him as Maya did to Romeo. Her back was to the camera, her long sleek blonde hair perfectly smooth against her bright red shirtdress. A red beret was pinned to the right side of her head and jewels dangled from her wrists. They all entered the elevator.

The next image of the couple was timestamped as the following morning. Chantal emerged from the elevator dressed in a black and white pencil dress, wearing an exaggerated big-brim black and white hat. Her black clutch purse was tucked under her arm. They looked like random strangers catching an elevator ride together. Not even their outfits matched. Gaylen stood in stark contrast to her style in khaki shorts and a casual, untucked button-up.

"It doesn't even look like they're going to the same place," Lydia remarked.

"Who knows," said Becca. "With their crazy relationship, maybe they aren't."

Later that Saturday, in the afternoon, the pair returned together and didn't leave until Sunday afternoon. Like the last time in reverse, the doorman-on-duty, a different one this time, greeted them at the elevator and took the suitcase from Gaylen. The three walked towards the front doors until they were out of sight. The doorman and Gaylen then returned after a few moments without Chantal. Jewell continued to wind through the footage.

"I hate to say this," Becca said. "But my eyes are too heavy to watch anymore."

"Mine too," echoed Lydia.

"Okay, let's carry on in the morning."

"My classes start tomorrow, and then I have to work in the bookstore," Becca said apologetically. "Say, speaking of school, Jewell, whatever happened to that professor you met at Rhita's?"

"Oh yes, I completely forgot," said Lydia. "What happened?"

"I'm a little busy here, you two," Jewell answered.

"Excuses, excuses," Becca said, and she and Lydia nodded in agreement, followed by Becca flapping her elbows and clucking like a chicken.

"Hey, don't you need to get your beauty sleep before your big day tomorrow?" Jewell asked snidely.

"Yep, I'll update you," Becca said. "And then you update me when you've called the professor."

"Ha-ha. I'll work on the surveillance video in the morning," Jewell said, determined to change the subject. "Seriously, good luck on your first day. Let me give you a hug." Becca came over and Jewell gave her a fierce good-luck squeeze. Turning to her mother, she asked, "Are you going to be here tomorrow?"

"I plan to be."

After Becca had left, Jewell sat on the sofa. This time, Lydia sat close to her.

"You're amazing," she said. "You're so intelligent. Just like your father."

"You were no slacker either, " Jewell said. "Hey, Della Rae said she might be able to pull off the party this weekend after all. She's itching to fill up her big house."

"Great. My goal was for us all to do something other than being consumed by the case. Not that I don't want to help Sherry, I do. I just don't think it's healthy not to do anything else."

Lydia reached over and brushed Jewell's hair from her face. It came as a surprise, but it didn't bother her.

"You look tired," Lydia said.

"I guess I am."

"Jewell, are you avoiding the professor? Christian."

"I don't know, maybe. But I *am* busy."

"Don't let a potential once-in-a-lifetime-chance pass you by."

The next morning, Jewell made her usual coffee-press brew and set up camp in front of the computer, determined to make it all the way through the security tapes until the date of Gaylen's death. She had opened the patio door to let Romeo outside. Maya lay on the patio chair, having briefly lifted her head to acknowledge Jewel with a meow. She would feed them both in a bit.

Bright eyed and alert, she started where she had left off, on the Sunday early in June. When Gaylen and the doorman-on-duty returned to the lobby, Gaylen said something to the man and waved as he entered the elevator.

Jewell realized how involved the doormen were in all the activities of the condo, and wondered why Detective Bowers hadn't questioned them. Or maybe he had? After all, Jewell and the gang were not exactly privy to all aspects of the investigation. She made a mental note to have Candi attempt to extract more information from one of the doormen if the security tapes came up empty.

Continuing on the same Sunday, Jewell watched Gaylen exit the elevator in the evening. She was learning his behaviors now, he never appeared without a grin and a spring in his step. Of course, he was wealthy and without worries, had a fiancé with supermodel looks and the whole week ahead of him to party away from her. Each weekday evening, he'd leave dressed for a night on the town and return anywhere from 1 A.M. to 3 A.M. with a beautiful woman, a different one nearly every night. They'd be laughing, playfully touching, passionately kissing at times. A far cry from his interactions with his ice-queen fiancé.

Jewell marveled at Gaylen's public displays. Surely word had gotten back to Chantal about his shenanigans. Why wasn't she the prime suspect? In fact, Jewell thought, she probably framed Sherry with full intent, happy to frame whatever random woman went home with him that Friday night in question. Sherry had just happened to pick the wrong night to go out.

Determined to gather evidence against Chantal that she could present to Detective Bowers, Jewell plowed through more footage.

Lydia entered the kitchen and poured some coffee from the press. "Good morning, darling."

"Good morning. Come look at this."

Lydia pulled a chair next to Jewell as she rewound the tape through the week.

"Wow, he was certainly a busy boy. A new girl almost every night. No wonder the weekend footage shows him and Chantal indoors most of the weekend." She laughed. "He was probably too exhausted to move."

The following weekend showed more of the same. Chantal entering fashionably with the doorman wheeling her luggage for her, a few appearances stepping on and off the elevator together until she left again on each Sunday.

"Now, let the fun begin," Lydia said.

That Monday started the same as the previous week. Gaylen exited the elevator into the lobby with his happy smile and night-on-the-town attire. He returned, as usual, with a fresh new woman. Jewell told Lydia she had noted that on some nights he didn't return at all, perhaps staying at the woman's home.

That particular Tuesday was different though. This time, Gaylen entered the lobby with another man. Lydia looked confused.

Jewell felt the explanation was obvious. "Lizzie, the bartender at Las Fuentes, said he sometimes took the night off from prowling. I don't remember him letting a friend crash before though."

"I guess even the best of them need a rest," Lydia said.

They watched as the two men waited for the elevator. Gaylen peered back in the direction of the doorman's desk, then slid his hand across the other man's backside and pinched it.

Jewell gasped and stopped the streaming.

"Did you see what I just saw?"

"I think so. Maybe they were just kidding around. Maybe he looked back to see if the doorman was looking so they could play a joke on him?"

"Or, if it was what we think it was, he looked back to make sure the doorman wasn't looking. Maybe he wasn't taking the night off after all."

"That would make him…" Lydia turned to face Jewell.

"Bisexual."

Jewell pushed "play" and the footage rolled on from the pinch. The elevator doors opened, the pair entered and then turned around to face the doors before they closed. Jewell leaned in and squinted. She stopped the tape and zoomed in.

"It's Travis!"

"Who?"

"The herbalist. I didn't recognize him from the back because his hair was up in that bun. It was like a mane the other time I saw him." Jewell paused the footage and faced her mother. "Do you know what this means?"

"It doesn't look good for Travis," Lydia said.

"But what would be his motive for killing him?"

"The green-eyed monster perhaps. It's landed many a man six foot under."

"But surely Travis knew about the parade of women Gaylen was working his way through. He wasn't exactly subtle."

"Maybe Chantal found out about this." Lydia waved vaguely at the screen. "She could live with him cheating on her with other women, but not with a man? Maybe it's her after all."

"Good point," Jewell said. "I'm trying to put myself in her place. I can't help feeling I would be more bothered by the multitude of women than one man though. In a way, I'd probably be less threatened if it was a man. I don't know, it's impossible to imagine."

"It is a tough one," Lydia said. "But infidelity is infidelity."

"I've got to get this to Detective Bowers right away."

"No, Jewell, you can't. How are you going to say you found the evidence?"

"Oh, crap, you're right. Then let's call the bar when they open and see when Lizzie is working. We can go and ask her if Travis and Gaylen hung out there. If so, we'll take the theory to the police station, say we heard information around town about how Travis has been growing deadly plants and that the two men seemed to be hanging out together in a more than friendly capacity. We can then also present the possibility of Chantal being the killer in light of Gaylen's activities with Travis, not to mention all the women. If he chooses to ignore us this time, we'll have enough cause to go over his head."

"Good idea, but can Becca go to the bar with you instead of me?"

"Oh, yeah, sorry. I'll wait until she gets out of the bookstore."

After checking whether Lizzie was scheduled at the bar, Becca and Jewell returned to Las Fuentes when Becca had finished her shift.

"Hey there," she greeted Becca and Jewell.

"We have a confession to make," said Jewell. "We weren't just curious about the Gaylen Spalding case. Sherry is one of our closest friends."

Lizzie's face tightened, though she tried to hide it by looking down as she wiped the bar. "You don't say."

"Yeah, sorry we lied," said Becca.

Lizzie's face appeared to relax, but Jewell wasn't sure whether it was natural or forced. "What can I get you? Want another Cosmo?"

"No," Becca said. "I think I'll stick with wine tonight. House white, please."

"Me too," said Jewell.

Lizzie returned with their drinks. "So, you have more questions, I assume." She went to wash some glasses. There was a sink under the bar, halfway between the bar and the floor with a ledge to turn the glasses up to dry.

"We do," said Jewell. "You said that some nights Gaylen took a break from...well, from picking up women."

Lizzie rolled her eyes. "Yeah, occasionally he left with one of his buddies."

A glass fell from the edge of the sink and crashed, shattering into pieces.

"DAMN IT TO HELL!" Lizzie yelled, then glanced around the bar. "Sorry, it's just going to be a pain to clean up."

Jewell shared a look with Becca and leaned in to whisper, "Clara."

Becca nodded in agreement.

"Buddies?" Jewell asked with expert casualness.

"What?" Lizzie shook her head as if to refocus from all the broken glass fanned out in front of her.

"You said buddies? Plural? As in more than one?"

"Yeah. Guy was popular."

Jewell used her foot to tap Becca gently.

"Do you know any of them?" Becca prodded.

"I do, but you don't really think for one minute I'm going to implicate any regular customers? You do realize how bartenders make a living? It's not from what the owner pays me."

"We understand."

"I don't mean to be rude," Lizzie continued, still staring at the mess on the floor. "But I'm on my own and I've got to pay my way through college."

"We're sorry," said Jewell. "When this is all over, we'll stop by for a friendly drink, I promise."

They dug into their backpacks and placed a hefty tip on the bar, then left.

They raced back to Jewell's and flew to the computer. Lydia and Romeo came in from the patio.

"How'd it go?"

"You won't believe it," Becca said as Jewell focused on the screen in front of her and pecked away at the keyboard. "Lizzie said there were 'buddies' who'd go to the bar with Gaylen. More than one."

"My," Lydia said. "I've never known anyone so busy in all my life. Hence the word 'playboy', I guess."

"Okay, y'all, let's look," said Jewell. "One of these days we'll get all the way through this."

"You said, 'y'all,'" Becca sang with a giggle.

"What?"

"You said, 'Okay, y'all.'"

"No I didn't."

"Yes you did," Becca sang under her breath. "We're rubbing off on you."

The video streamed and the three women hunched in as closely as possible. They weeded through weekends with Chantal and the weekly flow of beautiful women. Then a week here and there where Gaylen wouldn't come home and some in which Travis made an appearance. Jewell's focus dulled from the monotony, until Becca shouted in her ear.

"There, look, it's not Travis."

Jewell refocused. Lydia straightened in her chair. Jewell moved the footage back to re-stream.

"You're right, it's not Travis." She used the controls to play the sequence in slow motion. Another man was laughing with Gaylen. They entered the elevator and turned around. Jewell paused the video.

"Don't you ever wonder why people always turn and face the elevator doors?" Becca asked.

"Right now, I'm wondering who this other man is," Jewell answered, sliding her eyes towards Becca.

"I don't recognize him," Becca said, shaking her head.

"Hmm." Lydia's eyes flicked to the ceiling as she formulated her thoughts. "What if Travis was in love with Gaylen? He could tolerate the never-ending array of women, but feeling he had to compete with another man, or other men even, drove him mad." She scrunched her lips to the side.

"Wow, Mom, you might be right."

Lydia looked at Jewell in shock, and suddenly tears were streaming from her eyes.

"What's wrong? I said you might be right. It's a good theory." Jewell said.

"No, it's not that. It's…you called me 'Mom.'"

Lydia leaped up to hug Jewell. Becca was watching them, beaming.

"Alright, it's not that big of a deal," Jewell said. "I can keep calling you that, if it means that much. It's nothing to bawl over." She chuckled, feeling slightly awkward.

"It does mean that much." Lydia gave her a wobbly smile.

"Now, can we go to Detective Bowers, or, better yet, his chief." Jewell said.

"I'll go with you," Becca said. "We'd better hurry though, or he may be gone for the day."

"Do you want to come, Lyd…um, Mom?"

"No, I'll stay here. I want to try a new recipe."

"Lucky us," Becca said, and the two younger women grabbed their things and rushed out.

Jewell and Becca entered the police station still unsure if they should summon Detective Bowers or ask directly for the chief.

"Can I help you?" asked the clerk on reception.

"We need to see…"

Jewell paused when she spotted Ethan Bowers leaving his office. As he neared them, Jewell felt the sarcasm rising in her. She leaned out to him and in as much monotone as she could muster, said, "I see you're on your way out to crack a case, solve crime, make this town a safer place, but can we speak to you first? It's urgent."

He looked at the clerk, his lips pursed, apparently feeling under pressure to be civil in front of a witness. "Why don't you two ladies come into my office."

They followed him in and each took a seat as he rounded his desk and dropped to the chair behind it.

"Okay, shoot," he said.

Jewell opened her notepad to a blank page. "Here's my notebook and pen, if you'd like to take notes? Or we can record it on our phones and send a copy to you so that you have a record, since…" Jewell looked pointedly from one end of his barren desk to the other, fed up with his dismissal of them, "…you don't seem to have anything for documentation."

He scowled and leaned forward. He spoke in staccato through clenched teeth. "Don't you two worry. I never forget a thing anyone says or does. Now why are you here? Again."

"We heard rumors around town—"

"Ladies, I can't base a case on rumors." He bent his right arm behind his head and leaned back again in his chair, laughing.

"We realize that," Jewell continued. "But it might interest you to know that there are rumors about how Gaylen Spalding had extracurricular activities with more than just women."

The detective's brow furrowed. "What are you talking about?"

"Men. Rumor has it he was also entertaining them in his penthouse. We, um, my friend and I talked to the bartender at Las Fuentes, the bar he frequented, and she identified one of these men as Travis Browdy. We did a little more digging and—"

"Now just who's the detective here?" he snarked.

Jewell wanted to blast him with a tirade of answers to that particular question, but chose to pass for the sake of getting her point across.

"You are well within your right not to care about Sherry as a person. But she is our friend and we know she couldn't, wouldn't ever do something like this. So I demand that you do *your* job and follow up on this information. Otherwise, it might be said that you deliberately passed on a chance to help you complete this investigation. Properly."

Detective Bowers seemed infuriatingly unfazed. "You don't say?" He swiveled in his chair to face Jewell squarely and raised his eyebrows. "Go on."

This might be her last chance to persuade him. She had to make every word count. "Well, my friend and I took the opportunity to visit this Travis. He's a farmer, of sorts. He gave us a tour of his greenhouse and I noted that he was growing deadly nightshade. You might know it as belladonna."

"So, you're here to tell me about plants?"

"I'm a scientist, I studied toxicology. This particular plant is deadly, if consumed in large doses."

"Why would he grow a deadly herb?"

"Exactly," Becca said decisively.

"Actually," Jewell continued, "it is used as a medicinal plant too. You just have to be extremely careful with dosage. I suspect, however, that if Travis was Gaylen's lover, and Gaylen was parading women and men through his penthouse on a regular basis, perhaps Travis became jealous and decided to stop Gaylen's carousing. Permanently."

"Well, it doesn't get any more permanent than that. Interesting," the detective said, suddenly seeming engaged. He screwed up his mouth and rocked his chair back and forth.

"Alternatively," Jewell continued, "it could be that his fiancé, Chantal, caught wind of Gaylen seeing men and killed him out of, I don't know, envy, disgust."

"Leave the damn theories to me," Bowers snapped. "It sounds more likely that it was that Travis fellow. Tell you what, I'm going to call the forensic lab and expedite the toxicology. If it's this plant, this bella-whatever, then looks like we've got him."

"Really?" Jewell fought to tamp down her enthusiasm. "That would be great. Thank you."

They saw themselves out, not that Bowers had offered otherwise.

"Sorry I didn't say much," Becca said. "But that guy makes me nervous, and you were doing such an outstanding job."

"No worries. I'm just thrilled he's going to expedite the toxicology. Although his sudden change in attitude was really odd."

"It was," Becca agreed. "This entire case has been bizarre from the get go."

"Hopefully the toxicology will show the atropine from the belladonna and it'll be enough to charge Travis. Or at least put Sherry in the clear. She doesn't know the first thing about plants."

They went back to Jewell's, where Lydia came rushing to the door. "How did the chief react?"

"Well, Bowers caught us before we got the chance, but he turned out to be uncharacteristically receptive. It was odd. All the other times we've talked to him, he blew us off, but when I brought up the potential evidence against Travis he latched onto it straight away. Says he's going to have the toxicology expedited."

"It's about time. But you're right, why would he suddenly start being cooperative?"

"I say we go to Sherry's and give her the good news. At least, the potential good news."

Jewell and Lydia headed to the car with Becca lagging behind punching the keys of her phone to summon the rest of the group to meet at Sherry's.

Della Rae was already at Sherry's when they arrived. Sherry flung open the door and hugged Becca and Jewell simultaneously. Her eyes were red and swollen again, her skin splotched with the same red.

"How can I ever thank you guys?"

"There's absolutely no need," Jewell said.

"I'm forever indebted to you."

They passed through the threshold and Jewell noticed the knowing nonverbal exchange between Lydia and Sherry. They seemed to share a bond and language through their plights with alcohol, like wounded soldiers returned from battle.

"Who else is coming?" Jewell inquired.

"I think everyone," Della Rae said she reckoned.

"Well, enough of all this nonsense," Sherry said. "It's time to celebrate. I already ordered pizzas for everyone. If I can't drink, at least I can eat. I know I might be jumping the gun, I mean, I'm not in the clear yet. All Bowers has agreed to do is speed up the toxicology."

"I'm sure the results will implicate Travis, or someone he supplied," Jewell reassured her.

The rest of the gang arrived, including Miranda, and they devoured the pizzas and Della Rae's unmatched sweet tea.

"How did you ever get him to agree?" Nicci asked.

"We have no idea, to be honest," Becca answered.

"He did a complete 180 midway through the conversation," Jewell said.

"I think he's bipolar," Z quipped.

Jewell had an uneasy feeling in her stomach. Something was off, but she couldn't wrap her head around it. Soon, she let herself get distracted by more cheerful conversations, and let the good mood overtake her misgivings. It's not like Detective Bowers had smashed a mug in his office while they were speaking or anything.

A week passed with no word on the case. That Wednesday at class, they begged Maggie to work on more moves using the ghost wrap and she conceded, telling them they would pick up on the other veil wraps later.

They proceeded on to Sherry's as they had the week before. This time, Lydia had baked a Black Forest cake for them with shaved chocolate sprinkled liberally on top.

"Wow, Mom, that's almost too pretty to eat…almost." Jewell was still trying to get used to calling Lydia "Mom."

On the drive to Sherry's, Jewell cleared her throat and said, "You know, Mom, I know I haven't said it yet, but I'm really happy you're here."

"Me too," Lydia said. "I love you with every inch of my heart."

Jewell smiled, and meant it.

They all gathered in Sherry's kitchen. Sherry, Della Rae, Lydia and Jewell sat at the island while Candi, Nicci, Gabby and Miranda sat at the table. Z and Becca stood at the counter between them. The air in the house felt lighter.

"Soon we can start going back to Rhita's," Nicci said.

"What?" Z answered. "No, I like Sherry's house and Lydia's cakes better."

Eleven

Chapter 11

With Detective Bowers finally taking the reins regarding Travis, Jewell wondered how she would fill her days now. She longed for a purpose. She had quit her job because of the overpowering feeling of wanderlust that had taken her over. She considered resuming her plans to travel the country, but now she had Lydia to factor in as well.

She wandered through the house, finally going to sit on her bed, staring blankly ahead. Christian's business card caught her eye from where she had been safekeeping it on her nightstand. She picked it up and called the cell number listed.

"You've reached Professor Harrington. Oh, who am I kidding, call me Christian and leave your name and number. I'll return your call as soon as possible."

She quickly disconnected without leaving a message and then thumped her forehead with the phone.

She went back to the kitchen where Lydia sat reading the paper. No news of the case, but that wasn't necessarily a bad thing. Was it? She needed to distract her mind. Maybe she could take up scrapbooking with Lydia.

Grabbing a bag of cookies, she plopped onto one of her bar stools and offered a ginger snap to Lydia. She dropped it in alarm when her phone rang.

"Uh-oh."

Lydia looked concerned. "Jewell, are you OK? What did you do?"

The number she had last dialed appeared on the screen. She mumbled that she was alright and then pressed the accept button, keeping her gaze fixed on her mother as she put the phone to her ear.

"This is Christian Harrington. Someone just rang me from this number."

She quickly weighed her options. Hang up and hope to never run into him again or speak with him like a normal person.

"Hi. Sorry, it was me. This is Jewell. Caldwell. From Rhita's. The other night, er day, I mean day."

"Hmm, I met a Jewell Caldwell once, but this couldn't be her. The one I met must have left town, or possibly the country. She was going to give me a ring for a coffee date, but then disappeared. I know she liked me, so there's no other viable explanation."

Jewell couldn't tell if this was his weird British humor coming through or whether he actually thought she'd forgotten about him. "No, it's me. I'm the one. I mean, the only Jewell Caldwell in town. I've been busy. Very busy."

"I see. Does that mean you want to make a coffee date?"

She wondered why he kept saying "date."

"Yes, I would like to get together for coffee, if you still do."

Lydia flashed her a huge smile.

"Aw, bummer. I got married last weekend," Christian said.

"Ah... Okay."

"No, I'm kidding. I didn't get married. I'm not even dating anyone at the moment."

"Ha, and you said I was the comedian." Jewell laughed with relief.

"I'm sorry. That was mean. I really was hoping you would call sooner. But it's good to hear from you now. What are you doing tomorrow? I could meet up right after my last class. Say 4 P.M.?"

"Yes, that works for me."

She became distracted by Lydia nodding her head fiercely while Christian told her he wanted to take her to a place she hadn't been to yet. They settled on The Cobblestone Express and arranged to meet just outside the entrance. He wanted to greet her outside to escort her in like a gentleman, despite the intense heat.

"So, tell me everything," Lydia demanded as soon as she hung up.

"There's not much to tell. We're meeting tomorrow at four for coffee."

"A coffee date!" Lydia brought her hands together into prayer position and grinned gleefully at the ceiling.

Jewell did not appreciate the pressure. "Why does everyone insist on calling it a date?"

There were times in Jewell's life when it seemed there were influences beyond this present world, like happenings in a spiritual realm stirring to affect circumstances here on earth. Serendipity. During those times she felt she got a glimpse of something greater than herself and a distinct feeling of serenity engulfed her. This was one of those times as she rounded the corner to The Cobblestone Express. She spotted Christian straight away, in a light green shirt, complementing his sparkling eyes. She had forgotten how stunning he was, his most notable feature being his wide smile that nearly took up the entire bottom half of his face. His dark hair also had just enough wave to keep it looking perpetually mussed. When he spotted her, his already wide grin, somehow widened even further. He rushed over to meet her, then took her hand to enter the coffee shop, where the satisfying scent of java immediately made her feel welcome.

"I'm so glad I can introduce you to somewhere. Are you up for going to the rooftop terrace? The view's incredible."

"I'm up for it," Jewell replied, feeling a little flustered.

He led her upstairs to the open-air rooftop. It was covered slightly by a trellis roof and vining plants. The sun shined casting shadows through the vines down onto the terracotta floor. Misting fans hummed all around them, keeping the atmosphere pleasant in the Florida heat. They quickly ordered and eased into small talk as if no time had passed since their first conversation.

Jewell watched his face as he spoke, wondering how he timed his shaving to ensure he had just the perfect amount of stubble by this time of day. Then her eyes drifted to his lips. They were full and soft-looking. She imagined kissing them.

"You need to know something," Christian said, pulling her from her fantasy. "I can't do casual. It's not in my DNA. I also have a son whose needs I have to put first. He's only going to be confused if his dad brings home a string of women, no matter how lovely they are."

"Oh." Jewell placed her right hand on her chest. "I completely understand." She considered her own history. Two boyfriends in her entire lifetime and one near-rendezvous with Andrea. She supposed she wasn't exactly the casual type either. "How old is your son? And what's his name?"

Christian reached for his cell phone as he spoke. "Johnathan is three. Here he is. My screen saver, of course." He passed his phone to Jewell.

She swiped to light up the screen again. "Aw, he's adorable."

"I think so too."

Still cupping the phone in her hands, Jewell looked up. "My turn to confess. I don't know much about kids. I don't have any experience."

"That's okay. I didn't have any experience either until he came along. Let's just see how things go between us first, shall we? That is, if you're interested in seeing how things go…" He raised his eyebrows ever so slightly, with an endearing mixture of confidence and uncertainty.

Jewell realized she had become so enthralled by their conversing she hadn't stopped to take note of the spontaneous warmth coursing through her body. The quiet peace she experienced in Christian's presence, or even when thinking about him, contrasted pleasantly with her body's more primal attraction to him. It was dichotomy at its finest.

"Yes," she blurted out, aware suddenly that she had taken too long to answer. "I am interested in seeing how things go."

He chuckled. "Good."

Christian filled Jewell in about his ex-wife, Elizabeth. How he had moved to the States with his folks when he was in what he called 'secondary school.' Her family was new to the States also so mutual friends from London suggested the families meet.

They dated through school and it had been she who pushed for marriage. He felt ready to settle down and had wanted children anyway, so he agreed. Plus they had their home country in common. A very practical idea, he called it. But his wife had never bonded with Johnathan the way he had. She stayed out more and more over time and became increasingly withdrawn from both of them. He said they essentially ended up living separate lives, him and Johnathan together and Elizabeth on her own. It didn't come as a surprise when she announced that she was leaving, he just never thought she would go as far as returning to London.

"That is so sad," Jewell said, feeling a connection with Johnathan as an abandoned child herself.

"It was, but things are much better now." He shifted in his seat and continued with a lighter tone. "Would you like to go sailing this weekend? My mum and dad are taking Johnathan to a birthday party, we could take the boat out for a couple of hours."

"A sailboat? You have a sailboat?" She thought back to her first crossing of the Stallion bridge into Southbridge, the breathtaking beauty of the view it gave her. Pure white sails gliding over the bluest water.

"Ah-ha, I didn't tell you about my other hobby, did I? It's just a twenty-footer, but it's enough for a fun day out."

"I would love to," she said. "Go, that is. Sail with you. Wait, do you play your trumpet on the sailboat as well?"

He laughed and shook his head. "I haven't, yet. But I may do so this weekend."

Later that day, the house was quiet. Lydia watched TV in her bedroom as Jewell sat on the back patio writing in her notepad. She was taking to writing lately. She journalled her experiences and took the liberty of embellishing a little along the way, much like Lydia did with her scrapbooks filled with stickers and flowers. It all added flare and made the stories more interesting.

She was enjoying the flow of pen on paper. Typing on the computer reminded her too much of work and hacking. The notebook was somehow freeing. She imagined herself in a simpler time, when writing instruments and paper were the only method of writing. Then she wondered why each generation believed life in previous decades was simpler.

Lydia called from her bedroom. "Jewell, come quick, the news!"

Jewell rushed to Lydia's bedroom, where she was turning up the television volume.

"Travis has been arrested."

Jewell sat on the bed next to Lydia, their legs stretched out in front of them. She noticed they had the same long, slender legs.

A newscaster stood in the forefront, microphone in hand. In the background, two police officers were guiding Travis into the back of their car. His hands were cuffed behind his back.

"This is really happening," Lydia said.

The group texts went on for hours, discussing Travis' arrest and Sherry's new freedom. Della Rae announced the party for that Friday night. It would be a "Hafla," an Egyptian tradition typically involving Middle Eastern-style music and dancing, not to mention food and wine.

The day of the Hafla, Jewell and Lydia drove over to the large grocery store that lay on their usual route to the beach. Lydia read through her list of ingredients for baked Penne with chicken and sun-dried tomatoes.

Jewell pushed the cart. "If you're happy to bake a cake too, I'll buy the ingredients," Jewell offered.

"I just so happen to have potential recipes in my hand," Lydia said with a wink, flicking the cards out like a fan. Jewell peeked across at them. "Carrot cake?"

Jewell scrunched her nose. "Vegetables in cake?"

"Okay then." Lydia flipped to the next card. "How about a date cake with orange blossom syrup?" Jewell shook her head hastily. "Then, how about apple spice cake with ice cream?"

"Hmm." Jewell cocked her head in contemplation. "Maybe."

"Alright. Last but not least, my famous layered coconut cream cake." She held the card for Jewell to view the picture of five, thick layers of yellow cake topped with fluffy white icing and coconut flakes.

"Now you're talking."

They strolled through the aisles in no particular hurry, enjoying being out together without a fixed agenda. Jewell grinned as they passed the boxed cakes. She no longer needed those, thanks to Lydia's baking. Warm surges filled her, realizing just how much her life had improved since those sad grocery store trips she used to make alone in Washington.

They returned home and Lydia began cooking and baking while Jewell put the remaining groceries away.

"Hey, have you seen the box of Penne pasta?" Lydia asked. "I laid it right here."

"Maybe I put it away already. Let me look."

Lydia continued to cook while Jewell searched for the box. Then Jewell stood up, scanning the kitchen in confusion. "I can't find it."

"Strange. I'll do what I can for now. It's not still in the car, is it?"

Jewell shook her head slowly, taking inventory once again of the items on the island and counter.

"Mom, there it is. By the stove."

"How? I looked there. I know I did."

Jewell viewed Lydia with a flash of concern, but then shook it off and proceeded with her task. When all the extra groceries were put away, she announced, "I'm going to let Maya in."

"Okay, honey."

When Jewell returned, she saw Lydia glancing around the kitchen with her fingertips pressed against her lips.

"What is it?" she asked hesitantly.

"Well now I can't find the baking powder."

"We didn't buy any. You said you had some."

"And I do. I pulled the can from the cabinet and laid it on the island next to the mixer."

"Are you sure?"

"Yes, I'm sure. I'm not going crazy, Jewell."

"Do you feel okay? Maybe you need to sit down. It was hot out."

"No, I really don't need to sit. I just need to find the baking powder."

Jewell went to the baking cabinet and immediately pulled out the powder. "Mom, you're scaring me right now."

Lydia pointed to a spot next to the mixer. "I promise you, I took it out and set it right there."

Jewell let out the breath she had been holding. "Maybe it's too much trying to bake two things at once. Let me help."

"Honestly, I'm used to cooking by myself, and I can get around a kitchen better without any interference."

"Okay." Jewell threw her hands in the air. "But I'll be right in here if you need me." She sat at her computer, angling the screen to allow a clear view of the kitchen in order to keep an eye on Lydia.

The cooking proceeded, filling the house with pleasant aromas of melting cheese and sweet cake. Romeo hung nearby. He was also watching Lydia, but for very different reasons than Jewell.

"My potholder. I need my potholder."

Jewell got up to help her look.

Lydia opened the fridge. "Oh, there it is. How on earth... Oh well, I've found it now."

Jewell texted Becca. *I'm worried about Mom.*

Why? She's great.

I know, but she keeps losing things. Just now, she put the potholder in the fridge!

She's probably just stressed getting ready for the party.

Maybe, she has been looking forward to it for a while.

See, so she's anxious. I'm sure she's fine. Are you nervous about doing a solo?

No, I'm just going to improvise.

Gosh, I wish I was good enough to improvise.

You are. I'm not any better than anyone else. I just had intense lessons with Aniela.

Whatever. See you soon.

Sherry opened Della Rae's door for them. "She's in there." Sherry gestured towards the great room with her head. "She's in rare form. Been freaking out all afternoon."

"Freaking out? Della Rae never freaks out," Jewell said.

"I better go help her," Lydia said.

"I'll come with you and drop off the casserole dish," said Jewell.

"Then come out on the patio with the rest of us," Sherry said. She leaned in to whisper further, "if you know what's good for you."

"Ten-four," Jewell said, nodding.

They went to the kitchen and found Nicci standing near the stove, her back to it, facing them. Della Rae was at the counter, her back to Nicci. When Nicci saw Lydia and Jewell, she made wide crazy-person circles near her ear and pointed at Della Rae.

Della Rae caught a glimpse of Lydia and Jewell. "Oh good. You brought your food. I'm running way behind. I've never been so behind. I agreed with you, Lydia, that it would be nice to have us all fix something rather than catering. But, from now on, we're catering."

"Why, what's wrong?" Lydia asked. "I can help."

Jewell turned, poised to leave, when she saw Nicci shaking her head and pointing to the floor, telling her to stay right there. Jewell obliged.

"I just don't know what went wrong," Della Rae almost wailed. "Every time I went to fetch an ingredient or a measuring cup, the dang things were gone. I spent more of the afternoon tracking down crap than getting any cooking done."

Lydia placed her hands on her hips and shot a sideways glance at Jewell. "See."

The doorbell rang, and Jewell took it as an opportunity to flee.

It was Maggie. "I brought soup from the deli, as promised. I'm not much into cooking."

"It'll be great," Jewell reassured her.

"What's all the chaos?" Maggie asked as she entered the kitchen area.

"Trying to get caught up," Della Rae called.

"Well, like I said, I'm not much on cooking, but I can help. It's not like you to be running behind, Della Rae."

Della Rae and Lydia filled Maggie in on their trials of the day.

Gabby flew in without sounding the doorbell.

"Y'all, I got my corn fritters with ham here, but they nearly didn't make it. Those dang kids must have kept moving my stuff around. Every time I went to use something, it was gone!"

"Clara!" Maggie shouted and looked up past the ceiling. She burst into a deep belly laugh, while the others looked around at each other in confusion.

"What?" Della Rae finally asked.

"Oh, she's your problem now," Maggie answered. "I got her out of my studio. I guess she's visiting y'all moving your stuff around now."

Della Rae chuckled, shaking her fist playfully towards the ceiling. "Very funny, you old broad. You got us good."

"You don't for one minute expect me to—"

"Hush, Nicci," Della Rae cut her off. "Even if our cooking problems are coincidental, let us have our fun. After all, this party is in honor of Clara."

Jewell leaned in and wrapped her arm around Lydia. "Thank God, I was scared to death you were getting dementia."

Lydia winked at her, spurring Jewell to glance from Lydia, to Della Rae, to Gabby, with squinted eyes.

"Okay, let's carry all this food outside," Della Rae announced.

"Woohoo," cheered Maggie.

They feasted outside on Della Rae's patio, with plans to return inside to her recreational room for the performances.

Later, after carrying in the leftovers and putting the refrigerator items away, Della Rae led them down the broad wooden steps to her basement.

"Whoa," Z said.

"Haven't y'all been down here before?" Della Rae asked.

"I think we'd have remembered this room," Becca said.

The entire far wall was stone, with an elaborate fireplace in its center. An overstuffed armchair sat next to it, glowing like the Rockefeller Christmas tree. Della Rae had hung a halo from the ceiling with shimmering silk falling around the chair. The back, the arms and the front of the chair were also loaded with glistening hip scarves, dripping their gold and silver coins.

Della Rae proudly sashayed to the chair. She swept her arm in front of it and stated, "This, my friends, is for our guest of honor, Clara Tessa Berg, a.k.a. Allya Raqs."

The group cheered.

"I say we make this an annual event," Maggie said.

"Agreed," Della Rae said.

The group cheered again.

"Okay, dancers, get changed. There's a room through those doors."

Maggie, Z and Jewell left to get into costume. Jewell was relieved to see that the floor was a smooth hardwood. When they had finished changing, the trio stepped back into the room covered by their veils, while ululation and sounds of "yip, yip, yip" rose up and echoed around them. Maggie handed her phone to Della Rae and instructed her to play her selection on the speakers, although to hold off before pressing play.

"You have music on your phone?" Jewell teased.

"Hey, we've all come a long way since you first strolled into my studio."

The first to dance, Maggie removed her veil, revealing a silver baladi dress that reminded Jewell of a priestess' robe. She situated herself in the center of the room with a silver cane on her shoulder, and her head covered in a silver-fringed scarf.

The eternal teacher couldn't resist explaining the origin of the cane dance before she performed.

"It comes from the Saidi region of Egypt and is grounded in folkloric roots. You will observe hops and cane twirls. I'll be teaching this style this fall when we complete the veil disciplines."

"Cool," Z said.

"Awesome, I can't wait," Becca echoed.

Maggie danced with her usual poise and grace and, when the music ended, swept into a low bow. Butterflies danced in Jewell's belly, knowing she had agreed to dance second.

She handed her phone to Della Rae as well, then paused. "Wait, let me change my selection." Once satisfied, she handed the phone back. "Give me a minute. I'll let you know when I'm ready. I'll be right back."

She went into the area where they had changed earlier. She had planned to start her veil dance in the saree wrap she had used as a cover up, but in honor of Clara now wanted to enter with a ghost wrap and a more haunting song. She traded her upbeat original selection to a ballad-like song of longing, carried out by string instruments.

Once she had her veil manipulated into a ghost wrap, she stuck her arm out the door and performed wrists circles.

Z must have seen her first because she heard her call. "Hey, she's ready."

The music started and Jewell entered with her face covered by the ghost veil. She sauntered slowly, lifting each leg high and then placing it to the side of the opposite foot, all the while leaning her upper body back and performing arm, shoulder, and wrist movements. Fortunately, her veil was white, so it didn't completely block her vision. She turned her back to the group with the veil still over her face, performing hip and shoulder lifts and drops to match the accents of the music. Then, as the music escalated, with her back still to the others, she flung the veil over her head, allowing it to cascade down her back in a dramatic fashion. It fell until it was hanging from the back of her belt. She smiled to herself as her friends oohed and ahhed.

She turned and performed a few traveling steps that fitted with the music, then spun around to free her veil. She performed the veil moves while traveling, covering the large stage area. She felt as graceful and beautiful as a ballerina, her veil floating and swirling as she commanded it to. She heard Aniela's coaching in her ear. "Lift, lift, higher than you think necessary."

When the music ended, she dropped to the floor, her veil falling around her. Her chest tightened and her eyes filled with tears as she stood to see her friends and mother on their feet, cheering, whistling, and ululating.

"I'm not following that," Z joked, and Jewell's tears quickly turned to laughter.

Twelve

Chapter 12

❧

J ewell woke early on Saturday morning, unable to sleep with the anticipation of her sailboat date. She rarely watched TV in bed, but today she sat up and clicked the remote to the channel broadcasting local news. The next segment shook her quickly out of her morning fog. It was a feature on the murder of Gaylen Spalding. The reporter spoke about his life and family, listing the plethora of contributions the family had made throughout Southbridge.

Then the reporter switched her focus to Travis, "the murder suspect." There was an aspect to his arrest which Jewell hadn't seen yet. Previously, she had watched as officers put him into a squad car at his home. There must have been even more reporters camped at the station when he was brought in.

A twinge of something she couldn't quite work out affected Jewell as she saw what appeared to be a sincere plea from Travis. There, followed clear footage of him exiting the car at the prison, hands once again cuffed behind his back and an officer on either side holding tight to his elbows. His tears were flowing as he cried out. "I didn't do it. I loved him. How could I have killed him? I loved him."

Jewell got out of bed and sat on the floor with Romeo. He climbed onto her lap, sensing she needed comforting, and she stroked his curly back.

"What was it about Travis, Romeo? What if… No, I can't think like that. It's not up to us anymore. I'm just emotional today. Maybe it's nerves about my date. That's all it is. Right, boy?"

Romeo whined.

"By the way, you're going to like Christian." Romeo's tail wagged wildly, as it always did when Jewell had her discussions with him.

She went to the kitchen, where Lydia soon joined her. They sat at the island, enjoying coffee and breakfast. For some reason, all morning long Jewell kept picturing herself on Christian's sailboat wearing white. But that didn't make sense. Wouldn't her clothes get dirty?

She consulted Lydia about what to wear, who took her by the hand and led her to the master bedroom and slid open the closet.

"Well, you need non-skid shoes for sure." Lydia pulled a white pair of rubber-soled sneakers from the closet floor. "Then Capri pants, I think." She rattled through the hangers. "How about these? I think a khaki pair is fine. Plus, they have pockets. That might come in handy. And you'll need to keep reapplying sunscreen." She sorted through more clothes before landing on a light blue blouse. "Here. This blouse and…" She turned to the dresser drawers. "Where do you keep your sweaters?"

"Sweaters? It's going to be in the nineties today."

"There will be a breeze. And maybe even a storm. You never know out on the water."

"Thanks. You sound like you've been sailing yourself."

"I have. As a girl. Before my dad left. He had a friend with a sailboat. A very wealthy man who preferred that I accompany Dad over Laura. Most people preferred Laura's more boisterous personality, but this man appreciated my shyness. I think he liked the quiet. Laura was rarely quiet." She smiled. "He continued to help me in the ways a father would after your grandfather, Miles, left."

"Nathanael's middle name. He dropped it, you know."

Lydia shook her head.

Jewell wanted to take the words back.

Romeo was barking, and then the sound of knocking at the front door reached the master bathroom.

"Oh no, I'm not ready," Jewell cried.

"You're nearly there. Let me finish your hair for you. Trust me, he'll wait."

Lydia fastened Jewell's hair in a tight ponytail. She had never worn it this way before. But, glancing in the mirror, turning her head back and forth, she admired the sleek look it gave her. She had cut a few inches off prior to her travel expedition, the trip that hadn't exactly lasted as long as she had anticipated.

"I like it," she said and stood to hug Lydia.

"This way it won't blow all about and in your pretty face." Lydia rubbed her palms together. "Now, let's answer that door."

Jewell opened the door and Christian wolf whistled approvingly. Blushing, Jewell opened the door wider to reveal Lydia standing behind her.

"Oh bugger, I shouldn't have done that."

Lydia laughed. "Don't worry. I'm aware she looks good."

"She clearly got it from you," he replied, not missing a beat. "Have I redeemed myself enough to come in?"

"Please do," Lydia said and stepped aside to make room.

Jewell introduced them officially, including Romeo, whose tail was darting to-and-fro ferociously. Christian fussed over him as Jewell scanned the house. "I have a cat somewhere too."

Soon after, she was heading out with Christian, feeling like a high schooler on her first parentally approved date. "See you, Mom." She said, her sweater draped over one arm and sunglasses in her hand.

"Good day, Lydia. It was nice meeting you."

"You too. Have fun."

"I like your car," Jewell said as they reached the end of her sidewalk. "It has character. What is it?"

"A 1971 Mercedes."

"From before we were born! And it still runs?" He opened the passenger door for her. She turned abruptly to him. "I'm assuming you were born after 1971 too?"

Christian looked puzzled and possibly mildly offended. "Of course. How old do you think I am?"

She laughed. "Just teasing." He poked her gently in the ribs, sending lightning flashes all over her body. He went around and climbed into the driver's seat.

"I know you were born well after the Seventies, but…" She scrutinized him as he adjusted in the seat and reached for his seatbelt.

"Oh," he said, as if suddenly realizing she was waiting for an answer. "I'm thirty-two."

"And I'm twenty-eight. There, we got that settled."

She was amazed once more as his already unnaturally wide grin grew even wider.

In a short while, they reached the parking lot of the marina.

"What's with the sweater?" he asked.

"Mom said I might need it. She has sailed before."

"Where did she sail?"

"Most likely in Wash- Oh gosh." Jewell blushed.

"You won't be needing that here, in Florida. You can leave it in the car. I won't tell." He winked and she felt less embarrassed.

"Shall we walk to the jetty?" Christian asked.

"The whatty?"

"The jetty where the boat is docked."

"Oh, you mean, the dock?"

He laughed, then came around to open her door. She followed him around to the trunk, from which he retrieved some supplies. There was his trumpet case, and something else that caught her eye.

"Wait, is that a picnic basket?"

"It is indeed."

It was a real picnic basket. Wicker with a handle and red and white checked liner coming out the edges. "I've never seen anything like this." He raised his eyebrows at her. "Okay, I've lived a sheltered life. I used to carry my lunch around in a brown paper bag."

He wrapped an arm around her and kissed the top of her head, then they began the trek to his boat. There were hundreds of them in the dock.

"Which is yours?"

"Over here."

It wasn't the largest in the marina, but not the smallest either. Jewell read the name painted on the side. The Sloop Johnathan J.

"What's the 'J' for?"

"Johna." He spelled it out.

"Johnathan Johna?"

"Yeah, I know. It's a 'blending of the families' thing."

"I see. It's certainly a nice boat."

Christian threw in their supplies and boarded ahead of Jewell, then reached for her hand. "Careful, these jet— these docks can get slippery. Oh, and I probably should have asked before, but you do know how to swim, don't you?"

She giggled. "What would you say if I didn't?"

His eyes widened.

"Nah, kidding, I can swim."

Once her feet were secure on the boat floor, he pulled her towards him, a little harder than necessary. She wasn't about to resist. The force crashed her into him, and they stood there, bodies pressed together, until he broke away to retrieve a life jacket. He set it down on a bench.

"Sit here." He indicated a spot on the bench next to the life jacket. "If we hadn't broken apart just then, I don't think we'd have ever shoved off. It'd be dark, and a search party would have found us like that. Not that I would have minded terribly."

"Oh, I don't know," Jewell answered. "We may not have been standing…" The tension crackled between them when he looked at her, and that butterfly feeling danced around her belly.

"You're mischievous, I like it."

Her spot on the bench provided a view of the open water and other boats.

"I just need to prepare a few things before we shove off."

"I studied a little, you know, on the internet. About sailing. Well, motoring."

"Brilliant. Then you know to beware of the boom, I take it? I'll call out when I'm going to execute a tack or jibe. I'll show you more next time. But for today, just sit back and relax. You'll be safe where you are."

He started the motor and used the posts of the dock to push off. The wind brushed over her face and part of her wished her hair was loose so that it could wave freely with the breeze. The sun warmed her skin as they rode in quiet unison, taking in the breathtaking scenery. It seemed to be a custom to wave at passing boats, so she did, flashing her best smile.

After cruising around a while, Christian allowed the boat to glide into one of the coves. "We'll anchor here for lunch."

"Ah, the fancy picnic basket. I can't wait." Jewell clapped her hands and sat up straight.

"You stay put. Let me wait on you."

He brought the basket over and sat opposite her. Their knees touched slightly, and she was careful to keep the contact as he handed her a plate. She flipped it back and forth. "A real plate on a picnic."

Christian pulled out a loaf of French bread and broke the end off for her. She laid it on her plate as he handed her a mason jar filled with what looked like homemade lemonade. She peeked over the lid of the basket, brushing her thighs over his. "How'd you keep it so cold?"

"Ice pack pouches."

"I'm very impressed."

He grinned and handed her another container. "Mission accomplished."

She popped the lid to find an assortment of cheeses. "Yum." Next came the tiniest bottle of olive oil she had ever seen. "That's so cute."

"And here's some hummus and olives," he said, handing her yet another container. "And some grapes."

"Oh my, stop."

She removed the mason jar lid and took a large swallow of lemonade. "It's great."

"Cold enough?"

She nodded and dug into the cheeses.

When they had finished eating, he placed everything back into the picnic basket, then shifted to reach for his trumpet. Their spot was secluded. The water lapped gently at the sides of the boat, rocking it rhythmically as Christian played a series of low, melodious tunes.

"Wow, better than Miles." Jewell smiled and batted her eyelashes.

"Ha, you're just saying that because you're captive on my boat."

Putting his trumpet aside, he moved back so that he was directly across from her, his thighs a little closer than before. They picked up their conversation from where they had left it back at The Cobblestone Express. The topic quickly turned more personal.

"Elizabeth came back, you know. For a bit."

Jewell wasn't sure how to react, so she just murmured to make it clear she had heard.

"Yeah. Johnathan and I had just adjusted to being the two of us, and then she came back. I thought it was the right thing to do. To try. But there was a…something had crushed the love between us. I couldn't live with that emptiness. It was like skirting round a huge hole every day."

"I completely understand."

"So, she went back to London. Again."

"I hate that Johnathan was abandoned by his mother. I know what that's like."

"You do? Isn't Lydia your mum?"

"Yes, but she…she did abandon me and my brother, Nathanael. When he was six and I was three."

"Blimey, do you remember it? I'm always worried about what it might do to Johnathan."

"I don't remember, actually. My brother did, and I think it broke him, in a way. For me, the problem was more my day-to-day reality from that point onward. I was shuffled around between foster homes quite a few times. My brother had it worse. In fact, funny tidbit, his middle name was Miles."

"Really?" Christian said. "As in Miles Davis?"

"Well, Miles Jameson, actually. Nathanael Miles after my mother's father. Who, believe it or not, abandoned his family."

"How odd, and here I've been going on about Miles being the best trumpet player ever and it's your brother's middle name."

"Was," Jewell corrected.

"Oh no, is your brother…gone?"

"No, he dropped the middle name not wanting any association with an abandoning grandfather."

Christian groaned. "Well, I guess Johnathan has fared better then. I'm sorry about what happened to you. But you've turned into such an amazing woman in spite of it. How come Lydia is back in your life then?"

Sitting on that beautiful vessel, in the peace of their little haven, Jewell told Christian everything. He leaned towards her, holding her hands in his, as she described her entire life from childhood until the present. She wasn't sure why, but she trusted him with every detail. When she got to the part concerning Josh and the medication, she shared the whole truth without flinching. All the details she hadn't shared with anyone else, not even Becca, or Kage or even her mother. She incriminated herself with the experimental drugs and the hacking.

She finished, suddenly apprehensive as she waited for Christian's response. Her palms rested wet against his but she didn't dare pull away. Her heart raced. She thought the silence would never end, but then he finally broke it.

"Have you ever been kissed on a sailboat?"

Her heart thumped even harder. Her mouth felt desert dry. "Can't say I have."

He slid over to her bench, and his left thigh pressed against her right. "And are you, perhaps, so inclined?"

"I am so incl—"

He stopped her words with his mouth.

They shared a long, tender kiss. Attraction and passion saturated her, but not in a feverish or frantic way as she had expected. It was as if the two knew they had their entire lifetimes ahead to fit in their lovemaking, allowing them to savor each step along the way.

Later, they sat, still turned towards one another, hands still tightly locked together. She studied his face as if she could read his soul through it. She tried to discern what was so different about him, this man. There was friendship and commonality like she had with Josh, but along with it, the strong passion and attraction she had felt with Kage. Nonetheless, it wasn't fair, she thought, to lump Christian into some meshing-together of Josh and Kage. In just a flash of time, it was like the words she had shared with Lydia about him had come into being. She felt like she had known him all her life, or from another space and time altogether.

Jewell lost track of the time as they studied one another. Christain scooted closer, pulling her towards him by her waist and swirling to face her. He placed his forehead against hers. The boat rocked gently, and the water sloshed around them. With foreheads pressed together, they spoke in low, intimate voices.

"This has been great," Christian said.

"For me too."

"But, sadly, I've got to be getting back."

"I want to meet Johnathan," Jewell whispered. "Sometime."

"I want you to meet Johnathan too," he whispered back.

"I know!" Jewell said enthusiastically, pushing herself back a fraction and raising her voice to usual amplitude. "Do you go to the annual Hot Air Balloon Festival on Labor Day?"

"Yes, doesn't everyone? It's next weekend I think."

"And what a great way for me to meet Johnathan without him thinking I'm anyone special. I can be just another acquaintance you happen to run into in the crowd."

"But you are someone special. Very special."

"Aw." She grinned. "I know. But just in case things don't work out between us, we can avoid rocking his boat. No pun intended."

"Admit it, the pun was a little intended. But you make a good point. Let's coordinate the night before."

Becca and Lynn were visiting Lydia when Christian dropped Jewell off. Or were they just visiting, Jewell wondered. The three sat congregated in the living room, seemingly engrossed in small talk. Jewell crossed the room to join them.

When the small talk lulled, Becca, in a pitiful attempt to sound nonchalant said, "So, how did your date go?"

"Oh, it was fine." Jewell answered, then sat quietly and let the others' nosy silence infuse the room.

The other three women exchanged glances back and forth until Becca finally blurted out, "Oh come on, you know we want details."

Jewell laughed. "Alright then. It was great. I get such a sense of peace when I'm around him. Even now, just thinking about him I feel serene." Her eyes trailed off into the middle distance as she recalled certain moments.

"Uh huh," Lynn groaned. "Who cares about peace and serenity? We want to hear about passion!"

Jewell delivered details in full velocity, barely taking a breath. "He has this really cool old Mercedes, doesn't that show character? Oh, and he packed a picnic lunch. It was cheese, and bread, and olives and hummus. Oh, and grapes and lemonade. And get this, the lemonade was in these mason jars, he'd made it specially himself. And the lunch was packed in a real wicker picnic basket, like in the movies. Then the boat of course was beautiful. And he's so skilled at sailing. Oh, and it's named after his son, Johnathan J. The "J" is for Johna. And we're going to be introduced on Labor Day at the Hot Air Balloon Festival, only Christian and I will pretend that I'm just someone in the crowd his dad knows. Christian knows a lot of people, so it won't look suspicious. Gosh, wait, am I sounding like Mindy Sigel?"

"A little," Becca said, recalling Josh's assistant, the chatty teenager from Washington. Lynn nodded in agreement.

"But I like this side of you," Becca continued. "I don't even know who that girl was I met in bellydance class last year." She smiled and winked.

"You can tell me the real good stuff later," Lydia said with a smirk.

"Oh no," Becca said. "That stuff is for the best friend."

"There was some body contact, I will admit," Jewell said. "And THE KISS."

The women leaned in.

"What? Just a kiss?" Becca asked.

"But a great one," Jewell sighed. "A long, smooth, amazing one."

Their absorption was interrupted by a chime from Becca's phone ringing.

"It's Della Rae," she said. She answered, "Hello. Uh huh. No way. Nooo way. Jeez, okay, we will."

"What?"

"We have to put on the news. Ethan Bowers and Phineas Darcey have been arrested."

"Who on earth is Phineas Darcey?" Lynn asked.

"Chantal Darcey's father," Becca said.

They flew to the TV and gathered in front of it as Becca turned it on, scanning for the news channel. "Darn. We missed it."

"Come on, we'll look it up online," Jewell said.

They crowded around the computer behind her.

"I've heard that, if the Spalding family is considered wealthy, we haven't seen anything yet," Becca said as Jewell searched for the relevant news segment. "Apparently they look like beggars next to the Darceys' wealth."

"Here's the recap video," Jewell said and hit play.

The four listened to the reporter spouting in front of their local police station. "Detective Ethan Bowers and Phineas Darcey have been taken into custody on suspicion of tampering with State evidence and impeding the investigation into the murder of Gaylen Spalding. No further details have been released at this time. We will keep you up to date as new information becomes available."

Jewell flopped back against her chair. Becca squeezed her shoulder, and Jewell swiveled to face the others. "Well, now we know. No wonder he was so obstructive."

"Yeah, no wonder," Becca echoed.

They moved to the sofa, Lydia taking the side chair as usual. No one spoke for a few moments. They all sat quietly staring ahead and digesting this new turn of events.

Jewell finally broke the silence. "What on earth was Bowers up to?"

"I can't put it all together either," Becca said.

"Let's keep following the story and see if the rest of the gang has any theories."

As Jewell got ready for bed that night, her phone rang. It was Christian.

"How are you?" he asked. "I just wanted to tell you again how much I loved spending time with you today."

"Me too."

"I can't wait to do it again."

"Me neither."

"Did we decide when?"

"The Hot Air Balloon Festival, next Monday."

"That's right. And as luck would have it, my parents leave Sunday, so that prevents them mucking up anything."

"Phew," Jewell said.

"As for our next *real* date…what about the following Friday? We could have a bit of a knees-up."

"You want my knees up? That's a little forward, don't you think?"

"No, no, a dance. We can have a dance."

Jewell giggled, pleased that her fake ignorance had worked on him again.

"You like giving me a hard time."

"I'd love to go dancing with you next Friday. I'll dream about it tonight."

"I'll dream of *after* the dance," he said. "Goodnight, my sweet."

Jewell breathed out, "Goodnight."

Thirteen

Chapter 13

The group was summoned to Sherry's that Monday morning. Montgomery Alex had information to share which he was happy to provide via phone conference, although Jewell was disappointed they would miss seeing him in person in his high-end suit and combed-back hair. Nicci had sent a text saying she couldn't possibly leave work, but asked for a full report, and Lydia and Jewell came in late because they had stopped on the way at the downtown bakery to pick up fresh donuts for the occasion. Jewell loved the blast of sugar-infused air derived from entering the bakery.

When they arrived at Sherry's, the dining room was already full. Gabby's four boys, Tyler, Tristan, Tabor and Teague, were running rampage through the kitchen, living room and dining room. Jewell considered how, even if Gabby and Kevin weren't very skilled in disciplining their sons, they were at least excellent at naming them.

Going into the kitchen, Jewell and Lydia opened the box of donuts and found two plates on which to arrange them. They carried the treats into the dining room, where Sherry had set out coffee and fixings. The call was already in progress. Lydia quietly took a seat and passed her plate of donuts one way, while Jewell passed hers the other, although not before snagging a cream-filled one herself.

Becca leaned in towards Jewell and whispered, "All you missed was him filling Sherry in on the process of closing her case."

Mr. Alex continued through the speaker. "Let me assure everyone now that all charges against Ms. McKenna have been dropped."

The group couldn't help but cheer. Sherry buried her face in her hands while her shoulders shook with relieved sobbing.

"Sorry, go on, Mr. Montgomery, I mean, Mr. Alex," Della Rae said.

"See, they're backwards," Jewell whispered.

"As I was saying, all charges have been dropped," he continued. Z provided a subdued imitation of a crowd roaring. "I have studied the police records and it appears that Detective Bowers was repeatedly redirecting the forensic team to prioritize cases ahead of the Spalding case. He collected no evidence from the scene and made no effort, at least no documented effort, to pursue the case. When he finally presented the forensic team with a potential cause of death, naming a specific herb, they quickly launched into the toxicology testing, but it also triggered an internal investigation as to why the testing had been delayed in the first place. An officer began following Bowers and saw him meeting Mr. Darcey in a suspiciously remote area on several occasions. Upon further investigation, they found that Bowers had been depositing substantial cash installments into his bank accounts, and had amassed quite a number of new cars and motorcycles in his garage. With subpoenas, they were able to prove the funds had been wired from one of Mr. Darcey's accounts."

"But why?" Sherry asked.

"It's common knowledge the partner of a murder victim is typically the first suspect," Mr. Alex said, as if that was explanation enough.

"Even if the victim is in bed with someone else when they're found?"

Sherry asked.

"Mr. Darcey didn't take enough comfort from you simply being on the scene. He wanted further assurance that his daughter would never come under scrutiny or suspicion of any kind. After all, Mr. Spalding being found in bed with someone else, and the pattern of behavior that might suggest, if anything would point to a possible motive. He felt it necessary to pay any price to keep his daughter out of the press and out of the police's ring of suspicion. Not to mention, keeping the family name untarnished."

"But she didn't do it," Della Rae said. "Or did she?"

"No, there is no evidence she did. Mr. Darcey was a protective father with an abundance of funds and found it more...well, cost-effective to be proactive."

"Detective Bowers sure caused me a lot of heartache," Sherry said. Jewell took her hand.

"They both will pay," assured Mr. Alex. "Well, at least Bowers will."

The call concluded and celebratory chaos filled the room.

"It's finally over," Sherry said. "And you know what?"

"What?" the others' voices echoed.

"I know this was rough, and I hate what you all went through to help me. But, for me, I'm a little glad it happened, because now I'm sober and loving my life."

They all clanked their coffee mugs, laughing as the boys raced through the dining room. With the case behind them, the troupe found reason relax once more.

With all their worries behind them, a few days later Jewell and Becca decided to make the friendly visit they had promised to Lizzie at the bar. She was, at first, justifiably wary.

"Hey, you're back. Who are you this time?"

"Ha, ha, we're ourselves," Becca said.

"You want your Cosmo?"

"I don't know, what else do you make?"

"Everything, but how about a martini? I can make a sour apple one."

"Yes please, sounds great."

"Just the house white for me," Jewell said. Then, a little more softly said to Lizzie, "Are you upset? You knew Travis, from coming in here, right?"

"Yes." Lizzie's tone was curt. "But if he did it, he's where he deserves to be." Jewell was taken aback. Only a second ago, Lizzie had been pretty warm again towards them. "I don't really care who did it, as long as they're in jail."

"Well, at least Sherry, our friend, is cleared."

"That girl can put it away," Lizzie said, half-engaged in the conversation. She held her cell phone swiping the screen in a pattern to presumably unlock it. "I don't know many women who can drink like her. But it's great to hear it's ended well for her." She laid her phone on the bottom rung of the liquor shelves. "I'd better get your drinks."

She opened the half-fridge on the back wall and retrieved a bottle of wine. As she closed the door, a bottle of liquor dropped from the shelf above and broke, its heady contents rapidly swamping the floor. Colorful expletives soared from Lizzie's mouth. Her outburst when the glass had broken during their last visit seemed placid compared to the hot phrases firing from this five-foot-three woman now.

"That's top-shelf scotch. I can't afford to have that shit come out of my pay."

Jewell gave Becca a sideways glance and Becca nodded.

Lizzie served their drinks then cleaned up the mess. A man and woman had entered while she squatted, picking up glass and dabbing the floor. The man tipped his cap to Becca and Jewell, then the couple took a seat in one of the booths. Lizzie stood up, straightened her shoulders, smoothed her apron and left the bar to approach the booth with new customers. Jewell watched as Lizzie quickly turned on her friendly demeanor.

How odd, Jewell thought. The way her anger comes and goes like the flick of a switch.

As Lizzie returned to prepare the couple's drinks, her bar rag fell from the bar too.

"What the f—! Why the hell is everything dropping?" Her irritation seemed a little greater than the occasion warranted.

Jewell nudged Becca. "I have to go to the bathroom."

"Me too."

The pair went to the ladies' room and checked under the stalls. No feet.

Jewell whispered, "Clara is trying to tell us something."

"I know, but what?"

"I don't know. Did you see Lizzie's phone lying on the back shelf with the liquor?"

"No, not really."

"Well, it was. I'm going to try to snatch it while she's out at the booths. Cover for me. I'll pretend to need to go outside and see if there are any clues on her phone."

"Are you sure we should be doing this? I mean, the case *is* solved."

"Is it? I've been having second thoughts ever since seeing how upset Travis seemed, and how adamant he was about being innocent. I'm starting to think he really did love Gaylen, and that maybe he…didn't do it. It's been keeping me up at night."

The woman from the couple entered the bathroom. Becca and Jewell smiled at her and left.

Back at the bar, Jewell waited until Lizzie was distracted, then snatched her phone and carried it outside in her pocket. Thanks to her photographic memory, she was able to mimic the pattern and it worked to unlock the screen. She scrolled through pictures of Lizzie and other women her age in and around the university. Then she landed upon a selfie taken with Travis. They were standing in front of his house.

She knows him outside of work.

She continued to scroll. The string of photos plastered across the phone made her jaw drop. Here was picture after picture of Lizzie and Gaylen. Selfies of them lying in bed, scantily clad, of Gaylen kissing her, of Lizzie and Gaylen on motorcycle trips together. None of them were at Gaylen's condo. She must have been more than his one-night stands. Maybe it was her place where he stayed those nights he didn't come home on the surveillance tapes. Jewell quickly texted the pictures to Becca, then turned around and deleted the message from Lizzie's phone. Returning to the bar, she nudged Becca to order another drink, distracting Lizzie so she could return the phone.

The request required Becca to chug her first martini.

"The sacrifices I make," she joked, smacking her lips.

With Lizzie's back to them, preparing Becca's second drink, Jewell wiped the phone clean with her shirt and slid it back to its original spot. Becca reached into her backpack as her phone pinged with incoming messages, but Jewell shook her head and motioned for Becca to leave her phone where it was.

"Later," she whispered.

Lizzie returned with Becca's martini. "You sure are thirsty today."

Jewell detected an air of suspicion in Lizzie's tone.

"Drink it up," Jewell whispered through pursed lips.

"What? The first one's going to my head already."

"Trust me." Jewell placed more than enough cash to cover the drinks on the bar, along with a handsome tip. "Let's go."

Becca sang loudly as they walked to Jewell's car.

"What are you doing?"

"Singing that Shakira song. I think we should choreograph it." Becca began dancing on the cobblestone street as they crossed.

"Becca, come on. What's wrong with you?"

She threw her arm around Jewell. "I love you so much. I mean I *really* love you."

"Are you drunk?"

Becca hiccupped and twirled when they reached the other sidewalk.

Jewell laughed. "I guess chugging martinis will do that. Sorry, that's on me." Jewell helped Becca into the passenger seat. "Come on. We've got a job to do."

Jewell pulled in front of the police station, her windows down to the max in the hope the fresh air would sober Becca a bit, not that it had worked. Becca played the radio on full volume, singing loudly above it.

"Gosh, you have to stay here," Jewell said. "And keep that down." She dialed the radio volume down. "I'll be back as soon as I can." She wound the windows up and was leaving the car running so Becca could have the air on. "Please don't touch anything."

"Oh, and Jewell," Becca slurred, snapping a picture of Jewell as she swung around.

"What are you doing?"

"To commemor...what's that word, commmmoomorute."

"Commemorate?"

"That's it." Becca flung her arm straight out in front, pointing at Jewell. "That's it, for Lydia's scrapbook."

Jewell thought it best to lock Becca inside, then entered the police station.

The clerk recognized her. "Can I help you? You know Bowers is no longer here."

"Yes, I heard. Who can I see in his absence?"

"Mary Adams took over. You can go to her office. Third door on the left. It's marked. She's not so much on ceremony like Bowers."

Jewell followed his directions to Detective Adams' office. The door was open, but Jewell couldn't see anyone inside. She knocked, almost jumping when a petite brunette stood up from behind the computer on the desk.

"How can I help?" the detective said, immediately reaching her right hand out to Jewell.

"Thank you, detective. I'm Jewell Caldwell."

"Call me Mary. Jewell, it's nice to put a face to the name."

"I've been reading through Bower's files trying to get up to speed. I kept seeing you crop up, as well as…" Detective Adams flipped through her notes. "Rebecca Steal, Lydia Caldwell, Della Rae Young and, of course, Sherry McKenna."

"Yes, Sherry's case is why I'm here."

"Oh?"

"Yes." Jewell's heart fluttered with nerves. "I think Travis Browdy is innocent."

The office was on the same side of the building where Jewell had parked. Her car sat in direct view, allowing her to keep watch over Becca and assure she was staying put. Right now, she appeared to be sleeping.

"Is something wrong?" Detective Adams turned to peer out the window too.

"No, everything's fine."

"Back to Travis Browdy then," Detective Adams said. "He hasn't confessed. In fact, quite the opposite. He continually proclaims his innocence. He'll have a trial, of course, legal counsel, and a chance to prove his innocence, if that's the case. But aren't you and Rebecca the ones who brought in the suspicion against him in the first place?"

"We did, but I think we were wrong."

"Then this is a statement? Hang on." Detective Adams picked up a clipboard with a form. She must have noticed Jewell's surprise. "He didn't record anything you told him, did he?" She shook her head.

Jewell recited the narrative she had composed on the ride to the station, despite Becca singing in her ear. Her original plan had been to show whoever she met at the police station the pictures she had sent to Becca's phone, but then realized that taking someone else's phone like that was illegal. She wasn't sure where the law stood on sending pictures from it in addition but figured it probably wouldn't sway things in her favor. She had decided to withhold the pictures unless the police didn't believe her, in which case she would admit her guilt in the hope it would be overlooked in the course of ensuring an innocent man didn't go to prison.

"We had been frequenting Las Fuentes during the case, as you probably know. We admitted we were doing some of our own information-gathering. We had promised Lizzie, the bartender who provided us with information, that we would return when everything was settled to pay her a friendly visit. But when we went there today, she seemed different."

"Different how?"

"She was tense. A bottle she referred to as top-shelf liquor crashed to the floor and broke, and she reacted in my mind erratically, cursing in front of customers and making a scene. She appeared almost distraught. Although, to be fair, she was scared it would come out of her paycheck. Then later, she was out waiting on the booths, and Becca, Rebecca Steal, and I were at the bar. I realized I had misplaced my phone, and then I saw what I thought was mine on the liquor shelf.

I figured I must have laid it there when we tried to comfort Lizzie about the bottle. Only then, when I swiped the screen to see if I had any messages, I was greeted with a picture of Lizzie together with Travis in front of his house. I was so startled, I swiped again to check I hadn't imagined it. Then there came pictures showing Lizzie lying in bed with Gaylen Spalding! Of course, I replaced the phone once I realized it wasn't mine, although I did wipe it down first. Didn't want to leave any marks on someone else's phone."

Jewell picked at her nail beds as she awaited Detective Adams' reaction.

"Wait a minute. Let me process this. Even if her phone resembled yours, didn't she have it passcode protected?"

"Um…she must not have." Jewell felt her muscles tense at the lie.

"I guess some people don't. Who knows?" Then Mary Adams leaned forward in her desk chair. "I really don't want to know how you came about this information, do I?" She paused and sat back in her chair. "Well, that is some information then. I appreciate it and will look into it, Jewell, thank you. Is there anything else? Like, can I offer you a job?"

Jewell laughed. "No. I'll just be glad when this is all over and the right person is behind bars."

Jewell returned to the car and found Becca still passed out in the passenger seat. She unlocked the car and climbed in.

Halfway home, Becca roused. "Hey, where are we?"

"Welcome back. Sorry, I hated leaving you in the car like that, but I didn't want you to get arrested for public intoxication." Jewell cringed, realizing that the front of the police station might not have been the best place to have parked.

"It's okay since we got evidence to help Travis this time. I didn't mind taking one for the team. How did the chief react?"

"Actually, there's a new detective on the case, and I think she'll get things done."

223

"That's great news."

They pulled in front of Jewell's house. Lydia greeted them at the door.

"Let's get you some coffee," Jewell said to Becca.

"Sounds good to me."

They all sat in the living room, sipping coffee, as Jewell filled Lydia in on the details, then texted the troupe with an update.

The news came swiftly of Travis' release and Lizzie's arrest. Jewell was still reeling from Lizzie's confession. They heard about it all from Montgomery Alex. How Lizzie lost it and blurted out everything. How her anger towards Gaylen built into a rage she could no longer contain. She wanted him for herself. She had turned out to be so hateful and it was disconcerting to think how they had been so fooled by her. Apparently, she had a criminal record stemming back to her teenage years, all involving assault. Becca applied her budding analytic skills to diagnose Lizzie with a narcissistic personality disorder.

"Do you think we should stop to see Simon on the way?" Becca turned in the passenger seat to ask Jewell.

"No, not this time. Let's get this task behind us. It might not be a pleasant one."

Jewell's moist palms gripped the wheel as she turned onto the dirt road and up the long drive. They decided to try the greenhouse first since Travis had said it was where he found joy even when he was distraught. Those words rang in Jewell's head as she realized he must have been grieving over Gaylen during their first visit there.

They stood at the door of the greenhouse and heard him humming instead of signing. Jewell couldn't make out the tune.

"Hello?"

"Yes? Enter." His tone subdued.

Becca pushed the door open and they entered. He walked out into the aisle and stood in front of them holding a potted flower with a hot pink bloom.

"It's my breed of an Anthurium. I'm going to enter it in the St. Isidore—"

His body went limp, he slumped, nearly falling until Jewell and Becca each deftly grabbed an arm. Jewell figured their adrenaline aided in keeping his six-foot body erect.

"I'm sorry," he said, still clutching the prized flower.

They eased him to the cast-iron bench and sat on either side in silence for what seemed an eternity.

"You two were busy after your last visit here, weren't you?"

"I suppose," Jewell said, twisting her lips.

"We—" Becca began.

"Do you see that?" Travis interrupted pointing at a statue in the greenhouse among his plants. His voice, surprisingly serene.

"Yes, it's Buda," Jewell said.

"I'm Buddist." He paused. " There are insects all over this greenhouse. They all belong here. Play their own role and serve their own purpose. You were helping a friend. You must love her."

"We do," Becca said and Jewell nodded in agreement.

"I love Gaylen. He had his faults, but man…his spirit. He was full of life. Ironic, isn't it?"

"We're here to apologize," Jewell said.

"I can't figure out Lizzie," Travis continued, passing over Jewell's plea. "I guess I see good in everyone. She must have snatched some of my hangover remedy."

"We are just grateful the truth came out and you are free," Jewell said.

"See, it's because of you two, I am free. So why the need to apologize?

It all came full circle. And I suppose we all learned what we needed to learn."

"But, you had to spend time in jail," Becca said.

"Yes, it wasn't easy, but it is behind me now and I appreciate life even more."

They continued to sit in silence.

Fourteen

Chapter 14

versize pastel aliens filled the sky. At least that's how the massive balloons appeared to Jewell as she and Lydia meandered through the cobblestone streets with Romeo. Last year, she had walked these same streets pulled tight against Kage. Things were totally different now. No Kage, but she had Lydia, and now Christian, plus the burden of resentment she had been carrying since childhood had been lifted. She had forgiven her mother, but more than that, she felt genuinely grateful to have her back in her life.

The plan was to walk as far as the field just beyond downtown, where they agreed to meet up with the rest of the gang. The heat was oppressive, but no one seemed to mind. A celebratory feel infused the air, and the food didn't hurt either. Italian sausages with peppers and onions infused a heavenly scent through town, and of course Jewell spotted her favorite, cotton candy, pure spun sugar to melt in her mouth. Not to mention, fried pickles and, of course, ice cream.

When they met up with the gang, Jewell noted a bright red patch on Z's cheek from the candied apple she held. When Jewell brought it to her attention, Miranda kissed it off.

"Get a room," Becca said, something she had chirped at Jewell and Kage in the past.

"You should talk," Jewell said. "I don't think I could get a sheet of paper between you two." She indicated Becca and Max.

"I'm just glad this crazy detective stuff is over," Max said and squeezed Becca tighter. "Do I get her back for good now, Jewell?"

They laughed. Candi and Tom soon joined them. Together they watched as Gabby and Kevin visited the game booths in the distance with the boys.

"Hey, get a gander of this," Candi said.

Jewell turned to see Della Rae and Sherry approaching. If she hadn't been with Della Rae, Jewell didn't think she would have recognized her. Sherry's hair was cut to her shoulders and curled, as well as being three shades blonder. Her new makeup and red shiny lips stood out even from a distance and her uncharacteristically tight skirt showcased her tan and shapely legs. Jewell couldn't recall ever seeing her bare legs before.

"Hey, lady, this is a private party," Z said when she approached. "The dark-haired one can stay. We know her."

Sherry grinned.

"O-M-G," Becca said. "You look amazing."

"I'll say," Candi said.

"Make that all of us," Lydia added.

Jewell pulled out her cell phone and her heart skipped a beat. It was 3 P.M., time for her staged meeting with Christian and Johnathan. Her palms were wet with anticipation as she looked around for them.

And then she saw them. Johnathan held a string attached to a mini hot air balloon in the shape of a spotted dog. Her heart melted instantly. She sidestepped away from the others, who had been made privy to the plan.

"Hi, aren't you a former science student?" Christian asked her innocently. After all, it wasn't a lie. Jewell had been a science student, just not his.

"Yes, Professor Harrington, good to see you again."

"This is my son, Johnathan."

Jewell fought against everything inside her not to drop to her knees and pull the adorable boy into a tight embrace. He had fine, straight brown hair with bangs down to his eyebrows. It had a child's shine. His face was round and perfect, with big dark eyes scanning the sky above them.

"I like your balloon," Jewell said.

"Look at those," he said, pointing upward.

"I know, they're so big and beautiful."

"Look, there's a T-Rex, and a cow."

"Do you like dinosaurs?"

"Everyone likes dinosaurs," he said with authority.

"You are so right."

"Are you going to get a balloon?" He asked Jewell.

"Oh. I don't know. I just might. What balloon do you think I should get?"

He studied Jewell closely with one eye closed. "I think a princess. You look like a princess."

Jewell laughed and placed a hand over her heart. Christian nodded approvingly.

"Hey, is that your dog?" Johnathan asked, indicating Romeo.

"It is and he really likes little boys." Jewell granted Romeo permission to approach Johnathan who then patted his head as he smiled up at Jewell.

"Well, we should move on," Christian said eventually.

Her heart sank. "Have fun." She had to restrain herself from showing him more affection.

With Johnathan ahead of him, Christian briefly grabbed Jewell's hand as he passed her and squeezed it gently.

With the staged meeting behind them, the gang spread out and explored the festival. Becca and Jewell paired up as usual. Lydia claimed Romeo and roamed the festivities with Lynn.

"Oh no," Becca said.

"What?"

"Don't look now. Nine o'clock. Kage and Anna."

Jewell took a deep breath and let it go. "You know what? I'm fine. I can be happy for them because I'm happy for me. In fact," she looped her arm through Becca's, "I'm happier than I've ever been in my life. Let's go greet them."

Fifteen

Epilogue

⁓⟋⟍⁓

hen they arrived home from the hot air balloon festival, Lydia announced she was tired and went straight to bed.

"Okay, Mom. I'm going to play around on the computer a bit first. I'm too wound up to sleep."

"See you in the morning."

"Goodnight."

Jewell found Maya on the back patio and opened the door to coax her in. Once Maya was settled on the sofa, Jewell sat down at the computer. She peeked around the corner to make sure that Lydia hadn't come back into the room, then pecked away rapidly at the keys. She had been making progress in her secret search, one she had instigated shortly after arriving back in Southbridge.

She had begun by researching the ins and outs of witness protection programs. Crucially, she had learned that, often, those in security programs are assigned their real first name, or at least something similar, to help them avoid making mistakes until they are used to their new identity.

Taking that as the best lead, she had put together a profile of everything she knew about him. Details such as physical aspects, skills and particular interests she could remember, groups he once belonged to etc. Tonight, she used these parameters to set up online searches, trawling through both public records and internet photos. She was able to dismiss a sizable proportion up-front by specifying gender, height, weight, race, age and so forth, but there was still a daunting amount of data to sift through.

After hours of exhaustive work, she had finally narrowed the list down to twenty-five potential candidates. Her eyes were growing weary and her head bobbed, but she shook off the fatigue, determined to finish the task tonight. She rolled the wheel of the mouse, then almost flung it away from her. She hadn't been expecting success.

But there, in one of the photos on the screen, stood a car salesman in Tennessee, in a city just below Nashville. She recognized the man's rugged good looks, his olive skin and thick dark hair, the sideways grin that stopped him looking too much like a Hollywood star, and a forehead creased prematurely with worry lines. Beneath the picture was a caption, not that she needed one.

Nate Miles. If he can't find the perfect car for you, no one can.

About the Author

Hi, I'm Cathryn Petit and I sincerely hope you have enjoyed reading the story of Jewell Caldwell and her new friends as much as I enjoyed writing it. Reviews are crucial for any author, and even just a line or two can make a huge difference. I would greatly appreciate a review on your favorite sites. In addition, your review can help other readers decide to pick up this book and enjoy it as well. Thank you in advance.

Please keep reading to learn about the other books in this series! Also, follow me on any of the links ahead for updates on the launch of the series audiobooks read by the talented Angela Petry!

You can connect with me on:
- https://www.cathrynlynnpetit.com
- http://bit.ly/2OKQZdt

Subscribe to my newsletter:

✉ https://www.cathrynlynnpetit.com/contact

Also by Cathryn Petit

Praise for the series: Sisters of the Silk Veil

"Aside from the fact that Cathryn's characters in the Sisters of the Silk Veil series are endearing and easy to get wrapped up in, the author has an unusual and refreshing approach to how she structures her stories. They read more like a quest than a book that has been written by numbers. I am someone who can usually spot a plot twist from a mile away, but in all three of her stories that I have read now, the turns the plots take genuinely take me by surprise, without making me feel cheated. That's quite a skill. In book 2: A Spell of Wanderlust, she also shows a natural instinct for crime narrative and this could be a potential selling point– romance combined with intrigue, as well as the redemptive character arcs she has built in."

—Antonia Reed, Editor https://reedsy.com/#/freelancers/antonia-reed

Prequel: Lydia: A Sisters of the Silk Veil Prequel

Series short-story prequel

The story of Lydia is empathetic and claustrophobic giving a stark insight into how easy it is to fall into a negative spiral. We follow Lydia as she struggles to look after her young family as the institutional and bureaucratic nets close evermore tightly around her.

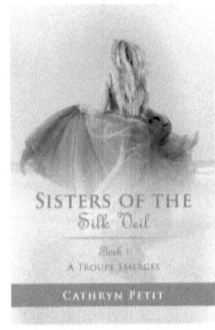

Book 1: Sisters of the Silk Veil: A Troupe Emerges

Torn between caring for her boyfriend who's crippled with phobias or breaking away to the life of her dreams, Jewell Caldwell, a beautiful you genius, contrives a plan to ease Josh's agoraphobia so she can move cross country to find the life of her dreams.

In the quaint Florida town she moves to, she stumbles into a bellydance studio and makes fast friends with the dancers.

When a handsome rancher struts into her life, she sees the chance for happiness beyond her wildest imagination. But, tragedy strikes, and Jewell fears she is the cause. Plagued by a blackmailer, guilt and grief, she plunges into despair and isolation. Will she learn to truly open up to others in order to regain her happiness or plod through life desperate and alone?

SOARS MY HEART,
Soft as Silk
A Sisters of the Silk Veil Series
Book 3

CATHRYN PETIT

Book 3: Soars My Heart, Soft as Silk
The Sisters of the Silk Veil Saga continues!
Return to the quaint town of Southbridge,
FL, for a fresh tale of passion, mystery, and
romance...

JEWELL CALDWELL'S search for her brother has finally yielded results... but tragedy and violence lurk in Nathanael's shadowy past.

Darkness from Jewell's own past plants seeds of doubt and rocks her blooming romance with CHRISTIAN HARRINGTON...but when he offers to marry her and build a life, how can she say no? Jewell finally has everything she ever wanted—that is—until a knock at the door turns her life upside down.

She's grateful for the distraction when her bellydance troupe with their proven record for solving paranormal mysteries springs into action. The Governor's mansion is being haunted, and it's driving tourists away. She soon throws herself into letters from the eighteenth century and grows obsessed with tales of a ghostly flamenco dancer and her romantic past.

But it's Jewell's own future that's in jeopardy.

Will Jewell allow a stranger to ruin the life she has built or conjure the courage to fight back?

Monthly Newsletter
#prizes #updates

Sign up for The Silk Veil Monthly Scoop

Sign up for the Silk Veil Monthly Scoop for updates on my writing projects and to enter drawings for giveaways!

https://www.cathrynlynnpetit.com/contact

www.ingramcontent.com/pod-product-compliance
Lightning Source LLC
Chambersburg PA
CBHW022007170626
46808CB00001B/316